A Step Into Darkness

Barb Shadow

ISBN: 0999837400
ISBN-13: 978-0-9998374-0-5

Book Cover Designer: Ivano Lago

From the Shadows Publishing
Forestburgh, New York

This book is dedicated to the ones who not only have always supported my writing, but have been my joy through the good times and my rock through the bad; the ones who believed in me before I had a clue. I love you. Kat and Bee!, Deanna, and Sean, who fuels me with his smiles.

Yes, Kat. You're a rock.

1

Jack pulled up alongside the old cement block building and put the Subaru into park. It rumbled loudly for a moment and then slowly expired as he took the key from the ignition. He exhaled. It had been a pain to find the twisted, overgrown drive and even on a sunny day in October, the asylum in front of him was imposing and stale. Not that it mattered. It added to the rumor and history of the site. He got out of the car, stared into gaping openings that should have held windows, and sighed. This would probably be another long night of sitting alone in a dreary place, waiting for something paranormal to happen. He had a long list of places with haunted histories that proved to be animals, folklore or downright fiction and didn't expect this one to be much different. He grabbed two large black cases labeled "Jack Barnes Paranormal" from the trunk of his car and paused to get some paperwork off the passenger seat.

New Castle Asylum. A small structure, hidden on the edge of a sleepy town, out of sight but not quite out of mind. A week before he had walked through the area, stopping to speak with shop owners and locals. Everyone nodded when he asked if they knew about the old asylum, but no one had wanted to talk about it. They were busy now, thank you. Or they looked at him as if he had three heads when he said he was going to investigate there. He only wanted a few minutes of their time and for them to volunteer some information, but sometimes in small towns that's the hardest thing to get. It had taken weeks to get all the i's dotted and t's crossed to be able to go in, and research revealed little. The typical institution history…abuse, neglect, despair…everything ripe for ghostly activity bordering on the demonic, or so everyone would have you believe. No one in the town had wanted to discuss the asylum, its history or ownership, and he had to track down the current owners in Oklahoma. They hadn't really cared if he wanted to go in, spend the night, hell, spend a month if he wanted to, as long as he signed off that if he broke a leg or something, it wasn't their fault. Great humanitarians. He smirked as he went inside and found a table for his cases.

He surveyed the space. An empty waiting room with broken glass and drab walls that might have been yellow years before they faded to a dull, dirty beige. Dingy, but he wouldn't have expected it to be brightly lit with warm, welcoming décor. It would do for a base of operations. He'd grab a folding chair from the car later, along with the rest of his gear. First, he needed to do a walk around the grounds and get some initial readings while he still had some sunlight. He had left work early, but the two hour drive had eaten up any "extra" time he might have had.

The warmth of the sun impressed him as he stepped outside. He started snapping pics around the perimeter of the building and noticed a partial foundation about 100 feet away. More pics. He had heard an outbuilding had burned some ten or twelve years ago. Rumors of a patient gone wild, a murderous intern, even a serial killer bent on taking out everyone whose name started with "A" had circulated at some point. Proof? Evidence? None. It was most likely some kid sneaking a smoke or faulty wiring that took that one out.

Jack circled the building, taking as many photos of the windows as possible. People loved those. Always searching for faces in the corners. Not that he didn't, too, but he hadn't found any. It was too easy to be deceived, anyway. Paredolia. Matrixing.

Reflections. There was almost always an explanation. Almost. He'd figure out that last bunch, though. Eventually. A ghost hunter who doesn't believe in ghosts? Yeah, it could happen. Let's just say the jury is out. Way out. He looked back up at the building, framing his next shot, and could've sworn someone, something, moved in a top floor window. Probably an animal, a bird. He'd check it out when he got back inside.

He stood for a minute, staring out at the trees that surrounded the asylum at a distance and noticed something in the overgrown grass toward the west. "Oh, now isn't this cliché?" he muttered as he came upon what appeared to be a small, unkempt cemetery attached to the grounds. A handful of gravestones, haphazardly placed, were in among the tall weeds and bushes. Dry, brown grasses and branches covered the stones and crunched with every step. They scratched as he moved them aside to see the stones. There was no, "Here lies," or endearing epitaphs on these stones. Only first names and a year. Carla 1947. Mark 1942. James… He took photos of each, so he could examine them in more depth later and get some research going. The breeze had changed a bit, a little stronger, and some clouds were starting to cover the sun. He needed to wrap things up outside. It seemed as though a fall storm was blowing in. Funny, he thought. Hadn't heard there'd be rain.

A brief stop at the car for the chair, a cooler, the heavy-ass batteries that would run his equipment for the night and he was back inside. He hung a sweatshirt over the back of the chair. A little cool now, but later it could get downright damp and uncomfortable. Jack stared out the window openings and slid his table to a far wall, away from the potential of getting rained on. He plugged a small banker's desk lamp into one of the batteries sitting under the table. He liked the old lamp. Gave the place a homey feel. Time to do a walkthrough and set up inside. Hopefully it wouldn't take that long. It was always best to get the cameras set and then settle in to observe once the sun goes down.

His flashlight was ready and waiting in his pocket, and the EMF meter was the first thing he pulled from one of the cases of equipment. A small digital camera hung from around his neck. It was only at this time that he ever regretted not utilizing a team. It'd help if someone would carry his things while he did a walkthrough of the premises. Well, you can't have it all. Solo work suited him best, even though everyone he spoke to thought he was nuts. "You're going to get hurt," they said, "and no one will be there." Well, it hasn't happened yet and he'd been on enough ghost hunts to know what he was doing. He understood their safety worries, and they had some truth to them, but he really wasn't concerned. He was smart. Careful. Willing to take a risk if it meant debunking stories of activity. People always seemed to get off on a good ghost story and usually let their imaginations run away with them. A whisper here, or some scampering there, and they would jump on the, "It's a GHOST" bandwagon. Gimmie a break. He shook his head and began the walkthrough.

His rubber soled shoes were very quiet as he made his way down the first hallway. Small pieces of cement from the broken floor slid under his feet, and he noted the chips in the plaster and peeling paint on the walls. It had been empty for about thirty years now. Kids throwing rocks at the windows, breaking in to hang out and vandalize, had really taken its toll. It didn't look like there was a solid window in the whole damn building. He pulled a piece of paper out of his pocket and glanced at a rough sketch of a floor plan. Although he gotten a blueprint from the property office, he had left it home in a stack of papers on the place. Well, he didn't really need it. Most of these sites were laid out pretty similarly. You'd have the morgue in the basement, business offices and common rooms on the first floor, maybe some patient rooms…and similar on the second floor. A doctor's office would be thrown in somewhere. Yeah, they were pretty much the same. Kinda like prisons.

The Mel-Meter was registering a pretty constant 55 degrees as Jack moved slowly and methodically down the hallway. For an unseasonably warm day, 74 degrees the last he checked, it was cool and dank inside New Castle. He passed a room that still had a half intact mirror on the wall and took a second to assess himself. Not half bad for a 50-ish, not quite balding, not quite gray haired investigator. At least he'd look good for the interviews. He sucked in his gut and walked on, watching for any unusual reading on his EMF detector and hoped that even one of the rooms would prove interesting.

It didn't appear that he would get his wish. The bedrooms on either side of the hall were typical. 10' x 12' rooms, some still with broken and bent bedframes. Any other furniture had long since been removed or ravaged by time. The common bathroom barely had any plumbing left. Vandals had pulled the sinks from the walls and smashed whatever was left. The stalls were gone; porcelain pieces scattered about. A small, walk in, shower was graffiti'd. At the end of the wing was what appeared to be an examination room. Or torture chamber. Jack shuddered. It certainly didn't look friendly. There were a few of the old, rolling metal tables, presumably to hold instruments, and a reclining…chair? Straps hung down from the arms and base of the thing, as if waiting for the next patient. Or victim. Geez. A thing like that could really make you think twice. Not of ghosts, but of what might have gone on there in years past. Ah, but that's just my imagination, Jack thought. Too many late night horror movies. He shook off the creeps that the room gave him and moved on.

More and more graffiti covered the walls as he walked deeper into the asylum. New Castle had had more than its share of issues with vandalism and thefts. Not that there was anything to steal anymore, but everyone wanted a souvenir. A chair, a piece of plaster, something to prove they had the balls to go farther than the last guy into the bowels of the building.

Behind what he thought was the door to the basement opened into what must've been the laundry room. Same dirty beige walls, but with a few rolling bins for soiled linens. Like the ones you see in movies. Nothing extraordinary, or even interesting. Except for the spike on the Mel-Meter. In the middle of the room, the meter jumped from 0.0 to 7.1 mG. Definitely not what he expected. It lasted only a second, but enough to notice. A malfunction? Battery issue? There should be no EMF in this place. No electricity, no appliances. The only thing with a chance of setting it off should be his own equipment…which wasn't set up yet. Even his phone was in airplane mode. He went back to the spot, but whatever had made the spike was gone. Jack made a mental note to put one of his cameras there.

He followed the graffiti to the end of the hallway and found what he was looking for. The door leading down to the basement and morgue was beside an old, unused and, more than likely, broken elevator. He pried the elevator doors about a foot apart and shined his flashlight into the shaft. Jack craned his neck to see into the space above him. Cobwebs and bugs, decayed wiring and dust. The usual. No groaning or growling entity bent on his destruction. The stairs were equally dull, with the barest echo of his own footsteps following him.

A simple wooden sign at the bottom of the stairs declared, "Morgue," in black letters. He touched the hospital-esque metal door. It was the kind with the wire mesh safety glass in the windows. They used to use it in old elementary schools. Jack gave the door a shove. For a moment, it refused to budge, then swung open with a scraping sound. The floor had probably heaved a bit over the years of disuse. It stuck wide open. He tested it a few times to see how easily it moved. He wasn't about to get stuck inside an old abandoned morgue, with no one expecting him anywhere until next week. You needed to be smart when you worked alone.

The morgue was small. Smaller than he had envisioned. Some counter space and cabinets lined the side walls, an autopsy table in the middle of the room, and on the back wall was the door to the cold room. Cadaver room. Whatever you wanted to call it. The place where they kept the bodies until they needed them. He figured the whole thing couldn't have been more than 12' x 14'. Jack walked around the room, leaving extra space around the autopsy table. Not because he was squeamish over the multiple bodies that would have had their blood drained there, but more because he was a germophobe. The thought of the bacteria that might be hanging around after all those years gave him the absolute creeps. He snapped some pictures of the table with a shudder and proceeded to give a quick look in the refrigeration room. Or what used to be refrigerated. Still, the whole area seemed a bit chillier than the rest of the rooms he had been in, but that goes without saying in a basement.

Adjacent to the morgue was another medical-type room with a connecting door. Stretchers and what looked like surgical equipment were scattered about. Odd that these things would still be there after so much time, but perhaps the vandals had chickened out before reaching it. He started opening the cabinet doors one by one. Empty. Empty. Empty. The last cabinet held a small, metal box. Locked. Jack turned it this way and that, examining the hinges, and he could hear something small, possibly metal, sliding inside it. He decided to bring it back to basecamp and see if he could get it open. Who knew? It might prove to be the most interesting find of the evening. Or at least a distraction.

On the hallway wall, more graffiti, peeling paint, and what might have been an old bulletin board. It was hard to tell anymore. Time and destruction had obliterated most of what might have been posted in the past. Jack stopped in his tracks and peered into the only other room in the basement. A waiting room of some sort; it was a large, broken tiled open area. He could see the men, women, amusing themselves while they waited for their names to be called. Some discolored drawings, probably done by patients, were still taped to the walls. They were faded images of flowers, stick figures, and the tape that held them was yellowed and brittle. The dust was thick and the air heavy. He didn't like this room. There was no reason; he just didn't LIKE this room. He turned on his rubbered heel and left.

As he went back up the staircase, he trailed a finger along the wall, watching some of the muted green paint flake and fall to the tile below. The whole area carried the scent of what he assumed were embalming chemicals, odd after all these years, but not entirely impossible. New Castle was in operation for nearly 40 years. Some smells you don't get out. Like smoke in an old hotel room or when your dog gets skunked. And this was worse, for longer.

Jack emerged back onto the first floor, half expecting the air to be fresher, but even though he could see the trees outside bending in the breezes, the air inside was still. Stale. The way you'd imagine an old building should smell; that odor of erosion that time seems to bring to all things abandoned. He checked his watch. 6:10. He'd need to move quickly through the second floor if he was going to have time to set up his equipment before dark.

Jack placed the locked box on his folding chair and headed toward the staircase to the second floor. He jumped when he heard it hit the floor. Not from nerves; he was calm to a fault. He just didn't expect the crash that it made from such a small box. He must've set it on an angle, somehow had it off balance when he put it down. Eh. He shrugged it off and went up the steps, leaving it on the floor where it fell. At least it couldn't fall from there.

More of the same awaited him on the second floor. Some patient rooms, the same dreary paint, plaster giving away, and graffiti scrawled across the walls. But as he continued farther down the hallway, the graffiti seemed more…serious. At the end of the hallway, it turned into symbols. Drawn, or painted, even carved into the floor. Assorted pentagrams, inverted crosses. "Huh," Jack muttered. "Guess they never heard of the Cross of Peter. It's not evil, guys."

Half burned black candles surrounded a circle on the floor, with what looked like animal bones in the center. Damn kids. Probably chicken bones to scare their friends into thinking it was an animal sacrifice to Satan or something. He looked a little closer and moved some of the items around with the toe of his sneaker. A book, some garbage they left behind. A cool breeze passed him. He glanced into the room to his right, out the window. The storm hadn't fully hit yet, but would soon. He'd snap a few more pics and head down for the equipment.

Jack snapped the final pic and turned. He nearly slipped as his foot landed on a board of some sort. "Shit," he muttered. "How did I not see that?" Picking it up, he saw it was a Ouija board. Great. Add this and the devil worship from story to definite. At least he could add this to his "reveal." The audience would be all over it. "Oooh, did you find a demon??? I've heard those spirit boards are EVIL. They open PORTALS, you know!" All the buzz words, no substance. That always bugged the shit out of him. He decided to bring the board back to his base of operations. He looked through the things the vandals had left and found the planchette. He could do some interesting experiments with it all and get it on video. Show the people that it's not what they all envision. Sheesh, it's made by Parker Bros., for God's sake!

Jack made his way back downstairs. The box was now in the middle of the room, square in the middle of the floor. Don't tell me those kids are back and messing around. That's all I need. He sighed, picked it up and put it and the Ouija board onto his table. "Stay," he told it. "If anyone is here, come on out! I've got too much to do to deal with your shit!" Nothing. Maybe they had gone already. Gotten bored waiting for him to show up. "I'll be here all night." He mimicked dropping a mic and got down to business.

He slowly got all of his equipment out and moved his chair to the other side of the metal table. He never liked to sit with his back toward a room. Somehow it always felt better to have a wall at his back. Instinct, he figured. Safety. He couldn't sleep with his head at the wrong end of the bed, either. The end closest to a doorway. Or let his feet stick out of the covers at night. He chuckled and got the DVR, monitor, and laptop plugged into the batteries; voice recorders ready. Everything on and running. He tested each camera, making sure the picture was stable and clear. Time to get everything placed.

Jack fed out the camera wire behind him as he walked down the hallway toward the patient rooms. 60 feet of wire per camera, not bad. He should be able to cover every room he wanted to. He'd leave some motion sensors in a few areas, and carry a voice recorder with him as he went. A few EVP sessions, then he'd settle in at base to do a few experiments and watch the cameras. Dinner and note taking. Coffee and camera watching. Yeah, definitely going to need some coffee.

Back at base camp, Jack checked the camera feeds. A four camera split screen with great views of the laundry, basement waiting room and medical room, and the second floor "demon" area shone on his monitor in the lamplight. He'd left the connecting door to the morgue open and could make out the end of the autopsy table. A voice recorder was running in the morgue itself, on the counter, of course. He wasn't touching that table if he didn't have to. He leaned back in his chair, hands locked behind his head, satisfied.

He watched the monitor for a couple of minutes and then pulled over his cooler. It was time for a thermos of coffee and a sandwich. Fuel up before heading into the dark to duel with the unseen. He chuckled again. Loved this. He took a bite of his hero, savoring the heat of the hot peppers with the ham and provolone, and washed it down with some, well, lukewarm coffee. Not quite a steaming hot cup from Dunkin Donuts, but it'd keep him going for a while. America may run on Dunkin, but he usually ran on gas station brews that would melt a spoon if you left it in too long. He kept taking bites of his sandwich, swigs of his coffee, all the while glancing at the monitor. He took a spiral notebook out of his bag and began to thumb through the pages.

Rumors. Folklore. Stories told out of parents' fears of having their children get too close to a place where the mentally unhinged resided. He pieced together some of the usual stories from the reticent townspeople. The ones who may have gotten close to the building, out of curiosity during the day, or on a dare at night. A few people had offered up some stories here and there as he poked around for information and he was able to find a newspaper article or two; some kids had gotten scared out of their wits when they sneaked in one night. Nothing substantial or substantiated. Shadows seen, noises heard. No stories of a lady in white here. More like crazed patients or axe wielding interns and maniacal doctors.

He had tracked down one of the teens, Danny M. They met at a diner and he bought the kid a burger. Danny kept his sweatshirt and denim jacket on the entire time, and looked as if he might bolt if things got too uncomfortable. He hesitated, at first, but then the words came quickly.

It was awful, man. That place is insane. I went up with my buddies one night, you know, just having some fun. We got there about 10, 11 o'clock. Had a couple of beers first, but we weren't drunk. I can tell you that. We all went in together, three of us. I wasn't scared, at first. We were all joking around, busting on each other, laughing. We had a couple of flashlights and were checking out all the rooms, making up stories about what must've gone on there… you know, I bet the doc's did some awful shit in there.

We went through the first floor like it was nothing. We didn't pull out that plumbing, though. Saw it, but didn't do it. A lot of kids have been there before us, you know? That wasn't us. We decided to go to the basement next. We really wanted to see the morgue. Everyone talks about it, you know? Like you've got balls to go in there. We were daring each other to go alone, but all went at once. It was creepy, especially that room at the end, but nothing we couldn't handle. It was fun, but kinda disappointing, you know? But that second floor, that second floor…. Damn.

You been there? We went up the stairs and it was pretty much the same stuff. Yeah, we did a little "urban redecorating," if you know what I mean. I had a can of spray paint and yeah, we wrote a little. You're not using my name, right? You said you wouldn't. I don't need trouble, man. Well, we were writing and I found that devil worship stuff. Saw it. Scary shit, man. I could've left right then, but we hung out there a while. Nobody wanted to pussy out, you hear me? There were these black candles and we lit them. Just to check it out, and Mike, well, he wanted to try that Ouija board as soon as he seen it. I wasn't good with it, but wasn't gonna be the one to beg out. Well, it scared the crap outta me. That fucking thing, you know that thing you put your fingers on, whatever they call it, that thing MOVED. I swear. I'm swearing, man. On a stack of bibles. Whatever you want. I SWEAR.

Jack remembered that conversation well. The kid was wiping his hands off on his shirt like he could still feel that vibration. As if he could smear away the feeling, get rid of that residual wrongness.

At first I told the guys to cut that shit out, but they said it wasn't them. It MOVED. I asked if something was there with us, to talk to us. Give us a sign. I swear it vibrated and then started to slide. Never again, man. I won't mess with that shit. We threw that board and backed off. Blamed each other for moving it, but we KNEW. I knew. We stiff walked outta there. Like a fast walk... almost a run, but that would've been a pussy move. And I know I heard footsteps behind us when we left that floor. I know what I heard, man.

He asked if they had seen anything, took any pictures. The kid paused and looked around nervously. Jack gave him time, let him breathe. He went really quiet.

I'll tell you this, and if I'm lyin' I'm dyin'.

Another pause.

I glanced behind us when we were down those stairs. The others didn't, but I did.

Pause.

There was a shadow. Had to be like 7' tall. Coming up behind us. Like a man shape. No face. Just a big, dark shadow. And it was gaining on us.

I pushed the guys and yelled, "RUN!" We booked down the steps and out the main entrance. But before I made it out the door, it TOUCHED me. My shoulder. It was the coldest thing I ever felt. It was like it went right into my bones. Like a hand of ice water, and it melted into my flesh. I can't describe it, man, but I'll never go near that place again. Don't even want to see it.

That thing TOUCHED me.

His eyes were wild with the memory. Jack sat in silence. The kid sat back and tried to relax. Jack could tell he believed what he was saying and wondered what might have actually touched the kid. After a night of scaring each other and walking through the dark, creeping each other out, he could see where imaginations could take hold. He wasn't ready to jump on the spirit/shadow man bandwagon yet.

He leaned back in his chair again, contemplating the kid's story. He knew there were things he couldn't explain, that he might deem paranormal. But he also knew he could debunk 99% of the stories of activity. Most people freaked out over nothing, attributed activity to everything except what it truly was...heat going through loose pipes, "fear cage" phenomenon from too much EMF in an area,… so many natural reasons. He was sure the kid had just gotten himself wound up. Pretty sure, anyway. Whatever it was, though, he'd figure it out.

He took off his glasses and ran a hand across his eyes and the bridge of his nose before replacing them. He could hear the wind picking up, but the rain still held off. "It was a dark and stormy night," he said, sighing. He smiled to himself as he stood up, picked up a voice recorder, KII meter, thermal camera, and put them into a small bag. He took his flashlight out of his pocket. Turning the flashlight on, he said, "Let's get this show on the road," and walked into the darkness of the first floor hallway.

Jack walked past the patient rooms, stopping only to snap a few pictures of the room with the mirror where he had assessed his appearance earlier. He enjoyed mirror photos. They always held a fascination with the public, as if they could see through them and into another world. People would look at his photos and always find odd little things to question. Is this a ghost? A demon? Are these EYES? He'd chuckle and explain away their questions with a scientific explanation and they'd be impressed with his expertise. It was a give and take, he felt.

The rest of the patient rooms held little interest for him; he might visit them much later in the night. He really wanted to start his investigation in the laundry room, where he had gotten the initial EMF spike. It was out of place and, as such, was like a knot in his brain. He needed to untie the knot, debunk the spike, so he could set it to rest in his mind. It could be as simple as an equipment malfunction, but, in case there was something in the room that set it off, he wanted to get down there first.

He approached the room cautiously, checking the doorframe, and then systematically going around the room, checking the walls, bins, floor, everything, to see if there was anything leftover from another time, a vandal, something, that could initiate an energy fluctuation. He found nothing. Knot still tied. He placed a motion sensor in the middle of the floor and sat down at the edge of the room, back resting against the wall. Of course. He turned on the voice recorder.

"Is there anyone here with me tonight? Anyone who would like to speak?" Other investigators had told him he should start with a prayer of protection or at least a visualization of white light, something. He could never bring himself to do that. It seemed hokey to him. Not his style. And, what did he need protection from? An errant energy from a deceased person who didn't know to find the light? Yeah, he didn't think so.

He waited, to give whatever might be around the chance to gather energy enough to project an answer. Unlike some investigators, he didn't sit there, earphones in, stopping the recorder, rewinding, listening, trying to discern an answer and then going on. He'd rather conduct the session, listen later, and do a proper analysis. Some swore by the "ghost box," radio communication. He couldn't be bothered with that. Too much static and controversy over what was being picked up... bits and blips of radio stations vs. spirits manipulating the radio energy to speak. Ehh. It did give some interesting...results? But, again, the jury was incredibly way, way out on that one. He'd stick to a voice recorder and the calm, quiet of the building. He had gotten EVP's before. Even debunked a few. The rest remained intriguing knots, still tightly tied, in his head. Voices from beyond. The ones he couldn't debunk were the best. Absolutely amazing.

"I'm not here to harm you. I only want to document your existence. If there's anything you want to say, now's the time. Just get as close as you can to this device," he held the recorder out in front of him, then set it on the floor. He turned the KII on, and its lights flashed across its face from green to red. "This device will let me know that you're around. The closer you get to it, the lights will light up in sequence. Let's see if you can get it to at least light up green." He placed it on the floor next to the recorder. And waited.

"How long have you been here?" Pause.

"What year is it?" Pause. He had a set list of questions in his head and used them for a lot of his investigations. He was thorough. The only time he waivered from his mental list was when there was some sort of historical significance to the type of activity reported...if it was tied to the prior owners or a specific tragedy or something. Like putting a recorder on the field at Gettysburg. You know you're going to ask about the battle and the soldiers. Here...what could you ask? Were you committed? He tried not to provoke. Not out of fear, but out of respect. He sort of figured that if someone was dead but still hanging around, they needed the same respect as anyone else. As if he were walking into a stranger's house, just because they were dead didn't mean they didn't have feelings. Or feel that you were the intruder.

"How long did you live here?" Pause.

"Did you work here? Do the laundry?"

"What is your name?" Pause.

Before he could ask the next question, the motion sensor gave out a long beep and the green light on the KII lit.

"Well, now. Thanks. Is that you, or do I need to change the battery on that device?"

It lit, again. A little brighter, and the next light lit.

"Cool. We're off to a good start. Maybe you could answer some yes or no questions for me." Pause. "I'll ask a question. You light up the lights for yes. Do nothing for no. Deal?"

The lights lit.

"Nice. Have you been here many years?"

Green.

"Were you male?"

Nothing.

"Were you female?"

Greens, a yellow.

"If you don't mind, I'll call you Miss. Alright, Miss. Were you a patient here?"

A pause, but then the lights came alive again.

"Did you like it here?"

Nothing.

"Was it a nice place to live?"

Nothing.

"Did you die here?"

The lights lit crazily and the KII slid about a foot across the floor, while the motion sensor kept blaring its awful beep. Jack's heart skipped a beat. He was thoroughly into this. Could someone be tampering with his KII? He didn't think it was possible, but there was a camera running in this room. There WAS a camera! He was thrilled to potentially have caught the equipment moving on video. This night could prove to be worth it after all. He leaned over and turned off the sensor. He'd let the KII do the signaling.

"If you can do that, I hope you're also talking into my recorder. Leave me a message, please, Miss. Tell me how you died.

Your name. The year. Whatever you can say. I'll document it. Write it up. Let people know. Can you try for me?"

The entire face of the KII lit up brightly, then slid across the room, hitting the wall, as if it had been kicked. "Hey! Treat the equipment nicely, please, Miss. It's not cheap." He went and got the KII, placing it back beside the recorder.

He sat in the dark for another half an hour, asking the occasional question, waiting for something more to happen, but the KII was silent. Hopefully, who or whatever that was hadn't broken it…and, hopefully, there was something more on the voice recording. He grabbed the thermal camera, took a few shots, and kicked himself for not grabbing it earlier, while the KII was acting up. It would've been amazing to see what he might have captured had he thought of it. Jack sighed. Well, you can't think of everything. Even in the field. Happens. It was a shame he didn't have someone he could share it with, but it always jazzed him to present his findings later on. HIS findings. He wasn't one to share the limelight or accolades. He guessed he wasn't a team player.

He then had an idea. He held out the KII and asked, "Miss? Is your name Carla?" He remembered seeing the name on one of the tombstones out back. There was a moment of waiting and the KII lit wildly. YES! He nailed it. Coincidence? Maybe. He couldn't wait to review everything he had captured so far.

"Thank you, Carla. Have a good evening. I'm going to move around to some other areas… you're welcome to come with me, if you'd like." He gathered his equipment and stepped into the hallway, keeping the recorder going as he walked. "Are you with me, Carla? You can still talk to me. I have this little device going," he held it farther ahead of himself, "and it'll still record your voice. I'll be able to hear you later."

"Did you used to take the elevator?" He went down the stairs, plaster pieces still grinding under his feet. It felt much darker as he went into the basement. The sun had long since gone down, but deeper into the asylum, devoid of windows, his flashlight illuminated his path and not much else. It was as though the darkness of the basement swallowed up the beam. The dark fascinated him. The lure of shadows made by the flashlight, how your eyes would make you think you saw things that weren't there. Or were they? He chuckled. "You with me, Carla?" He didn't mind trying to encourage the spirit, or whatever it was. If it was something that could be encouraged and not something he'd end up debunking. Either way, he couldn't wait to review the recordings later.

Jack went for the morgue first. With the KII and the voice recorder safely on a counter, he took some thermal photos around the room. Nothing jumped out at him. He smiled at the thought. "What do you think of this room, Miss Carla? Were you ever here?" Nothing. No lights. "Did I lose you, darling?" He thought he saw a shadow go by in the hallway and quickly moved to the doorway to look out. Must be his eyes.

"Anyone else here with me tonight? Any friends of Carla?" Only darkness. "Pretty dead in here tonight," he muttered. Now the KII reacted. "You like my humor? Good. At least someone does." He sat down to continue questioning whatever was energizing his meter. The autopsy table reflected the light from his flashlight too brightly and he turned it off.

"Do you like the dark? That light was too bright." The KII lit. Not as strongly as earlier, but it was definitely picking up on something. On what, was anybody's guess. At least it was making an interesting night.

"Were you a doctor here?" Nothing.

"Was your autopsy done here?" Nothing.

Jack started to wonder if he had any true responses at all, or if there were somehow some random spikes of EMF running through the place. He'd need to go online and see if he could find some reference to the wiring of the building. Maybe talk to the owners, although they probably had no idea. He would've thought that all the wiring was gone or destroyed by now, and, with the electricity shut off to the building, there should be no EMF anywhere. Well, he'd look into it.

He strolled into the adjoining medical room. "Anyone here? Were you examined here?" He stood for a minute, peering through the gloom. Again, he thought he caught motion in the hallway out of the corner of his eye. And, again, he moved to the doorway. Nothing. "Well, I'm going to move on. It seems something wants my attention farther down."

KII and voice recorder in hand, he stopped in the hallway, staring into the large, open waiting room. There was no way he wanted to go sit in the room and talk to anything. He shook his head. That wasn't like him. He never got cold feet on an investigation. Time to stop watching horror movies, he guessed. There was no killer clown hiding behind a support beam waiting to axe him. Still, he had to will his feet to move. Sheesh! He'd have to see a shrink or something. How ridiculous!

Step by step brought him closer to the room, and he realized he was inching along. Okay, time to grow a set. He took a deep breath and forced himself on. He started snapping pics, figuring it would get him back into control again. It worked. He was there to do a job. He was there to figure things out. Not vice versa. He was there to debunk and document, if there was anything to document. There… he was nearly back. So odd that he waivered, though. He took a deep breath and noticed, peppermint? It was fairly strong. How had he not noticed it earlier? Damn, he was off his game tonight. Maybe he was coming down with something. That might explain it. He was getting sick and hadn't realized it yet. Something.

"Did you like peppermint, Miss Carla? Did your friends?"

"Did they give you peppermint while you waited to see the doctor?" It was more likely they gave it out to try to hide the other smells in the basement. How sick was that? He could just see a room full of people, some sitting, maybe rocking in their seats. Others pacing, nervous. Maybe drawing to pass the time until…what? And that smell of peppermint,…maybe they sprayed it somehow? Why had he not noticed it before? He walked more determinedly around the room, forgetting his initial discomfort, as he searched for the source of the odor. As quickly as it had hit him, it was gone. Perplexing. If he had been in a building with electricity, heating, he could have passed it off as a scent coming through a vent. Even an old spill of a peppermint liquid could rekindle itself under the right conditions, even years later. But this was odd.

"What did you do here?"

"Can you give me a sign that you're here? Move something, bang on the wall?" After about 30 seconds, he thought he could hear a faint rapping from the distance. Tap tap tap.

"Was that you tapping? Or a squirrel dropping a nut? Can you do it again for me? Can you come a little closer? Do it a little louder?" Again, the wait. Again, a faint tapping from father off in the building. "If that's you, you've gotta be pretty far off. Are you answering me or playing around?"

SLAM. He jumped. It sounded as if the morgue door had slammed shut, or a large book had dropped from about eight feet in the air to the floor. He half ran, half power walked down the hallway to the morgue. The door was still open, exactly how he had propped it earlier that day. No other door was shut. Nothing had fallen. He did a quick walkthrough of the medical room and even forced open the elevator doors. Nothing. There had to be something he missed. Something that had slipped, fell, closed. He thought for a moment that it could've been a door upstairs, but knew that would've been a much duller sound. At least it would be on the voice recorder, and if something fell that he couldn't account for now, it should be on the video. Fingers crossed, he thought.

"That was a great sound. Carla! Did you throw something?" He was back to the investigator he always was, bold and ready for anything. "What'd you slam? Come a little closer and let me know."

He walked back into what he now thought of as the "Peppermint Room." He let the camera rest on his chest and pulled out his thermal cam. "I'm taking some special photos, Carla. They capture the heat energy that's around. If you're here, let's see if we can get a pic. Can you make an area cooler? This cam will pick it up. Try for me, girl."

He snapped 15 or 20 pics before deciding to move on, fairly satisfied with himself. "I'm heading upstairs now," he said to no one in particular. "You coming?" He waited, politely, and went back up to the first floor.

Before continuing on, he stopped at his equipment table. He checked the monitors for a few minutes while he uploaded the audio file and pictures from both cameras. Jack grabbed the thermos and swallowed the rest of the coffee, room temperature at best now, so pretty chilled. So much for the thermos. He'd have to get a new one. After pawing through his cooler, he settled back in his chair with a bag of cookies. "Get some trail mix or some power bars," his friends told him. "Something healthy!" Hah! Give him some caffeine and a sugar rush and he'd be fine. Chocolate chips...the fuel of investigators everywhere! He smiled to himself. He jotted down a few things in his notebook about the first session in the basement. After some time on the second floor, he would go back to the morgue area and see if he could kick up some more activity.

Jack turned his attention to the box on the table. He shoved the Ouija board out of the way to make some room in front of him. He examined the box, turning it slowly in his hands. It was only about a 4" x 6", beat up, gray metal box. Nothing overly remarkable, nothing to make it stand out in any way. But why had it not been found before now? Opened, taken as a souvenir? He tried the small, silver colored lock with his finger. It was the kind that needed the little silver key, like the boxes they sold for ten bucks in Walmart. Cheap. He pulled his key ring from his pocket and snapped open a little folding knife. One good stick with that and the lock popped open.

The box itself stuck shut, but he pried it open without any difficulty. The only thing inside was a ring. It was gold, and definitely a man's signet ring. He leaned closer with it under the lamp. Engraved. JPB. He sat back, surprised, yet not really. Coincidences happen all the time. Was kind of a cool that it'd have his initials. JPB. Jack Phillip Barnes. He turned it over a few times in his hand before slipping it onto the ring finger of his left hand. Fit like a glove. Or a ring that was made for him. He chuckled. "Like out of an obviously written movie." He pushed himself back from the table. "Well, it works for me! Time to go explore." He flipped the lid of the box closed with a clang and grabbed his bag.

Maybe once this investigation was done, he could get himself an intern. Someone to train, who would put in the hours of evidence review that were necessary after each investigation, who would carry things. Like a golf caddy! Yes. He would get an investigation caddy. Chuckling, Jack tucked the last few cookies back into the cooler and dropped the lid into place. A shame he didn't bring a second thermos of coffee. He had some bottled water, though. Not the same, but at least he wouldn't be thirsty. Still, it went against his grain to buy bottles of water, just like he hated to pay for television. Water is free, signals should be, too. But, before he started ranting in his head about paying the cable company, he started repacking his bag to head upstairs.

As he stood, he noticed a dark shadow move across camera 1's field of view. Not a shape, but a darkness that partially obscured the video for a second and then was gone. He quickly noted the time in his notebook so he could check it out in review later. Camera 1 was the one recording on the second floor. He slung his bag over his shoulder and, at the last second, grabbed the Ouija board and planchette. "This could be interesting," he said, and headed up the stairs.

The first thing he noticed as he topped the stairs was the smell. Decay. As if an animal had died and was now becoming worm food. He cocked his head toward one of the glassless windows and could hear rain coming down. Maybe an animal came in to get out of the storm and had died? He exhaled. Nope. Nothing could smell that bad that fast. He'd have to check each room. Maybe he missed something on the first walkthrough and the wind and dampness were recirculating the odor.

Jack stopped at the first doorway and shined his light into the little room. The wind had picked up a bit and "it was a dark and stormy night" was echoing in his mind. He went to the next room. It didn't matter how long it took, he had all night. As he moved along, the smell seemed to subside. Either that or he had become habituated to it. He snapped some pics as he went, especially of the graffiti, and some long shots to the "demon area," or "dark area,"...he needed to come up with a good name for it. Something to intrigue his followers. "The area where worshippers of the dark lord tried to conjure his minions." He cracked a smile. He did amuse himself at times.

"Are you with me, Carla?" he called out. The patient rooms were getting pretty boring; shining a light, seeing nothing that would lead to a smell, going on. He spent some extra time in the bathroom, giving a thorough look through the plumbing, or what was left of it. Maybe the kids who had been in doing the Ouija stuff had taken a shit or a piss. He didn't know how recently they had been there, but it probably wasn't that anyway. Then, it occurred to him that the odor might belong to whatever the bones were at the end of the hallway. That's got to be it. Maybe there was more to that pile of bones than he had thought. Jack quit checking the bedrooms and went straight to the "minions of Gozur area." He shook his head. No Ghostbusters references, please.

"Do you know anything about what happened here?" The green light was still on his recorder, so everything was working. "Can you tell me what those kids were trying to do here?"

The decaying odor had gone. He pushed the animal bones around with the toe of his sneaker, but no smell rose up from them. He decided lighting some of the candles would add an eerier feeling to the video. He lit one after another, carefully setting them down, watching the way it changed the lighting in the hallway. The shadows and flickering lights danced with each other. Definitely creepier, he thought. Jack turned on the motion sensor and sat down to continue his EVP session.

"My name is Jack. What's yours?"

"Have you been here long?"

"Were you a patient here?"

"Did you have something to do with what the kids were doing?"

"Did they bring you in from somewhere else?" He paused. For a second, he thought he could hear footsteps at the end of the hall. "Is that you, Carla? Did you come up to visit?"

He waited. Everything was very quiet. He almost thought it was too quiet, but he hated that term. How could it be "too quiet?" Things could only be as quiet as was possible for them to be. No noise, no movement, nothing to make a sound...it would just be quiet. It couldn't be too quiet. The cold of the floor tiles started to seep into his ass. He shifted and put the Ouija board on the floor in front of him. He set the planchette on the board.

"Well, now. Let's try a little experiment."

"I've never done this, so, if you have, feel free to help." He shined the light on the board. It was your stereotypical Ouija board. The same beige background and dark, fancy lettering. Yes and No in the corners, the alphabet across the main part of the board. Everyone he knew who was into the paranormal was against the "spirit board." They felt it opened portals to other dimensions, other planes. From

Parker Bros.? What'd they do, make a deal with the devil? "Here, sweetie. Take this toy, go to your room and summon the devil and all his minions. Run along now, Mommy loves you." Give me a fucking break. But it'd make a great experiment for the video camera. He shifted again, making certain everything he did would be center frame for the recording.

Jack propped his flashlight up so he could use both hands and still see the board. He lightly placed his fingers on the planchette and asked, "Okay. Is there anyone here who would like to communicate tonight?" Another flit of a shadow in his peripheral vision.

"Is that you? You can talk to me through this board, you know." He sat listening to the pouring rain, calmly waiting for something to happen. "I don't want to bother you. Just want to prove that you're here. I've never used one of these things. Can you tell me what to do?"

"I found this great ring in a box in the basement. Was it yours? What are your initials?" At that moment, almost imperceptibly, he thought he could feel the planchette vibrate; there was the slightest motion on the board.

"Is that you? Or my imagination? Something psychological, maybe it's me. If it's you, can you muster some more energy to communicate with me?" The vibration was more noticeable now. It was as if an energy was flowing into his fingers from the planchette. It was an unusual feeling. He was trying to pin down a description of it in his mind so he could write about it later.

The planchette began to slowly slide across the board.

"J." Slide. "P." Slide. Pause.

"Come on, you're killing me…" Jack said under his breath.

Slide. "B."

"Bingo! So…" he paused. "How do we tell if this is you, some supernatural… something… perhaps from beyond the grave, or if it's just me, influencing the results?" He thought for a moment. He'd probably end up at a psychologist's office, interview the guy and research the likelihood that it was his own mind, sending a vibrational "desire" to his fingertips. At least that'd be a great debunk for the night. He'd have to book an appointment when he got home tomorrow.

"Well. It looks as if we have the same initials. I guess it's not you, eh, Miss Carla? Well, hello, whoever you are. Can you spell out your name for me?"

The planchette slowly circled the perimeter of the board, circumventing the alphabet. It made about three loops and then settled on the word, "No," in the corner.

"Either you're not willing to share, or it's just me, not knowing what to make up. There's GOT to be something you can tell me to prove you are what you are. What can you tell me from the spirit realm?"

Again, the planchette slid. A little faster, a little more forceful, if he could call it that. Determined. A little more determined, perhaps.

"G. E. T." Pause.

"Get? Get what?" He was thoroughly enjoying this dynamic and hoped the camera had a good focus on the board itself.

"O."

"U."

"T." It stopped.

He rolled his eyes. "Get out. Well, that's fucking original." Jack muttered. "Give me something better than that."

"D. I."

"Yes? Go on. D…I…"

"E."

Jack rolled his eyes again. "Die. Nice. Not Caspar the friendly ghost, are you. All right, I think I'm done talking to you. Carla. Are you here?"

"I'm trying to talk with Carla from the laundry room. Are you here?"

He had just about given up on this game when the planchette started to move once again. It slid straight to the "Yes," in the corner.

"Good girl! Now, we have something. Carla. What can you tell me about yourself? How old are you?"

"1." Slide. "6."

"16? You were quite young. Do you know this J.P.B. character? Or what his name is? Whatever you can tell me would be amazing." He sat, waiting for some sort of response, as the cold from the floor seemed to reach up and move through him. He shivered. Should've grabbed his sweatshirt before he came upstairs. He didn't expect to be this cold yet.

The planchette moved. A pause, a slow circle of the board and, without warning, flew straight off and hit the wall. Jack was startled, maybe slightly uncomfortable, but not unnerved. "I take it, Carla, that either you or JPB aren't amused. Well, hopefully, we have some of your responses on the voice recorder. I think I'll go back downstairs for a bit and get warmed up. No worries, though," he looked around. "I'll be back." Jack stood, stretched, and grabbed his bag. He then gathered the planchette and the spirit board, blew out the candles, and began the long walk back to the stairs. "But I expect more communication and less throwing things when I'm back!" He called over his shoulder.

A footstep. A feeling. He whipped around, as if trying to catch someone behind him. Nothing but the graffiti on the walls and the candles, still with faint spirals of smoke above their wicks. He snapped a few pics and tried to the shake the feeling as he went down to the first floor, but it kept creeping up on him. Sliding into his thought and personal space. As if whoever JPB was, he was making sure that Jack got out. Before he got halfway down the stairs, he could hear the motion sensor's hideous beep going off on the second floor. He paused on the steps and waited for it to stop.

At base, he resisted the urge to pull up the video of his time on the second floor. There'd be time for that. Right now, he wanted to go back through the two newspaper articles and the interview with Danny to see if it was possible he missed something. There were only two articles that he had come up with; one in the Daily Sentinel and the other was in Willow Tree Weekly. He rolled his eyes. Not quite the New York Times. Filled more with Jean Simmons' award winning Blueberry Buckle recipe and that Norma Radley's granddaughter got engaged. Not that he had anything against hometown, homespun weekly coupon shoppers. He had grown up in a small town and they had a sweet, memory triggering hominess to them. But… they hardly qualified as reliable journalism sources when it came to the goings on in the area. They did, however, have their finger on the pulse of the community.

He read and reread the articles finding nothing new. One was on the asylum closing, the other was a passing Halloween piece… don't go near abandoned New Castle or you may see things that can't be unseen. Ghouls, goblins and things that go bump in the night, and you'll also be arrested, no trespassing. "Hold on a second…" he leaned in closer to the lamp light. There was a picture attached to the story, showing New Castle "back in the day." It was captioned, "James Paul Borden, employee, died on premises. Is it James who haunts New Castle Asylum?"

He slapped the paper onto the table. "NOW we have a direction. Oh, we're going to have a conversation, James, you and I." Jack leaned back in his chair, hands again behind his head. "Oh, yes. We will." Geez, he was a creepy looking dude. Although the photo was old and distorted in the way old copy machines did to pictures, the guy was truly creepy. Tall and lean, resting on a shovel and staring directly at the camera as if he was challenging the photographer to snap the shutter. He looked like an undertaker waiting to dig the next grave, or dig one up for parts.

He wished that there was some internet he could tap into to try to find out what had happened to Mr. Borden. He hated being without access to some good WiFi. It really crimped his style. If he could just jump on and search some local records on the guy… aargh. He was torturing himself. But, back to Mr. Borden. What claimed you, James? Innocent heart attack? Freak accident? Killed by a patient? Was he autopsied on the table in the basement? Jack shuddered. He guessed he'd have to spend some more time in the morgue.

He sighed. He'd have to take a quick break from it all. Nature was calling. Damn, it figured he was in a building without any working plumbing. He eyed the wind and rain outside. And that didn't make what he had to do any better. He didn't want to pee right outside the building, get soaked, or pee into unused, broken plumbing. He sure as hell wasn't going to pee in his thermos. He looked outside again, and quickly changed his mind. Well, the thermos was done anyway. Probably wouldn't even keep his pee warm for more than a minute or two. He laughed to himself. God, he felt like an asshole. He opened the thermos, unzipped and heard the loudest SLAM of the night. Metal on metal, with force. "Shit!" Nearly lost the thermos mid-stream. "Thanks, James!" He called out. "Not!" After finishing, he carefully screwed the top on the silver metal jar and placed it next to the door. He'd take it out in the morning.

He kicked himself for not being in front of the monitors watching when the slam happened. He'd have a lot to look for on the review. It would've been really cool to see, and then he'd be able to go and probably debunk it. Now, he only could figure that it probably happened on the second floor. Sheesh. This place was turning out to be more interesting than he thought. New Castle had potential. Paranormal potential? Even he had to give in to what was going on. Still, he'd debunk what he could…and research the hell out of what remained. There are more things in heaven and earth. Shakespeare had it right.

He put on his sweatshirt, grabbed a cookie and got ready to head to the basement.

Jack strode into the morgue, a man with a plan; recorder going, KII held out in front of him. "James? You here?" He paused, in case there was an unheard response. He walked the perimeter of the autopsy table. "I think we need to have a talk, James. What happened here? How did you die at New Castle?"

He put the KII down on the counter and grabbed his camera. He took a pic of his hand. "It looks like I'm wearing your ring. These are your initials, right?" He took another pic. "Come on, James. Let me help. Let me tell your story. What can you tell me?"

Jack leaned against the wall, waiting. "What do you think, James? Or are you a Jim? What was your job here?" After about twenty minutes, he said, "How about the waiting room, you like that better? Let's go." He pushed off the wall and the KII spiked to yellow. "You want the waiting room? Is that you?" The morgue door that he had stuck open, closed with a bang as he stepped into the medical room, and Jack tripped into the wall. "Thanks, a lot." He rubbed his shoulder. A little uncomfortable, but not deterred, he walked back into the morgue to check the door. It probably hadn't been secured enough and finally gave way, but as he pulled and pried, it wouldn't budge. He took the long way around from the medical room and, with all his force, it wouldn't move an inch. A few more pics. He stared at the door for a minute, considering. He wasn't sure how it could have swung back hard enough to have settled in so tightly. It was almost as if, almost, something was holding it closed. Or stuck. He'd go with stuck. For now.

"Okay, guys," he said, under his breath, as he walked into the waiting room. "Show me something." The room didn't feel quite as uninviting as it had earlier in the day, and the peppermint smell was gone. Nothing. No KII hits, footsteps, bangs, slams. He yawned, more from boredom than sleepiness, and checked his watch. 2:30 a.m. With only a few hours of night left, he decided to get back up to the second floor for one last try at James. He grabbed the Ouija board on the way past base camp. Second time's the charm.

He came out of the stairwell and the air on the second floor hit him like a wall. Stale, thick, and just a hint of the decay smell he had gotten on his last visit. "James, James, James..." he whispered. "You here, James?" The dampness from the rain coming in gave his sneakers a little squeak, squeak as he walked down the hallway. He felt watched, as if with every rubbery squelch he was calling attention to himself. Like wearing corduroy pants and walking through a crowded room. Swoosh, swoosh. Embarrassing.

The temperature seemed to be dropping as he got down to the end of the hallway. A cool breeze circled him and he picked a piece of the floor to set up shop, his back to the wall, of course. He wanted to try this session with the Ouija board at a different angle to the camera. Always a scientist at heart, another angle for an experiment couldn't hurt. He set the KII and voice recorder on the floor beside him and put his hands in the kangaroo pocket of his hoodie. It was getting cold.

"Is there anyone here with me tonight who would like to make his presence known? Carla? James? Anyone else?"

You had to have patience when investigating, he'd found. Hours of sitting in the dark, waiting for anything to happen. Most of the time, it didn't. It was almost as bad as reviewing recordings, watching hour upon hour of video, unwavering staircases, unmoving chairs. Tedium at its best. But still it fascinated him and drove him to keep searching for the unknown... or, debunking the debunk-able, he chuckled, and enlightening the gullible. He wanted that one undisputable piece of evidence that would blow the doors off the paranormal world. Damn, it was cold. He blew on his fingers.

"Are you making it cold? There are easier ways of letting me know you're here." Other investigators swore by temperature changes as a spirit manifesting and "sucking" the energy out of the atmosphere for their own devices. He'd run into traveling cold spots before, but so far, nothing had truly correlated between temperature changes and the moments of activity he'd experienced. But if this kept going, he'd have to find some gloves. Or a parka. He glanced out the window to make sure a freak snow storm hadn't kicked up.

"How about this for a test… how about you make it warmer? I wouldn't complain."

He heard, something. Something at the end of the hall? He shined his flashlight as far as the light would reach, but needed something more powerful. He shook his head. All the kick ass equipment he had and a crappy dime store flashlight in his hand.

"That you? Come a little closer. I'd like to get you on camera."

A…footstep? He peered into the darkness. Done messing around, he pulled over the Ouija board. "Okay, James, if that is your real name. Let's start a dialogue." He put his fingers lightly on the planchette. "Are you James P. Borden?"

That now familiar vibration started under his fingertips. Still not sure if he was the cause, but leaning toward NOT, Jack continued. "Are you James P. Borden?" The planchette slid to, "Yes."

"Thank you. Finally. I heard you worked here." A quick, small circle, and back to the, "Yes."

"Did you like it here?" Nothing.

"How did you die?" Nothing.

"Did you know Carla?" A pebble sized piece of plaster stung him on the check.

"Really, James?" He grabbed one and threw it back in the direction his had come from. "You wanna play games now?"

Another piece of plaster, a little larger than the first and flung harder, hit him in the chest. It came out of nowhere, or at least he couldn't determine the direction in the dark. Maybe it wasn't James. Maybe those kids had come back, or at least one of them, and was messing with him. They could've sneaked in while he was in the basement and were pissed he had been in their things.

"Hey! You kids! If it's you, bring your pussy asses out of the darkness now. I'm not scared and I'm not leaving. You want a piece of me? Quit hiding!"

A sound came out of the shadows, like a combination between a metal chair being dragged across the cement and a growl. An animalistic, low, deep GROWL. He held his breath, as if something huge and mean was waiting to pounce on him. He waited. The temperature had dropped again, and he was shivering. Shaking. Not what he expected from the shadows, or from himself, for that matter, but he knew when it was time to pack up. He took the KII and recorder off the floor and that was when it jumped him. A full force body slam that sent him and his equipment flying. He hit the wall like a rag doll and whatever it was held him there. His back was flat against the wall with such a pressure on his chest he almost blacked out. When it released, he sat crumpled against the wall gasping for air. The flashlight had rolled down the hall and he had no idea where his devices ended up. He scrambled on the floor, trying to get his bearings, when another blow connected. He was on all fours; his feet slipping as he tried to get some traction and make it to the stairs. Fucking sneakers! Holding his side, he ran down the staircase and to the first floor to the main entrance. There was searing pain and silence, except for his panting. Cold fear sweat dripped down his face.

When he recovered a little composure, and was fairly sure another attack wasn't imminent, he lifted his shirt. There, across his side, were three slashes, each about three inches long. He was still breathing hard and was in no mood to roll his eyes or call it cliché.

He'd have to chalk this up to a true, invisible attack, and damned if it didn't fucking hurt. Thank God it was on camera. He was unnerved, but excited. He had it. He goddamned HAD it. To actually have what he'd been searching for for so long, on video! There were no words. He stood in the doorway, still unwilling to move from this "safety" zone, with a smile growing on his face. If he could survive breaking down the equipment and loading the car, he would be gold. He held his side and waited.

The equipment table seemed miles away. He stayed in the doorway for what could've been five minutes or five hours, he had no idea. He only knew he had been staring at the lamp light, trying to will his feet to move and somehow they were mired in quicksand. Each foot was attached to a thousand pound weight. He looked at his side again. The bleeding had stopped, but the scratches hurt like a bitch. Burned. Stung. He'd be bruised, too, from that hit he took. He glanced toward the stairway, senses heightened since everything had transpired. He had never known fear could be so…solid…before. A physicality he hadn't expected. A wall that he couldn't will himself through to a table that was only twenty feet away. He swallowed. He waited. He stood in the doorway of the New Castle Asylum until the sun came up over the horizon. And then some.

With the sun up, and his stomach starting to growl, he slowly crossed the distance to the table and switched off the lamp. He looked at all he would need to break down, and sighed. It was always a pain in the ass to go back around the buildings to collect his equipment, but this time it was tinged with dread. Well, he guessed this was what investigating was all about. Start to finish. Now get going, Jack. Get back what belongs to you. He grabbed a case to take with him.

"Today, Jack, you ass," he chided himself. "Nothing's going to jump out at you. Yeah, right." He moved down the hallway toward the laundry room like a scolded child.

"Well, here we are again," he stated, more to hear his own voice than anything. He took down his camera and wound the cable neatly around his arm. "One down, three to go." In the daylight, it looked like any other room in an abandoned building. Nothing new, disturbed or touched by Satan. He chuckled. Perhaps his sense of humor was coming back and he'd be his old self soon. Perhaps what happened wasn't as bad as he remembered it. Perhaps he overreacted. "Yeah, right."

Walking into the morgue for the video camera was easier. Slightly. He got the cable wound and into the case with only minimally prodding himself. "Never used to talk to myself so much," he said. "They say it's a sign you're losing your mind." He looked around. "Hear that James?" He almost winced when those words came out. He'd really prefer not to run into James today. Or Carla, for that matter. Fuck 'em. The waiting room was next. Bolder and a bit more confident, he had that set taken down in no time. Things were running pretty damned smoothly again. He was fine. Guess he was lucky he didn't shit his pants last night. What an idiot he was! If anyone had seen him, standing statue still in a doorway through the last hours of the night, they would've had him committed. He laughed and rolled the case back to base camp.

He propped the case against the table and looked at the next one. "Jack Barnes Paranormal" in silver lettering stared back at him. He was half temped to take the loss on the KII and voice recorder and leave, but he needed the camera from that hallway. It may hold the key to not only his experience, but give the field some unparalleled evidence. He had to get it back.

The sun shining in through the glassless windows brightened his disposition and he wondered how long it would last once his feet hit the dark staircase to the second floor. "Balls to the wall, Jack," he said to himself. "Balls to the wall," and grabbed the case. He took the stairs two by two, but still, the staircase seemed longer than it had the night before. Now, he moved steadily, but only because he knew he had to get his things.

He breathed out slowly and stepped onto the second floor. There was sun coming into the windows of the bedrooms, streaming in the east side of the structure. It highlighted the dust and plaster bits that were everywhere. Calm. It felt calm. Empty, almost. The way an abandoned building should feel. Even the graffiti seemed less imposing. He moved a bit more quickly. He told himself it was confidence, that he wasn't afraid, but truly knew it was from a need to get off that floor as quickly as he could. The video camera came first. That was most important and if he had to get out of there fast, it was going with him.

He wound the cable around him arm while glancing back and forth from the hallway to the "demon site." The title was much more appropriate now and he wasn't laughing. He placed the camera and cord into the case and noticed the KII about 8 feet away from where he hit the wall, closer to the elevator. He swiped it up and started searching for the voice recorder. He found it in pieces; its batteries scattered. "Ah, damn," he said, but scooped up the pieces. Turning them around in his hand, he wondered if he could do something with it at home. He dropped them into the case. The motion sensor was nowhere to be seen. That was that, he was done. So done. He wanted to walk out slowly and confidently, but as he got closer to the stairs, he was practically jogging. He didn't care. He wanted out.

He barely slowed down as he got to base camp, grabbing the other case and going straight out to his Subaru. He almost regretted having to go back in to get the cooler, lamp and chair. Almost. He left the box that the ring came in. Someone might want it. Or not.

As he got everything into the trunk, he slammed it shut and, keys in hand, opened the driver's door. The Ouija board was on the passenger seat, along with the planchette. He stared. He could swear he hadn't put it there, hadn't carried it out to the car. Hell, he didn't remember taking it off the second floor. Not that he had been in his right mind, but he would've remembered that. He thought. He got into the car and turned the key, shaking off the confusion. He must've brought it with him. Must've tossed it in without thinking. It couldn't have just appeared, right? The ignition sprang to the life and he quickly backed up, swinging the car in an arc facing down the hill he had driven up less than twenty-four hours earlier. He gave a fast glance over his shoulder and shivered. In two hours he'd be home, in his own bed for a long nap, and then a whole lot of evidence review. A little '80's radio would help kill the miles. He shifted into drive and maneuvered the car down the asylum's overgrown drive. It was time to go home.

Barb Shadow

42

2

He woke to the phone ringing and almost hit it off the nightstand, scrambling to get it unlocked before whoever it was hung up. "What, what, hello?"

"Jack! How'd it go last night? Find anything?" It was his buddy, Parker.

"Park, you woke me up, you pain in the ass."

"Yeah, yeah, whatever. You sleep too much anyway. So how was the asylum, man?"

"Geez," Jack rubbed his eyes and looked at the clock. 2:00 p.m. He'd only been asleep two hours. "Park, let me call you back when I'm human. The asylum was...." His voice trailed off. Although never at a loss for words, there was no right word for anything that happened that night.

"What? It must be really good if it's got you stumped. Go back to bed. I'll be over later with beer and we can look at the evidence together."

Before he could protest, the line was dead. Parker was a great friend; they'd known each other easily fifteen years now, and he was, let's say, an "enthusiastic" paranormal believer. Nothing was too farfetched for him, and he was always willing to jump on the ghost bandwagon. If Jack didn't push him out the door, Park would jump right in and start loading up audio and video files to watch. He preferred to do his review alone, but...Park was pretty thorough. And even though he was ready to call every shadow an entity, he accepted Jack's debunking with disappointment, but few complaints. Jack chuckled. Their friendship had even survived Park dating Jack's ex-wife for a bit. Yeah, Park was a good guy and he learned from his mistakes. Jack rolled over and went back to sleep, dropping his phone onto the bed beside him. Caesar, his Russian blue, curled up on top of it.

He woke about an hour and a half later to pounding on his side door and a cat in his face. "Park! What the fuck, man?" He opened the door to his friend, who walked in like he owned the place, arms full with a pizza box and a twelve pack of Budweiser. "You know I don't like Bud!"

"Deal with it," Park smirked. "You'll keep your mind on the review." He looked around. "You don't have anything set up yet? Sheesh!" He cracked a beer and pulled out a kitchen chair for himself. He put his foot on it and rested the beer on his knee. Jack grabbed a cold one for himself.

"Tell me what you found."

Jack watched Park as he opened the pizza box. He pulled a couple of pieces of pepperoni off the pie and stuck them in his mouth.

"Quit it," Jack shoved his friend. "You'll eat 'em all and I'll be left with a plain pizza."

"Give. You found something, didn't you? The tip was good. Damn it, I knew it!" Parker had been the one who told Jack about New Castle. He had heard that there was something going on there. Satan worship shit or something, and he KNEW there'd be activity. Reports of shadow people, sounds. "You know I wanted to go with you."

"You know I work alone." Jack half regretted not having Parker along with him on this one, but was also happy he hadn't involved him. He liked the limelight, but wasn't ready to put his friend's safety in jeopardy, either. He worked alone. Always.

"You work alone when you drive the bus, you shit. Investigators should never work alone."

Jack sighed. They had had this discussion before. So many times he couldn't count. If he didn't love Park like a brother, he would've beaten the snot out of him long ago over this one.

"Yeah, yeah." He stared at his beer. "I gotta look at the evidence first. Check it out."

"Would you just TELL me already?"

"I won't know until I look at the footage," Jack said, in a totally unconvincing tone. "Look, you know me. I'm not gonna talk out of turn."

"Yeah, and you know me. I'm the best friend you have on this planet. Probably your only friend, you egotistical, narcissistic shit."

Jack laughed. Park had him there. He paused for a moment and the smile faded from his face. "Here." He put his beer on the Formica table top and pulled up his shirt.

"Whoa! What the fuck?" Park reached out to touch his friend's ribcage and Jack jerked back.

"Still pretty sore." He let his shirt fall back into place.

Parker was shaking his head. "That's bad, Jack. Really bad."

"Yeah, hurts."

"You know what I'm talking about. Whatever did that to you. It's freaking evil."

Jack chuckled. "Nah. You should know better than to jump to conclusions, especially around me. Look, I found a picture of this guy who used to work at the place…and he had the same initials as this ring I found." He held out his hand for Park to inspect.

Parker slid his chair back along the green kitchen tile. "You TOOK it?? Some dead guy's ring from an asylum where you were SCRATCHED by something demonic and you brought home his ring??? Are you fucking NUTS?!" He slapped his hand down on the table, almost spilling their beers. "I can't believe you. I know you're the "King of Debunk" or whatever the hell you refer to yourself as now, but even YOU should realize there's bad shit out there…and you messed with it."

Jack was silent for a minute. He loved his friend and knew he had some valid points. The ring was cool, though. He had really grown to like it, and, even though he wasn't a thief, he had no issue with liberating the ring from its forty or fifty year tomb. It was obvious no one else wanted it. The dead aren't wearing jewelry. And, as for the scratches, well. The jury was out. He had had a scare, but…the jury was still out.

"I don't think it was demonic."

"Give it up. Just stop. Nothing ghostly, no apparition or any spirit interacting on this plane, causes that." Park motioned toward Jack's chest. "And if it wasn't evil, what the hell do you think it was?"

"I don't know. I need to see the video, listen to the recordings. Maybe it was this guy… James… who was pissed about something. Maybe he felt the ring was still his, I don't know. I'm going to find out, though."

"James. You're on a fucking first name basis with this guy? If I were smart, I'd walk out that door right now. But you know I'm in it with you, you god damned fool."

"Help me get my shit out of the car and maybe I'll let you look over my shoulder while I work."

"Fuck you." They both laughed.

Park stood up and they both went out to the carport. A fine October day greeted them, with a bit of a nip in the air. Leaves were blowing and collecting along the edges of the house. Bright reds and golds were piling up and the trees were going to be bare soon. Jack loved the crunch they made as he stepped down the three steps to their cars. Fall was the best time of year in his book.

Jack popped the trunk and grabbed the cases while Park went to the side of the car. "Anything in here you need me to get?" He let out a whistle. "Where did you get this?" He picked up the Ouija board and looked it over closely.

"Asylum, second floor."

Park dropped the spirit board back onto the seat of the Subaru. He leaned his head down on the side of the car, resting on his arm. "You're a fucking paranormal investigator and you don't know the first thing about the stuff you're dealing with. You're all Mr. Scientific and debunking Mrs. O'Leary's bumps in the night, but you have no fucking idea of what is out there. This shit can haunt you, Jack. Excuse my pun. It can go really bad."

"It's a TOY for god sakes, Park. Everything else is conditional, environmental, scientific, something. Here and there you get the voice of a ghost, an object moves, fine. But this is a god damned toy. Look at the Parker Bros. seal."

Park pushed off the car and stared at his friend. "Yeah, a god damned toy. That people use to focus their intent. The mind is a powerful thing, Jack, and there are energies waiting to be let in. I swear," he paused. "I swear, Buddy. You don't want to get into this."

"You're being fucking dramatic."

"Am I?"

"Yes."

"What did you run into? What gave you those fucking scratches?"

Jack paused.

"Right. Get rid of the board." Park shook his head. "Before you end up using it."

Jack stood just inside his screen door and looked at Park.

"AND, you fucking used it." Park's arms fell to his sides and he stared at his friend.

After a long minute of silence between the two, Jack offered, "You want pizza or not?"

Park smirked and followed his friend inside, letting the screen door slam behind him. "You're an asshole and I'm gonna hate you for this."

Jack dropped his car keys into the bowl on the counter and patted his friend on the back. He smiled and said, "Yeah. You probably will."

They set up the monitor, DVR and laptop across the kitchen table. It was also the dining room table, the bill paying table, the…

well, whatever he needed at the time. Besides, the kitchen had the best light…and the house was too small for anything else. As they got all the cables plugged in to the various inputs, outputs and power strip, Caesar jumped up and sat in front of the monitor. Jack had been out all night and Caesar was having no part of his getting down to business yet.

"Spoiled cat," he muttered, scratching behind Caesar's ears. A deep loving purr sprung up and Caesar sprawled across the laptop's keyboard. "Oh, no, you don't," Jack said, scooping up the gray ball of fur and guiding him to the floor.

Jack popped out the side door and was back in the kitchen in under a minute. He held the Ouija board in his hand. He slid it onto the table in front of Park.

"Nope! Not funny." Parker was obviously not amused.

"T.O.Y. It can't hurt you."

"Why'd you bring it here? Got a death wish or something?"

Jack rolled his eyes. "Give me a break. You know I don't believe that shit. I thought I'd mount it on the wall. Kind of a paranormal souvenir."

"You're pulling my leg."

"No. Really. I thought over here." Jack took the board and held it up high on the kitchen wall, to the left of the only wall clock in the house, above the table they were working on.

Park shook his head. He couldn't believe that Jack didn't get it. Spirit boards weren't the problem, they were the tool. People would get caught up in the debate of whether or not the boards were evil. They're not. But when you use a tool to open communication with the spirit realm, you're making a portal. A point of focus. You're asking things to come through…and unless you know how to close that doorway, you're screwed if the wrong thing comes through. And you never know what thing will choose to come. He kept it to himself, for now. They'd been through it all before, at one time or another. He'd be beating a dead horse.

Park noticed the pieces of the voice recorder. "How'd you do that?"

"Dropped it."

"Okay, fine. Don't tell me. Yet. Bet I'll find it on the video."

Jack chuckled. "You might just."

Park smiled. "Okay," he said. "How far into the video did everything happen?" His hands were poised on the mouse, ready to fast forward the DVR and get right to it.

"No."

"What?"

"No. We'll start at the beginning and go through it step by step. I'm not skipping anything."

Park let out an annoyed huff, but knew he was stuck. "You're the boss."

"Damn straight, I am. Now, you start on the video and I'll hit some audio." Jack put headphones on to start listening, while examining the pieces of his broken voice recorder. Caesar wove between Jack and Park's ankles.

Jack took the headphones off and went over to one of his kitchen drawers. He began rummaging through, pawing through pens, screws, and paperclips. He pulled out a plastic, hinged container with some tiny screwdrivers in it, then changed his mind and tossed it back in amid the chaos of the junk drawer. He dug through more of the contents until he found a spool of picture wire and a little tub of screws. He deposited everything on the counter in front of him.

"Hand me that board, Park," he said without turning around.

"What?"

"The Ouija board. Beside you."

"You're not serious," Park replied, hand hovering over the board.

"Like hell, I'm not. I'm gonna hang it."

Park reluctantly handed him the spirit board. "I'm registering my complaint now."

"Pussy."

Park shook his head. "Asshole."

Jack attached the picture hanging wire to the back of the board and strategically attached the fine wire to the back, as well. He hung it down over the front of the board and tied it to the planchette. After marking a spot on the wall and driving in a nail, he hung the board. When you stood back, you couldn't see the wire holding the planchette. It sat neatly in the center of the board, as if waiting to be used. It looked great. He stood back to admire it and gave Park's shoulder a shove.

"Come on, you know it looks good, Park."

Park had to admit, to himself, it kind of did. But he wasn't going to share that with Jack. It felt wrong…not the hanging of the thing, but the having it. God, he wished his friend hadn't come across it. He handed Jack a beer and turned back to the monitor. "We have work to do if we're going to figure out what happened to you."

"Right." Jack turned his attention to the broken pieces of the voice recorder. He knew there was no fixing it. At least he had only lost what happened on the second floor. Everything else was already uploaded to his laptop when he was attacked. Hopefully the video will have caught any EVP's. He shivered a second. He was totally excited to see the footage of it all, yet was holding back. Odd for him. He never thought he would've been this shaken over anything. He stepped on the lever to the garbage can, popping the lid open, and dropped in the recorder pieces. It wasn't like he didn't have more.

Headphones on, Jack brought up his audio editing software. At least it gave him a sound wave to look at as he listened to the recordings. It could get pretty boring, listening to empty air for hours on end. And Park was staring at videos. He laughed to himself. Video review was the worst. 99.9% of the time, nothing changed. He'd watched a staircase through five hours of recording once. Nothing moved. Let me tell you, that's when you start questioning your sanity. He opened the notebook he always kept in his equipment case and turned to a blank page.

October 17, 2015. He dated the page while he listened to his footsteps on the way to the laundry room in New Castle. It always amused him to hear his voice on recordings. As patiently as he could, and a bit on the edge of his seat, he waited for his session in the laundry room. He could hear the slide of the KII and shortly later he heard it hit the wall. Excited, he sat back in his seat. He really needed to sync his listening to the video. Park was still a few minutes behind him. He watched over Park's shoulder, checking out all four camera views.

"Going too slow for you?" Park asked, turning slightly in his chair.

"Yeah…but you're almost there. I had the KII slide across the floor in the laundry room. Camera 2. I want to see if something interacted with it." He slid his chair next to Park and leaned in close. Park clicked to full screen on cam 2 and turned up the volume.

With eyes glued to the screen, they heard Jack's questions, but the KII was obscured by a laundry bin. "Geez, Jack. Why didn't you move those things?"

"Damn it!"

The glow of the KII lights was evident, but you only heard the device slide. When it hit the wall, they saw the hit but not what initiated it.

"For all we know, you kicked it, Jack."

"Fuck. You and I both know that didn't happen."

"Yeah…but it's the first thing someone is going to say when they see it."

Jack was visibly pissed that he missed such a great piece of video. He knew he had just brought that piece of equipment into the room with him and there was truly no way it could have been tampered with. Even he knew in his heart that if it had been caught on video, there wouldn't have been anything to debunk. That thing slid on its own. Twice. But he couldn't prove it.

"At least you're getting a LITTLE analytical." Jack prodded his friend.

"Bite my ass." Park smiled and snapped the tab on the next beer.

"Yesssss." They both heard it and turned to the monitor.

"Rewind!" Jack commanded. Park clicked on the rewind button in the on screen menu as quickly as he could.

"Miss, is your name Carla?" Pause. *"Yessssss."*

Park put the clip on repeat and hit play.

"Miss, is your name Carla?" Pause. *"Yessssss." "Miss, is your name Carla?"* Pause. *"Yessssss." "Miss, is your name Carla?"* Pause. *"Yessssss." "Miss, is your name Carla?"* Pause. *"Yessssss."*

"Okay, okay." Park hit stop and high fived Jack. "Nice one! Kinda manly, though, if you ask me."

"What?" Jack had been lost in thought. He had made a note of the time, question asked, response, in his notebook. It was a Class A, kick ass EVP. So many times, the EVP's were C quality; you know something's there, hear what you're sure is a voice, but there's no way to make it out. Even Class B's could be a pain… you hear it, but different people make out different things and tend to put their own spin on what it says. "Yes, dear," versus "I'm here," versus "My spear," or "My beer." He hated when the voices could be debated. But Class A evp's were the gold standard. No mistaking what they said.

"The voice. Pretty deep and raspy for a woman."

"She's dead, Park," Jack laughed. "How would you sound?"

"I suppose," Park smiled. "Just sayin, I wouldn't want to meet up with her in a dark alley. Damn. Nice catch!"

"What you'll like even better is that I have a picture of a headstone from a cemetery on New Castle's grounds with the name Carla on it."

"Get the fuck out."

Jack nodded. He knew that'd get Park's engine running even faster. The guy had a thing for the paranormal maybe even stronger than his own need to debunk. He minimized the audio program to bring up the pics he'd captured before Park could even ask.

"I've gotta see it. Where's the shot?"

Jack laughed, "Hold on, hold on. I'm finding it."

He had taken hundreds of pics, with probably a third of those outside. They started clicking through from the beginning, searching for the cemetery shots.

"Holy fuck, man. Stop! What's that?" Parker pointed at the screen. Jack had snapped at least thirty shots of the asylum itself. The window shots, he called them. Always a win with his followers...and the paranormal community as a whole. Parker was looking at just such a shot. Up on the second floor, at the far end of the building, was a so called "window shot."

"Come on, Jack. Don't you fucking tell me you don't see it."

Jack looked closely. He remembered thinking he saw something at a window, but there it was. Which it couldn't be. He knew better and didn't get excited.

"Park," he started.

"No. Not this one. Look!" He zoomed in on the window. In the glassless rectangle, high up on the side of the building, you could see the edge of a curtain. It had that flow to it, of threadbare linen in a breeze. And blocking part of it was a shadow. A black shadow, but what else would a shadow look like in an abandoned building? It was the shape of a man, slightly leaning in front of the curtain. Slightly. Facing him. It had that sinister look you see in the stereotypical ghost pics. The old, broken brick building, with ivy, no longer green, but dried brown and brittle, lifeless. The shadow was lifeless, as well, but with a dark energy of its own. Jack shook his head, rubbing his eyes, trying to rub the sight of this shadow gone. There was something unhinging about it.

"Park, come on. It could be a thousand things."

"No. It can't."

They zoomed in a little farther. If ever a shadow looked like a man; if ever a dark mass could look back at a camera with…intent. If a shadow could even have intent. This was it. But he knew it had to be something else. Where was that window anyway? He felt his face go a little pale and he sat back.

"Oh, fuck me. What? What, Jack?"

"Print that one. Print it," was all Jack said. He didn't know what was wrong with himself. He was a dichotomy of feelings. This could be the best investigation of his history and he should have some major proof of the paranormal, but as eager as he was, he was nearly as hesitant. He'd never been afraid in his life and certainly never walked away from a fight. But this was different. This had gone a little deeper. This had touched a spot inside him that he didn't know he had. Or at least had thought he'd sealed off a little better. He took a deep breath.

Jack took the mouse and clicked the next picture. It was the same window, but the figure was gone. Definitely gone. 100% gone. He always took at least three pics of everything, so he could compare them, with the very thought that if this happened, you'd have it nailed. It happened. He nailed it. He felt great and terrible all at once. Thrilled and nauseated. Exhilarated and terrified. God, what was wrong with him?

He clicked print on that second photo, too. Both printed at 8 x 10. He needed to see them up close and compare…he needed to have something physical in his hand, even if it was just a piece of paper, to prove to himself what he was seeing. The printer whirred to life and slowly spit out two pictures, each on photo quality paper. If you were going to do it, you needed to do it right, he always felt. It didn't matter if the good paper cost a little more.

Jack grabbed them out of the printer before Parker could get there. He looked over Jack's shoulder at the photos. They were great quality, perfectly framed on the building, the dead ivy, the background of trees. If it weren't for the leaves on the ground, you would've sworn it was a cold winter shot. But their eyes didn't see any of that. It was the window and only the window that had their undivided attention.

The pictures were shaking a little in Jack's hands. Fear? Excitement? They were nearly one and the same, especially at the moment. It also didn't matter what it was or why. It was there. There was no discussion, no question in his mind. That was the scariest thing. He could debate and debunk pretty much anything and this, this…stunned him.

"It's standing in the area where I was attacked."

"Attacked. Not just scratched. Fucking attacked."

"Yeah. Something like that. The fucker hit me, slammed me into the wall, once or twice."

"God, Jack. No wonder you're not on your soapbox over debunking the fucking bumps in the night. You okay?"

He touched his ribs, the spot where the scratches still burned. "Yeah."

"No, you asshole. Are you OKAY?"

He looked at his buddy and didn't know if he could answer truthfully. "I think so. Yeah, I guess I am. Just shocked me to see it."

They laid the photos on the counter, under the light by the sink.

"Cool shit, though, Jack. Best pics ever."

Jack smiled. "I know."

Parker went back to the laptop and started pouring over all the outdoor shots. "I assume you want me to print the cemetery ones? Carla? Any others?"

"Yeah. Carla. And James. I'm pretty sure he was damn active last night." Last night. Hell, it was only 24 hours ago. It felt like minutes and years all at once. He could still smell the peppermint in the basement and hear that... growl... in the demon spot. After the outdoor photos were printed, Jack attached them to the picture of James Borden and put the case file away.

"I've got to quit, Park. I'm exhausted. Investigation hangover."

Parker waved him off. "Go get some sleep. I'm going to keep reviewing for now. I'll let myself out and lock up later."

"Suit yourself. Don't wake me if you find anything," Jack chuckled. He walked into the bedroom and sighed. He was bone weary. He needed a good seven or eight hours sleep and to be back in tip top shape again. The room was a peaceful forest green. He always felt it was like camping out among the trees, something he had loved as a boy. He stripped to his boxers, stretched and crawled between the sheets. He pulled the comforter up around his chin. The bedroom, at the far side of the house, was always a little cooler than the other rooms. Most of the time he appreciated that. Cool air is the best sleeping air. But tonight he was a little too cool. He reached over to the sweatshirt on the chair near his bed and tossed it over his feet. Then he settled into sleep.

Parker continued to scrutinize the still pictures that Jack had taken. Each photo fascinated him; it was actually a beautiful place, even if Jack didn't see it. There was art in the way the ivy twisted along the bricks, and in the broken windows. It brought a sadness to the place. A deep emptiness. A darker realm. He loved the darker side of things; old abandoned buildings, cemeteries, anywhere with a mention of ghostly activity. That picture of the shadow on the second floor. My God, what a capture! He glanced at the photo, still on the counter. Jack had neglected to put that in the file.

The pictures were giving him a good idea of the asylum. The deterioration, like the ocean eroding a beach, time was chipping away at the building. Slowly and, eventually, completely. He wanted to get through as much as he could while Jack slept. He really wanted to find what had happened to his friend, but would respect Jack's desire to go, start to finish, through the evidence. He could understand that... but if it had been him, he'd have been on that evidence immediately. There would have been no stopping him. He sighed. He wished Jack wouldn't investigate alone. It was too dangerous.

Parker had gone through about seventy pictures from the main floor when he noticed something. *Something.* Right there, behind Jack. A shot that he snapped of himself in a mirror. Parker could swear there was a ...form? Shadow? It stood, head and shoulders behind him. WTF? The printer whirred, again, while he zoomed in. And he knew Jack wouldn't be able to debunk this one, either. When he laid it next to the first photo on the counter, they matched. They fucking matched. It had probably been with him the entire night. And it didn't look like any "James." Parker stared at the two photos for the longest time and then went back to the still pics. He had to find more.

Jack woke up and stretched, while Caesar stayed curled beside his pillow. He could see the light of the sun around the edges of his window shade. He threw off his comforter and headed for the bathroom. "Park? You still here?" No response. Well, the shower called. He dialed up the heat and pressure, and let the steam fill the room while he shaved. The damp heat felt wonderful. He unwrapped a new bar of Ivory, and stood under the hot water. The lather smelled great as he worked from his arms, to his chest. He stopped for a moment to examine the scratches. Still sore, but scabbed over. They'd heal quickly, he hoped. He continued to lather. When he got down to his balls, it crossed his mind to stay there a while and enjoy his hands, stroke a bit. It'd been a while and he could certainly use the release, aside from the fact that he was really fucking horny, but quickly got rid of the idea. He was sure Park had probably stayed over and that would be too weird. He quickly lost the hard on he had cultivated. It was a damned shame, too, to waste it. Never one to be shy, he liked the fact that he was rather hung. Always a plus, in his book.

He felt for the towel on the rack and dried his hair quickly. Not that it took long. He smiled. Ah, that wonderful aging process. He toweled off his chest and legs, stepping out onto the green shag mat. Standing sideways to the mirror, he checked out his physique. Gut sucked in, gut pushed out. Sucked in, pushed out. He laughed. He still looked good, even at fifty-something and was proud of it. Walking into the bedroom, he grabbed a pair of jeans and a tee shirt from the clean clothes basket. He'd get around to putting them away at some point. Maybe.

He strode into the living room feeling great. "Wake up, Park. Let's get breakfast." He shook Parker's shoulder.

"I've got stuff to show you," Parker said without opening his eyes. He sat up. Around 4 a.m. he had finished the photos and, exhausted, collapsed onto Jack's sofa. It wasn't as if he hadn't done that before. It was somewhat comfortable, more so when he'd had a few drinks. He wished it was a little longer. He turned his head and cracked his neck.

"I want coffee. Come on, we'll start fresh after."

Parker nodded and followed into the kitchen. In mid-step through the doorway; Jack dropped his hand into the bowl on the counter to grab his keys. It was about the only thing his wife had left him in the divorce. His hand hit the bottom of the bowl. He fished around for a second. "Where're my keys?"

"How should I know?" Parker yawned.

Jack quickly patted his pockets. "Where the fuck would they be?"

"You probably left them in the car."

"I always drop them in the bowl. You know I do. I've done it a thousand times."

Parker shook his head. "Check the car, man."

"You know I don't lose my keys. Hell, I drive for a living. I don't lose keys." They got out to the Subaru and there they were, hanging from the ignition.

"See?" Parker asked. "You left them in the car."

"I swear I didn't."

"Then how'd they get there? Come on, you were exhausted and obviously shaken. You just missed it, is all."

Jack looked doubtful. He knew he would never leave his keys in the car. "Yeah, I guess." He ran his hands through his hair, got in and turned the key. "It's just not like me."

"Forget about it. You'll feel better after you buy me breakfast." Parker clicked his seatbelt and settled into the passenger seat like a kid.

"You're a jerk," Jack chuckled.

"Yeah. But I get breakfast." They both laughed out loud and it felt good.

It was only a five minute drive to Jack's favorite restaurant. It was a little, out of the way place called A Touch of Home. As he expected, the parking lot was packed. SUV's, station wagons, family cars. This was the place to get a breakfast that would stick to your ribs. Not fancy, and not your typical diner food. This had soul. And flavor. He was nearly a regular here, or at least he was getting to feel that way. Some of the waitresses knew him by face and had coffee ready when they saw him coming.

When they walked in, it was fairly full. Morning chatter, children bickering, utensils clanging and clattering, all the hustle and bustle of a Sunday morning brunch. He loved it. And the aroma! His mouth was watering before they were halfway through the door.

They asked the hostess for a booth. She grabbed a couple of menus and steered them to one toward the back. They had families on either side and were near the kitchen. Not that it mattered. It was more private than a table or the counter, and they had things to discuss.

"What'd you find in the pics last night? Anything good?" Jack slid into his side of the booth and moved the silverware out of his way. He leaned forward onto his arms.

Parker looked down at his menu, "What are you having?"

"Park. Focus."

"I am. You're buying and I'm starving. Gimmie a minute."

The waitress arrived at the table with fresh, wrapped silverware. Jack didn't recognize her. She was a cute brunette, thirty-ish, hair in a ponytail. Jack sat back.

"How are you both today?"

"Great, great. How're you?"

"Oh, I'm fine, thanks. Looks like a beautiful day. Are you all set to order?"

"I'm ready," Jack said, "but he's a little slow today." He locked eyes with her for a moment. She smiled what he thought was a beautiful smile and asked what he'd like. He had to bite his tongue. "I'd really love some scrambled eggs, bacon, and toast."

"Well, I'm sure I can dig some up for you." She turned toward Parker. "And you?"

"Hmmm… the same, please."

She walked away, but with a glance back at Jack.

"Did you see that?" Parker asked. "You're such a fucking flirt."

"I didn't do anything but ask for my breakfast," he smiled. Park knew him too well. But, damn, he thought she was gorgeous.

"Must be the way you asked for it then. She's coming back already," Parker smirked a bit.

"I'm sorry. Did you want anything to drink with your breakfast?" She kept her eyes on Jack.

"Coffee would be great. Thanks, Doll."

"You're very welcome."

"Um, me, too," Parker stated.

"Of course!" she smiled again, at them both, but mainly at Jack, and left.

Jack watched for a moment as she walked away. "Now that's something to think about," Jack said quietly to Parker, but then shifted gears. "So, what did you find in those pictures?"

Parker leaned forward. "I've got more shots of him. The shadow guy. Sometimes a shadow that doesn't make sense, sometimes a more settled shape. But it's him."

"Him?"

"Him."

Jack felt something cold go down his spine that sucked the enthusiasm out of him. Him. "What makes you think so? Shadows...you know how I feel about shadows. It's like orbs. Everyone sees what they want to and 99% aren't anything paranormal."

"You'll have to see when we get back. There's one with him looking over your shoulder. You took it of yourself in the mirror."

The waitress came back moments later with two cups and a hot pot of coffee. She poured, smiled and left.

Jack looked a little uncomfortable. He grabbed the metal container of milk and slowly poured it into his cup. He opened his silverware bundle, found his spoon and stirred the milk into his coffee. Slowly. His throat was dry and he had to clear it a few times to get the words out. "Where," a bit raspy, a sip of coffee, "Where else?"

"Second floor."

Jack slid backward into the booth cushion as the waitress served him a steaming plate of food. When she handed Parker his, she asked, "Can I bring you boys more coffee?"

"Thanks, Doll. We're good."

"Great. If you need anything, let me know. Oh, and it's Laurel." She smiled sweetly; Jack winked and she moved on to the next table.

"Second floor?"

"At the end. It looks like he's kind of looming down there. As if he owned it, you know…larger than life. I printed them, along with the headstones."

"How do you know it's the same shadow?"

"When you look, you'll see. Unmistakable." Parker dove into his breakfast. He looked up to see Jack shoving his eggs from side to side. "You gonna eat your bacon?"

"Take it."

"Now I know you're sick or something's gotten to you. This isn't like you, man."

Jack sipped his coffee and looked over to the next booth. The mom was trying to juggle what looked like a four year old and a toddler, plus actually get to eat something herself. He gave her a half smile and a shrug, as if to say, "What can you do?" She smiled back. Parker took his bacon.

"You really should eat. It's delicious."

Jack continued to shove the food around his plate. He took a bite of the toast, but, today, it tasted like cardboard. He washed it down with some flavorless hot water. He was sure it was delicious; their coffee always was. But for now, his taste buds had crawled up his ass. Nothing tasted good.

"When we get back, I want to start going through the video. You go through the audio, that's your favorite, anyway. We need to correlate the time stamps with that shadow and see if we can get any cross evidence."

"Yeah," he took a long mouthful of coffee, swallowed slowly. "Definitely."

Parker finished his eggs and sipped his coffee while they silently people watched. Jack had pretty much quit talking after he had brought up "him." Not like Jack at all. But he let him have his space, for now. The mom left with her kids and was soon replaced by an elderly couple. They looked to be in their early 80's and had probably been together since the beginning of time. Sunday brunch brought in everyone.

Laurel arrived at the table to see if they wanted anything else. She was clearly hoping they weren't ready to leave yet. "More coffee? You obviously weren't happy with those eggs. I'm so sorry. Can I bring you something else?"

"Oh, no, the eggs were fine. Thanks. Just the check. Laurel," Jack flashed her his baby blues, not totally unintentionally. Women had always complimented him on his eyes. Not that he dated much. It'd probably been at least six to eight months since he had even seen a movie, let alone taken someone out. When she cleared the dishes and went for the check, Parker told him to quit it.

"What?"

"God, you were going to melt her on the spot."

"That obvious?"

"OMG," Parker fluttered his eyelashes, "Take me now, Jack, you big hunk of man!"

Jack laughed and threw his napkin at him. Laurel deposited the check on the table and wished them a great day. Jack looked her over as she walked away. "Let's go, you jerk. You leave the tip."

"Yes, dear."

Jack punched his friend in the shoulder and paid on their way out. At the car, Laurel came running out. "You forgot your jacket!" She caught up with Jack by the door of the Subaru.

"I didn't have a jacket, sorry, Doll."

"I know," she said, quietly. "But it was the only way I could give you this." She put a piece of paper in his hand. "I don't usually do this, but I just had to," she smiled nervously and ran back inside.

"Her number?" Parker asked.

"Yeah," Jack smiled to himself. "Still got it."

"Yes, dear," Parker ducked and dove into the car.

"Once more time and you're walking, I swear it, Park."

Parker clammed up, but couldn't get the smile off his face. "Gonna call her?"

"I might," Jack said. He tucked the paper into the glove compartment of the car, put it in drive and felt a little better. Some of the dark cloud he had been under had lifted.

They pulled into the carport at 11 Ridley Road, and Jack shifted into park. He turned the key and let the engine do its usual rumbling around before it decided to quit. Parker looked at Jack with an "are you ever gonna get that looked at" gaze.

"At least she runs," Jack said. "Come on. We've got a lot of work ahead of us."

The two went up the steps and into the house. "Shit," Jack said. "The board fell. The wire must not have been strong enough." He dropped his keys into the bowl and bent to pick up the Ouija board.

"You sure? Check the nail."

Jack checked. The nail was in the wall, and the wire was still tight into the board. He couldn't figure out how the thing had fallen.

Parker had started to go on a Ouija board rant, but Jack cut him off. "I don't want to hear it. I didn't hang it well enough."

"Whatever, man. Just saying. I don't trust those things and you shouldn't, either."

Jack readjusted the Ouija board on the wall. "Come on, Park. Let's see those pictures." He had some of his usual confidence back. Not his cockiness yet, but that would return soon, he figured. Parker was on it before he could change his mind, sorting through the photos he had left on the counter.

"Here. Check this out. The one you took in the mirror."

Jack was stunned. There, behind his reflection, was the unmistakable shadow behind him. A head and shoulders, but still a dark shadow, was just behind him. He pushed back the feelings that wanted to reclaim him. He held his breath and forced back the fear that wanted to grow in him. This was his passion. He couldn't let anything get in the way of that. If he did, his days of investigating would be over.

"God damn," he whispered. "You're right."

Parker could hardly contain himself. It wasn't often that Jack offered up that bit of praise. He held out the next photo. The one from the second floor. Looming. That was the only word to describe it. It loomed. Jack scrutinized the pic. Then set it on the counter and leaned back against the refrigerator. He folded his arms across his chest. The cool metal door grounded him. Rooted him in the physical. "Let's do this."

They worked in earnest for the next three and a half hours; Jack on the audio, making notes and every so often handing Parker the headphones for his input. Parker did the same with the video, stopping only to confer with Jack. The starting, stopping, going over, playing and replaying sections of audio and video always took forever, it seemed. That's what separated ghost hunters from true paranormal investigators. Ghost hunters wanted to chase activity and have the experiences. Paranormal investigators put in the research and the hours of review, even when knowing that most of the time there'd be nothing paranormal to find. Not everyone had the patience for the work of it.

Aside from the KII hits and the noises in the basement, they found no more EVP's. It was somewhat disappointing to Jack, but not out of the norm. After all, the KII could've been triggered by stray EMF from…something. He'd have to go over the video himself to see if there were any clues. He wished the KII sliding and hitting the wall had been dead on camera.

Parker paused the video on the second floor as Jack came into camera range. He waited till his buddy finished checking the audio section he was working on to show him where he was on the recording. "I kinda thought you'd want to watch this together." Jack nodded and Parker hit the play button.

Jack lit the black candles around the pentagram on the floor. He stepped back and watched the flickering lights cast shadows around him and sat down. The candle flames caused shadows and shapes to dance on the walls.

"My name is Jack. What's yours?"

Although they could hear the questions he asked fairly well, Jack cued up the audio with the same time stamp. He played it through the laptop's external speakers and synced it to the video as best he could.

Jack rubbed his arms, and shifted on the floor. After a long pause in his questioning, he reached for the Ouija board. "Well, now. Let's try a little experiment."

Paker shifted uncomfortably, but refrained from berating Jack over it. The time for ranting was over. Now was the time for finding out what had happened and...damage control.

"I've never done this, so, if you have, feel free to help."

Although the board was lit by Jack's flashlight, you couldn't get the details from the video. He was too far and at the wrong angle. They might be able to zoom in, but it wouldn't be tremendously clear.

"Okay. Is there anyone here who would like to communicate tonight?" Jack looked over his shoulder, as if he was trying to pull something out of the darkness. As if he stared a little harder, he'd make out what was there.

Parker leaned in closer to the monitor. "I kept hearing what I thought were footsteps down the hallway," Jack offered. "Could've been the rain."

"Rain doesn't generally sound like footsteps."

"Is that you? You can talk to me through this board, you know." His pauses grew longer between the questions. "I don't want to bother you. Just want to prove that you're here. I've never used one of these things. Can you tell me what to do?"

"I found this great ring in a box in the basement. Was it yours? What are your initials?" Jack's attention to the board suddenly became much more focused. His face was intent on the planchette.

"Is that you? Or my imagination? Something psychological, maybe it's just me. If it's you, can you muster some more energy to communicate with me?"

"It was weird," Jack said, eyes glued to the monitor. "I swear I felt like an energy running through the thing. Like it vibrated under my fingers."

The planchette began to slowly slide across the board.

"It spelled out James' initials, but it could've been me. You know, power of the mind and all."

"Uh, huh."

They watched the session with the spirit board as what it spelled out came swifter and more forceful.

"You got a little snarky with your comments, Jack. Sarcasm with a ghost? Telling him he's not fucking original? Calling him Caspar?"

Jack looked at him out of the corner of his eyes. "I said he wasn't Caspar." They locked eyes and laughed.

Jack shifted on the floor again. He seemed much more uncomfortable, physically, as he continued to talk to the board. When he exhaled, you could almost see his breath. Almost. A bit of vapor in the candle light. After a few quiet moments, the planchette started to move. It was a slow, methodical circling of the board, and then it flew into the wall.

"Play that back!" Jack commanded, but Parker had already highlighted that section and hit the button. They watched it, over and over, first at regular speed and then slowed. They slowed it x2, x4… and kept trying it until they reached the machine's maxed step by step playback.

"That's so cool!" There was nothing he could debunk in that video. He had nothing to do with the way that planchette took off and hit the wall. You could see it pull away from under his fingers, with force and angle that he couldn't have caused.

"It'd be cooler if it wasn't a Ouija board and it wasn't you, man, but, yeah. That's a great catch!"

They continued.

Out of the camera frame, Jack's footsteps stopped, then started again, and trailed off. Within seconds, the motion detector went off, lights and an ear piercing BEEEEEEP BEEEEEEP BEEEEEEP.

"It felt like someone was following me. A really eerie sensation. Like someone was making sure I got out of there."

"Obviously he got you out and went back to his area by the pentagram by the way the motion sensor went off."

"Could be a malfunction in the unit. I'll make a note to check it."

Parker rolled his eyes. "Always good to check, but come on, Jack. Sometimes you have to let the evidence speak for itself."

"That's where you're wrong. I've got to try everything to explain it naturally, or I'm doing a disservice to the field."

"Yeah, yeah. I get it. But you're going to find that thing works just fine."

"Eternal paranormal optimist."

"You know it, man. I live for the ghosties."

"To really twist your brain, we can test it right now," Jack reached for the case that was closest to the kitchen table. He popped the latches and took out the REM pod. It was a round, heavy device with lights at the four compass directions and sensors. He flipped the button on the bottom to on and set it in the middle of the kitchen floor. After a 30 second reset, it was "armed." Park, sitting about four feet away, waved his arms. BEEEEP BEEEEP BEEEEP. The light lit in his direction.

"Well, we know it can see me."

Jack moved to the archway to the living room and waited for the device's reset. He waved his arms in big arcs and it went off again. They tested it off and on until they couldn't stand its high pitched wail any longer. Jack sat back at the table.

"Onward," he said, pointing at the monitor. Parker hit play.

They continued on the way they had been, audio playing through the speakers while they both watched the video. Parker startled when a slam came out of nowhere. Jack started laughing, his head in his hands.

"What now?" He paused the playbacks.

"I was in the middle of a well needed piss, into my thermos…"

"THERMOS??"

"No plumbing, man, and a storm raging outside."

Parker shook his head.

"That slam happened mid-steam and I almost peed across the place."

"Remind me never to drink from your water bottles. EVER." Parker paused. "Did you remember to dump it?"

"Oh, shit." They broke down in laughter. "It's in the car, Park. Just…just throw it out."

"You know I'm not going near that shit. You're on your own, buddy."

Jack's hunger had finally come back and his stomach was roaring. He got up and opened the refrigerator. BEEEEP BEEEEEP BEEEEEP.

"Didn't you turn that thing off?" Parker complained.

"Guess not," he said through a mouthful of pizza. "You want?"

"Nope, thanks."

Jack grabbed a second slice and sat down. He rested it on his leg, licking his fingers.

"Ever hear of using a plate?"

"Then I'd have to do the dishes."

"At least you seem more like yourself now," Parker said. "You've unclenched your ass a bit."

The pizza hit the spot. He wished he had enjoyed the breakfast earlier, but Park was right. His ass had been clenched all the way up to his throat. He was getting back into his groove again, review was moving steadily. The evidence he'd gotten so far was excellent and he felt better by the minute. He wiped his fingers on his pants.

"You're a slob, you know that?"

"Yup," Jack smiled. "Hit play."

Jack had to catch up on the audio to Parker's video so they could stay in sync. Once he did, Jack was already at his re-visit to the morgue.

"That place is so creepy," Parker volunteered.

"It looks like I'm wearing your ring. These are your initials, right?"

"You know that's provoking, right? It's like passive aggressive provoking."

"I was connecting with him. On his level."

"Uh, wrong," Park said.

"Uh, bite me."

"Not on a fucking bet, you asshole."

BEEEEP BEEEEEP BEEEEEEP

They both jumped out of their chairs, Parker hit his knee into the table. "Shit!" He yelled. "Turn that fucker off!"

Jack grabbed it and hit the power button to off. "What the hell? It shouldn't have gone off. We weren't moving."

"Who knows? Maybe you moved your arm or something."

"I didn't.'

"You don't know. You weren't thinking about it."

"I DIDN'T."

"Fine, you didn't. Maybe I did."

They sat back down and continued with Jack in the morgue. Once he was on camera, in the medical room, they heard the morgue door slam shut. It was off camera, though. "What the fuck?!" Jack was entirely annoyed. "Why is everything that happens just off camera?! I can't prove, disprove or anything with that!" He was so frustrated. What the hell is the point of investigating if you can't get anything on camera? A slam means next to nothing if it's only heard.

It could be anything; it could even be set up. The world wouldn't recognize that as any type of evidence. Damn.

"Did you know Carla?" A piece of plaster hit Jack.

"Really, James?" Jack reached for a piece of broken cement and threw it in the direction the plaster had come from. "You wanna play games now?" He was hit, again, by something bigger. Whatever it was wasn't playing games. "Hey! You kids! If it's you, bring your pussy asses out of the darkness now. I'm not scared and I'm not leaving. You want a piece of me? Quit hiding!"

Jack was tense. No, not even tense. He was taut, watching the footage leading up to his attack. God, this was sick. If it had been a TV show, he would've been yelling at the TV. "Don't do it, Buddy! Are you an IDIOT?" They heard the sound before they saw anything.

A growl. Not just a breath or a sound that could be confused came out of the shadows. A GROWL. Jack lurched backward into the wall and the devices went flying. He stayed, suspended, against the wall for what seemed like forever, before sliding down.

Jack scrambled. It looked like a scene from a cartoon, where his feet were moving, suspended above the ground, before he finally fell. There was no humor, though, and before he could get his bearings, he was hit, again. Slammed. He was trying to run for his life when his feet finally got traction. He moved as quickly as he could down the hallway, out of camera range. A barely perceptible shadow formed and was gone.

Parker hit stop. "My God, Jack. Should I...?"

It was just a whisper, "Rewind."

They watched the section again. And again.

Parker couldn't believe what he was seeing had happened to his friend, and Jack was stunned, watching what had happened to himself. Finally, they both sat and stared, neither knowing what to say to the other. Parker got up, opened the refrigerator and asked, "Want a beer?"

"Yeah."

It didn't matter what time of day it was, or if they had eaten. It wasn't a matter of drinking to escape or to get drunk. It was a beer, in silence, with a friend who knew. Who had seen. Who understood.

"Jack?"

"No. I can't answer any questions right now."

"Fair enough."

"Great footage, though. Right?"

"Yeah. So cool."

"Park? Save it to the computer and let's go take a walk. Rake leaves or something."

Parker did just that, and shut down the DVR and computer. They were done. It didn't matter what might be heard or seen on the footage, they had seen enough for one afternoon. Jack ducked into the bedroom to grab a sweatshirt and shove his wallet into his back pocket. Caesar jumped up from his spot on the bed and meowed. Jack paused to give him a quick pet.

As they went out the door, Jack dipped his hand into the bowl on the counter and felt his keys at the bottom. All was well with his little piece of the world. For now. He took the keys and locked the door behind them as they left.

Parker let Jack take the lead. They walked down his driveway and turned right at his mailbox, heading up the street. The day was overcast, with some dark clouds on the horizon, but no rain in the forecast. A typical late October afternoon in New England. There were a few houses on the street, but the closest to 11 Ridley was about a tenth of a mile ahead. Jack lived at the termination of a dead end and liked it that way. Close enough to have neighbors, but far enough for peace and quiet. Trees lined the road, branches overhanging it in spots, but mostly trimmed back to leave room for the electrical lines. He used to lose power a lot before the road crews stepped up to keep the lines clear. Still, having a shed with a generator could sure came in handy. He walked along, staring at the trees, absorbing the cool crisp air.

They got to an intersection and Jack turned right. Still silent, hands pushed deep into the pockets of his sweatshirt, he crossed Jones Street and went into the park. There were a few people out for the afternoon, a couple of joggers doing laps on the path, some guys shooting baskets at the far end. Jack leaned on the merry-go-round.

"It was cold, Park. Really cold. As if something had drained all the warmth and life out of the air while I sat up there."

Parker looked at his friend.

"I can't wrap my head around it. Whatever it was, it hit me with such a force... I couldn't fucking breathe, Park. It was on me and I couldn't take a fucking breath, and then it came again, like a sucker punch. What the fuck was that?"

"Do you want my opinion?"

"Go for it."

"When those kids were in there, doing whatever rituals and shit they were doing, they brought something in. Dark. Negative. It saw you coming and took advantage."

"It rattled the shit out of me. You know me. I'm not scared of anything. Never have been. This thing could've killed me right there. Park, it was fucking real."

"I know, man. I know."

"But you know what gets me more than that?" Jack glanced away. Getting this emotional wasn't like him, either. But, FUCK. This shook him to his core.

"What?"

"Why didn't it?" He hit the metal bar of the merry-go-round. "Why didn't it snuff me out right then and there? I couldn't breathe, it had me."

"I don't know, man. They say those things get off on fear. Maybe it was mad you were up there, disturbing its personal space or something. Gave you a warning."

"I'm definitely warned. It can keep its space. But this has my mind twisted and I can't unknot it," he shoved the merry-go-round, watching it spin.

"You'll go nuts if you keep trying."

"Of that, I'm sure."

They walked for a while, chatting here and there about nothing in particular. It felt good to get out and get some fresh air. Jack could've pointed himself in a direction and kept going. Fear sucked.

By the time they got back to Jack's house, Parker had to leave, but Jack was okay. He needed some downtime. As much as he cared for his best friend, it was good to be alone. He dropped his keys into the bowl. Guess it was time to go in and hang with some crappy TV and ignore the world. Juggling a slice of pizza, a beer and a bag of pretzels, he made his way into the living room. His favorite chair, a big, overstuffed recliner, was waiting for him. Calling to him. And he answered with his ass. The remote was on the arm of the chair, well-worn and he clicked "on". He flipped channels for a bit, landing on the Discovery Channel. He didn't have a brain, or stomach, for that matter, for anything SyFy or paranormal. Not yet. That may take a while. He fell asleep in the chair, waking up in the night long enough to stumble into the bedroom and fall into bed.

Monday morning came early. 5:30 a.m. His alarm clock was like a nail to the brain. That was the one thing Jack didn't like about his job, starting so damned early. He'd shower, dress and get coffee downtown, maybe a breakfast sandwich, and be driving, well, driving for everyone else, by 6:30 a.m. His route was an easy one and boring as hell some days. It all depended on his passengers. Many times it'd be senior citizens going to the local Walmart, others it'd be students headed to the library or the college, all on his route. He'd stop at regular intervals, they'd get on, pay, sit. Some would chat, others would barely look in his direction. He didn't mind. He'd throw on some '80's music, which annoyed the college guys, and enjoy the day. But he did hate getting up early.

He hadn't always been a bus driver. He'd picked up the job after the divorce. He and the, happily now ex, wife had poured their time and money into a little mom and pop business. A homemade pie company, how the hell did he let her talk him into that? It fell through as the marriage died and he left with the clothes on his back, basically. Scooping up the bus job was a godsend. No one telling him what to do, his route ready and waiting every day. Fabulous. When 4:30 p.m. rolled around, he was done and only fifteen minutes from home.

He slowly got out of bed. The shower always woke him up, started the day fresh. He stumbled into the bathroom and turned on the water. The steam slowly filled the bathroom. He got in and stood, letting the water run down his back for a few minutes. Warming his old bones. He chuckled. Perhaps he was getting back to himself after all. Slightly, anyway. He still had the knot in his brain and that wasn't likely going to go away soon. But he could live with trying to work it out. The bone chilling fear couldn't touch him under the steam of the shower. Even his scratches were less noticeable, less painful.

Once showered, he was usually dressed, shaved, and out of the house in about fifteen minutes. He shook the Friskies box and waited for Caesar to come running, but when the cat got to the doorway to the kitchen, he stopped. "Whatever, Cees," Jack said, pouring some cat food into the bowl. He set it on the floor next to the water bowl. "Can't be late."

His drive to work took him past a Dunkin Donuts, a McDonalds, and other quick breakfast stops. He preferred DD for his coffee needs, but hit the drive through at McD's for an egg sandwich. Faster and easier than cooking at home, and there he'd have to do dishes. This way, he could throw his "dishes" out. It worked. He hit a second drive-thru at DD's for a hot, light and sweet. He sipped as he drove. It looked like a beautiful day.

Jack finished the last bite of his sandwich as he pulled into his parking space at Houghton's Bus Service. He wiped his hands on a napkin, tossed it on the passenger seat and swallowed the last bit of coffee in the paper cup before depositing it in the cup holder. The rest of his morning garbage went into the cup to throw out later. Bill, another bus driver, pulled in beside him.

They greeted each other and walked into the office of the bus station together, after Jack hit the clicker and locked his car doors. Not that he had anything to steal. It was just a habit. He was full of habits. Bill and Jack walked up to their manager's desk and waited for their "assignments." They always drove the same routes, but once in a while a stop was added or deleted. Like when a new store would open or an event was going on at the college. Still, pretty regular and routine. He glanced at a mirror that the boss had hanging in the office and made sure his uniform was neat. Bill looked at him and raised his eyebrows. "Women love a man in uniform," Jack replied to Bill's stare. They both laughed, grabbed their clipboards and assignments, and went out to their respective buses. Other drivers would be in later, to stagger the shifts.

Jack flung himself into his bus seat with his usual flare, checked his instruments as if he were piloting a plane, closed his door and turned the key in the ignition. The blue bus roared to life. He checked his mirrors, made sure everything was just the way he liked it, turned on the music and started to roll.

He only drove about half a mile when he got to his first stop: the senior citizen apartments. He wouldn't have many today. Tuesday was the day that all the shops gave senior discounts in his area. They would all get on, chatty and friendly and looking forward to discounts on denture cream, cookies and frozen lasagna. Today was more likely one or two would be going to the doctor, maybe a stop at the pharmacy. "Hello, Mabel," he offered up when a sweet little old lady slowly and delicately moved up the bus steps, holding onto the railing. There was always a hat with a flower on the side and he rarely saw the same hat twice. They never matched her long, dark blue wool coat with the big round buttons, either, but they didn't have to. She was a pip. "How's the hip today?"

"Oh, fine, fine. Shoulder's a little sore, though," she dropped some coins into the fare box and adjusted her hat. He nodded, closed the door, and waited until she took her seat to put the bus into motion. He didn't mind the boring bus route. It was pleasant enough, and he got to see the scenery, watch the seasons change. He didn't even mind when the weather would turn bad. He rather liked a slide here and there. Kept his skills up. He gave a little sigh. It wasn't what he pictured he'd be doing after he got his master's degree, but life gets funny sometimes. At least it paid the bills.

Jack saw that there were a handful of kids, well, they were probably twenty-somethings, waiting in the college's bus area. He swung it in and waited for them to gather their backpacks and belongings and decide to grace him with their presence. He smiled at them as they dropped their coins into the metal box beside him.

"I don't see why we have to pay bus fare," said one bohemian looking guy with a knit beanie. "It stinks of bureaucracy." He touched the side of his nose at Jack and went to find a seat.

"It stinks of gasoline, upkeep, repairs when something's wrong so you can catch a ride when it's cold or wet or you want to get to the store," Jack needled the guy a bit. He rode fairly often and was a good kid. The others got on in silence. Nothing new. They had no use for a bus driver. They'd be surprised to find out he had more education than they did and this wasn't what he had aspired to be all his life.

When Jack was small, he wanted to play ball. Football. Basketball. Soccer. Anything that would get him outside and running. Football was his first love. He tried to join the team in high school, but you had to be good or your mom had to know someone, be PTA involved, or something. He never could make the team. Finally, he quit trying. Pfft. In retrospect, he probably wasn't that good. He chuckled. It didn't matter in the scheme of things. It really hadn't affected him. He went to all the games, and still was the one who got all the girls. He smiled to himself. Yup. Still got it.

When he had gone to college, he hadn't known what he wanted to do with his life. Typical. He liked his classes, but had no drive or motivation. If he liked the subject, he did well. If not, he either dropped it or squeaked by. School had always come easy for him. Until he met Grace. She had been a dark haired beauty who walked into one of his classes the first semester of his junior year. He didn't even remember which class. Might have been math. She was gorgeous. Long, dark hair and eyes browner than brown, with a body that was built for sex. Well, that was the only way he had ever thought to describe her. He thought that long before he had ever asked her out. They hit it off and were inseparable from then on. He found a major, business, that would mesh with her desire to be a small business owner. She'd create the product, he'd keep everything flowing in the background. They were married right after graduation and dove into starting her business. He would have done anything for her.

They had stayed married for seven years. That was it. Wow. He'd been divorced longer now than they'd been married. It was an odd realization to hit him just then. Huh. It didn't bother him anymore. They parted somewhat amiably, although his heart ached for a long time afterward. It's never easy to leave someone you shared a home and bed with. It was right, though. They had grown apart before they had had a chance to grow completely together. He didn't like the word whirlwind, because that would imply rushing into things. Nah, it was more of a whirl-weed. Like a quick little tumble weed. It would blow around, happy and carefree, but was gathering dust and dirt and in the end was brittle and nothing special. He liked that. Whirl-weed.

"What's the fare?" A middle aged man he hadn't seen before had stepped on.

"$1.25."

"Highway robbery."

"Cheaper than owning a car," Jack offered.

"Yeah, right," the man muttered, sliding into the closest seat. "Do you go to Midtown Medical?"

"Absolutely."

The man sat back, somewhat satisfied, and Jack continued through his route, passing by the shops and offices, Walmart, DD, here and there pulling up to a curb and rotating the passengers on, off, on, off. Bus drivers seemed equally liked and disliked among the masses, but more liked than the parking enforcers. He laughed. A little ditty from the Simpsons television show went through his mind. "Hail to the bus driver, bus driver, bus driver, Haaaaaail to the bus driver, bus driver man." Damn… now he'd be humming it all day.

The guy with the beanie got up and stood behind the white line while he waited for Jack to pull to a stop. He knew the drill. He and Jack had danced this dance before. "You need to change up that music, man. That '80's shit, it's…" He shook his head as he started down the steps.

Jack laughed. "Have a nice day!" The guy gave Jack a finger gun and walked away. "It takes all kinds."

His day rolled on, an endless array of faces and stops, until he pulled up for the last stop at Midtown Medical. Mabel was patiently waiting. She took the stairs gradually and deliberately.

"How's the shoulder doing, Mabel?"

"Oh, fine, fine. Hip's a little sore, though." Jack smiled. She was his one constant in her own inconsistencies. He had a soft spot for the little lady.

"Shopping tomorrow?" he asked as she found her seat.

"Oh, yes, yes."

He nodded, closed the door, and pulled away from the curb. He'd drop Mabel off and be at the station in no time. It had been a good day.

Jack walked in the door and dropped his keys into the bowl. What a day! He slumped into a kitchen chair, took his cellphone out of his pocket and opened the small, yellow piece of paper. He stared at it a few seconds, turning it over in his hand. He wanted to call, but needed to put his feet up and tune out the last 48 hours. A drink, some mind numbing TV, some music. Anything but staring at that damned monitor. Perhaps she'd be a well needed distraction. A shower first, then he'd call. Get rid of the sweat and tedium of the day. He dropped the paper on his end table next to his bed and stripped.

He looked closely at his face in the bathroom mirror. Tired eyes and five o'clock shadow. Not bad stubble, though. He liked the way it looked. Kind of a "just stepped out of my pickup and wearing Wrangler jeans" kind of face. He smiled. He'd shave in the morning. The heat of the shower was what he was looking for. He turned on the water and got the steam nice and high. He took a minute to pee as the mirror fogged, then happily stepped into the tub.

The soap smelled great as he lathered up, a manly scent. He chuckled. Well, that was the advertisement said. He generally bought whatever he grabbed first. No big deal. He scrubbed his face and arms, stomach, and the heat was gone. What felt like ice water was pelting him, pouring down his face and torso. "Shit!" he yelled, trying to jump out of the way and, at the same time, swatting the faucet. Somehow the knob had swung all the way around to the cold setting. "What the fuck!" He flipped it back to hot and in a few seconds was re-warming himself. How the hell did that happen? He finished lathering, rinsing and decided the knob had to be loose; he'd check it later. He had better things to do at the moment.

Jack, still wrapped in a towel, sat down on the bed and grabbed his phone and the slip with Laurel's number on it. He dialed.

"Hello?"

"Laurel?"

"Yes?"

"Hey… it's Jack. Jack Barnes. From the restaurant yesterday? I hope I'm not bothering you."

"Oh, Jack! Hi. No, you're not bothering me," she laughed a nervous laugh. "I gave you my number, so how could it be a bother?"

He smiled. "I thought maybe you'd like to get dinner with me one night this week? Get to know each other a bit?"

"Yeah, that'd be really nice."

"Would it be weird to go to A Touch of Home? It's my favorite. If you'd rather go somewhere else, that's fine, too."

Laurel laughed, "No, that'd be fine. I'm off Thursday night. I could meet you around 7:00?"

"Great. That'd be great."

"Great."

They could both feel the conversation getting awkward. The blessing of not knowing the person you're making a date with. Life was funny that way.

"Okay. Time to feel a little awkward on a first call. I can't wait for dinner Thursday. See you at 7:00."

"Great," she laughed. "See you then."

They hung up and Jack felt…well, great. He was really looking forward to Thursday's dinner and getting to know Laurel. What a pretty name, he thought. He leaned back in bed, slid off the towel, and started something else he hadn't done in a while. And damn, if he didn't feel he deserved it.

He relaxed on his bed for a while after he came, absently petting Caesar and just feeling good, until his stomach started growling. "Well, Cees, let's see what's for dinner." He wandered into the kitchen and, again Caesar stopped dead in the doorway. "What's the deal, Caesar?" The cat stared at him, turned and walked back into the living room. His bowl of food hadn't been touched. "Now, that's weird," Jack muttered. He checked the freezer.

He didn't mind cooking, but lately he'd fallen into the bachelor frozen food mentality. From freezer to microwave to stomach. Ah, he was getting tired of it. But quick and easy is quick and easy. He took out a turkey pot pie. That was almost like cooking. Almost. It had oven instructions on it, but he'd throw it in the microwave anyway. 7:00 minutes and dinner was served. He took the steaming hot bowl out of the microwave with oven mitts, grabbed a fork and put it all onto his coffee table. Caesar immediately jumped onto the coffee table, meowing up a storm. "Oh, now you want MY food?" Jack smiled. He clicked the TV on with the remote, sat, and found a couple of little pieces of turkey to let cool for Caesar. His cat devoured them and begged for more.

"You're a royal pain," Jack commented, taking more turkey bites out of his meal. "Why didn't you touch your crunchies?" Not that crucnchies were better than bites of well, frozen processed, turkey. "We all get off our feed once in a while, eh, Cees?" The cat purred while it happily chewed. Before the cat could decide to settle in his lap, he made a quick stop in the kitchen for a bottle of seltzer. He got back onto the sofa, put his feet up, and was joined by his favorite, furry buddy. He reached back, over his head, to the end table and felt around for his book. There was nothing on TV, really. Reality shows, trumped up paranormal shows (those he liked to categorize as the "Oh, I HEARD A NOISE IT MUST BE A GHOST, RUN! shows), and general crap. Even the news wasn't much lately. He clicked it off.

He turned the book over in his hand. Ah, classic supernatural tales. He loved them. Everything recently was all special effects and no plot. He thumbed through until he found where he had left off what seemed like ages ago, and began to read. Caesar climbed onto his lap, kneaded his leg a little…Sheesh, Cees…and finally went to sleep. He read until he started to doze himself, but was brought out of it by a loud bang. He jumped; Caesar dove under the sofa.

Jack ran into the kitchen, the direction the noise had come from. It had sounded like a crash, as if an entire drawer of silverware had slammed to the floor. He searched. Nothing. Nothing had fallen or broken. He flipped on the outdoor light in case something had happened outside. Maybe someone had hit a light pole. Nothing. All was quiet and calm. He shook his head and ran his hand through his hair. He gave a quick look through the rest of the house, his bedroom, the basement. Could he have dreamed it? No. He was sure he didn't. File that under odd happenings. He checked his watch. 11:30 p.m. "Come on, Caesar," he called. "Let's get to bed." The cat stayed under the sofa. He wasn't coming for anything.

He woke with a start at 5:40 a.m., the alarm blaring. 5:40?? He checked the clock. Must've hit snooze, although he didn't remember it. Damn. He felt as if he'd barely slept. Almost as if he'd been in a bad dream that he couldn't remember, but that robbed him of a restful night. He rushed through his shower and skipped his breakfast sandwich, but ordered an extra-large coffee at DD. He had a feeling he'd need it.

Bill was already in the office when Jack pulled up. "Morning," Jack reached for his assignment while taking a large mouthful of coffee. He got right to his bus and on the road as quickly as he could. He hated being late, and if he started late, he'd screw up everyone's day who needed him to get them where they had to go. He almost chuckled as he closed his bus door and headed for the senior center. Maybe if he was the kind of guy who could wake up earlier, have a leisurely breakfast and actually start his day, say, an hour earlier than he did, things would work better. He just couldn't bring himself to do it. He stifled a yawn.

"Morning, Mabel," he said, routinely, when she started up his steps. "How are you today?"

"Oh, fine, fine. Knee's sore, though." She moved to her usual seat.

"Where are you headed today?"

"You just drive. I'll get off when it's time."

Jack smiled. She was still in control of her faculties and liked to be in charge. He didn't mind. It was like having his own mother around again. He missed his mom now and then, even though she'd been gone ten years. Ah, well. The next stops awaited. The coffee helped, some. He was almost jittery, and was getting hungry on top of it. Never a good combination. He wished he had stashed a power bar or something snacky somewhere, but he always ran out of the house too fast in the morning to think of it. Especially today.

As he drove through the seemingly endless stops, the weather turned. From overcast and chilly to raining and cold. His mood was starting to echo the day. When his bus was empty and he was between stops, he parked alongside the McD's and was able to run in for a sandwich. It helped him physically, but the weather still gave him a bit of a low. It was always so somber when it rained in October. Like the dead days of winter were at hand. He liked winter, but some days had that stark, empty feeling. When the trees first empty their leaves and wait. Wait for what, he wasn't sure, but they seemed to wait. For snow to cover them and seem more holiday-esque? For spring? He was unsure. It was a long wait, though. He didn't like the empty trees.

He sighed. Even the pumpkins and jack-o-lanterns looked lonely in the rain. Halloween was coming soon and that didn't cheer him, either. Oh, it wasn't that bad, he wasn't a scrooge or anything, and you'd think it would be his favorite holiday of the year, given his profession. But, as busy as he usually was during the month, for obvious ghostly reasons, he just didn't like handing out candy. OH, what a cute little witch; OH, what a great little Spiderman. It wasn't him. The last few years he left his outside light off. He got very few trick or treaters, anyway, living at the butt end of a dead end road. It worked for him, he guessed.

Maybe he was just damn tired on a rainy, dank day. He pulled his bus into the parking lot and ran into the office to hand in the day's paperwork. He had hoped that the rain would ease up while he was inside, but no such luck. Not today. He pushed the glass door open and half-ran to his car, stepping in a puddle and soaking his foot on the way. "Damn it!" It was like a Charlie Brown moment. "I got a rock."

When he got home, Jack saw that Caesar still hadn't touched his cat food. Perhaps there was something wrong with the bag. He dumped it into the garbage, scrubbed Caesar's bowl, and refilled it from a new bag. "That should do it. Cees?" He looked over his shoulder, expecting a ball of fur to come barreling in from the living room, but nothing. "Cees?" He looked around the corner into the living room and Caesar was sitting on the recliner, staring back. Jack shook the cat food box. Nothing. Geez, what a day. Everyone was out of sorts. He walked over, picked up his cat, and brought him to the food bowl. Caesar scrambled as fast as his paws would carry him, back to the living room. "Fine," Jack muttered. "You'll eat when you're ready." For himself, he hit the speed dial for Yang's, the local Chinese food hotspot. He was not even going to try cooking tonight. Or microwaving. Whatever. He ordered some General Tso's chicken and won ton soup. That should be good on a shitty night. He turned on the TV while he waited.

A knock at the side door brought him out of a documentary he was listening to about the disappearance of bees. He walked into the kitchen, switching on the light. He swung open the door to the delivery guy's surprise. "Whoa," the kid said. "Where's the other guy?"

"Other guy? What other guy?"

"The guy that was just here. I saw him through the window as I drove up. He would've been standing, there. In front of the sink." The guy pointed and was trying to look over Jack's shoulder.

"Buddy, there's no one else here. Must've been a shadow or something." Jack pulled out his wallet.

"$14.75."

Jack handed him a $20. "Keep the change."

"Yeah, thanks, man," the kid was still glancing around, uncomfortably, as he went down the steps.

Jack brushed it off. Was probably a shadow from having on the TV. He opened the cartons and closed his eyes, breathing in deeply. Just what he wanted. He poured the soup into a big mug so it'd be easier to carry, put the Tso's on a plate and set it all on the coffee table next to the dish from last night. Ah, yeah. He'd need to do his dishes soon. Caesar pulled himself out from under the sofa. "What were you doing under there?" Jack asked. The cat stretched and jumped up next to the plate of chicken. He sat. Expectantly. Knowingly. And, of course, he got.

Curious, Jack went out to the kitchen and brought back Caesar's food and water bowls. Caesar dove into the crunchies, after the chicken of course, as if he had never eaten before. "What's the deal, cat?" He scratched Caesar's ears. "Why won't you touch them out there?" Jack shrugged. It could be easy as Cees not feeling well the other day and maybe now, with some spicy Tso's, he's feeling more like himself.

Jack's phone rang. Parker. "Yeah," Jack said between mouthfuls.

"What's for dinner?"

"What are you, a stray cat?"

"Yeah, that's me. What's dinner?"

"Chinese."

"Got any extra?"

Jack looked at the half gone plate and said, "Sure. If you get here before Caesar has at it."

Parker laughed. "5 minutes. Keep his whiskers out of it."

Jack smiled. He wondered what Park had up his sleeve tonight. Ten minutes later, Parker was in the car port. He gave a passing knock on the door as he walked in. "Where's…"

"Caesar finished it."

For a split second, Parker looked concerned, but then he knew better.

"Grab a fork and have at it." He handed Parker the plate. Happily, Parker helped himself to silverware and then sat in the recliner near Jack and Caesar.

"What's doing? How's work?"

"Exciting as ever. What's up with you?"

"Was passing by. Checking in. Making sure you're still alive and kicking."

Jack laughed. "And looking for a free meal."

Parker smiled. "Always." He stopped to chew. "Did you call the waitress?"

"Yup."

"What'd she say?"

"What's she supposed to say? She wants to take it on all fours and have my babies."

Parker almost choked on the mouthful of food he had. "You're such a shit."

"Yeah, I am," Jack laughed. "We're going out Thursday night. Dinner."

"Nice. Where you going?" Caesar circled Parker's legs, rubbing and looking for attention. He reached down and scratched under the cat's chin.

"Forget it. I'm not telling you."

"Why not?" Parker tried his best attempt at innocence.

"Because you're a fucker who'd show up. Been there, done that. Not again." Jack walked into the kitchen to get a bottle of seltzer. He drank out of the bottle itself. It was better than washing a glass. He brought it back with him.

"Come on! I'll sit at a distance."

"You won't be there. Lost one date over your antics."

"Antics?" Parker was amused. "She was awful, man. Not your type at all." He motioned for the seltzer and Jack tossed it to him.

"Yeah. She was pretty bad."

"So, I saved you from the biggest mistake of your life."

"And got us banned from a movie theater. For life! Not happening. Laurel seems really nice."

"Fine, fine."

"You sound like Mabel now."

"How is the dear grandma?"

"Everything hurts, but still going strong."

"…and," Parker paused. "How's your side?"

Jack lifted his shirt a bit. Parker could see that the scratches were barely visible. He nodded. "Been concerned about that."

"Well, I was, too. But everything seems to be getting back to normal. As normal as it ever was, I guess."

"I hear that. When do you want to get back to review?" Parker tossed the plate onto the growing pile of dishes on the coffee table and finished the seltzer. He looked around. "Where's dessert?"

Jack rolled his eyes. "I didn't get any. And as for review, I don't know. Maybe on the weekend?"

"How do you not get dessert? Don't they always at least throw in some fortune cookies?" Parker went into the kitchen and went through the bag the cartons came in. "Bingo!" he yelled. Jack shook his head as he heard the rustling of plastic as Parker opened and ate each cookie. He walked back into the living room. "You didn't want any, did you?" he asked with his mouth full.

"You are such an asshole."

"Born and bred. Hey, want to catch a movie?"

"Nah. I've got to get up in the morning. Some of us work, you know."

"Yeah, yeah. I work."

"Banker's hours."

"Hell, yeah. Well, if you're not in, I'm out. Places to go, people to see. You know."

Jack laughed. "I know. Go. I'll call you at the end of the week."

"Thanks for dinner!" Parker called out as he went down the side steps.

"Anytime, you jerk. Next time at least take off your jacket!"

As Parker drove off, he gave Jack a thumb's up out the window. Jack was glad he came by. They were like brothers. It was always a feel good time when he was around. Well, mostly. Since they were so close, they pissed each other off to hell and back sometimes. But it never mattered.

Jack looked at Caesar and then at the dishes. "Guess it's time to get it done, eh, Cees?"

The cat stretched and strode over to the recliner. He hopped up and settled in to nod off. Jack gathered up the dishes.

Thursday night couldn't come quickly enough. Jack finished his shift and rushed home. There were a couple of hours before he would be meeting Laurel and he planned on taking advantage of them. A hot shower was first on his list.

He walked in the door and was hit by an odor. Foul. "Cees! Whatever you left in that litterbox, damn!" No wonder the cat wasn't eating well. That definitely didn't smell like anything normal. He opened a few windows to air out the place. "You're not sleeping next to me tonight. Find yourself somewhere else, farty cat."

He dropped his keys in the bowl. "Now, what the fuck?" Two of his kitchen drawers were opened. Wide open. How did Caesar do that? He shut them both. What was getting into that cat? He'd watched Caesar open the cabinet doors before, but this must be a new trick. Maybe he climbed up on the counter and wedged one of his paws down and in… it didn't seem feasible, but there really was no other explanation. Unless he was losing his mind and actually left them open himself. That didn't happen. It had to be Caesar. That cat was getting a little weird.

"Cees?" Jack called for him. He walked into the living room. "Caesar. Where are you?" He got down on his knees and looked under the sofa. Two bright cat's eyes stared at him from far back by the wall. "You crazy little cat. What's the deal?" He reached in to pull him out and Caesar hissed. Hissed! Another first and not one he liked. "All right. Stay under there if you want. But something's gotta give."

The shower called. It'd been too long since it was a refresher for a night out, rather than an unwinding for a night home alone. He debated shaving, but decided clean cut was best for a first date. He dug through his medicine cabinet and found some cologne. Cool Water by Davidoff. He loved the scent. Oceany. Clean. A quick spray and he was set. Just had to get dressed and then pace the floor until it was time to meet Laurel. He smiled. This felt good.

Jeans. A blue, button down shirt. Casual, yet...casual. Again, he smiled. That summed him up in a nutshell. He owned a couple of suits, but could barely remember the last time he wore one. Probably his mom's funeral. Yeah, that was it. Not quite the best suit memory. He'd stick to jeans. They felt more natural. He checked himself out in the mirror over his dresser. Yes. Acceptable. Even presentable. He chuckled. Hell, he felt like he was twenty again. The nervous boy at the door. "Hello, Sir. I'm here for your daughter." At least he had more confidence than that. More like, "Hey, I'm taking your daughter out tonight. Deal."

The clock on the night stand seemed to be moving way too slowly. 5:45 p.m. Fuck. An hour to wait before he would even leave the house. "Okay, Cees. It's you and me, buddy. Gonna come out?" He was back on his knees, peering under the sofa, trying to coax him with some tuna. Caesar had relaxed a little, sniffed the fish, and at least got close enough that Jack could gently reach in and slide him out. "Good boy, Cees. What got you so upset?" He pet Caesar until he had to change his shirt. Never knew gray cats shed so prolifically. At least he had more than one blue shirt. He deposited Caesar on the bed and got changed.

"Well, that killed fifteen minutes." He looked around to see if there was anything, ANYTHING, he could do to waste some time. Picked up a book, put it down. Clicked the television on, turned it off. Folded some laundry. This was ridiculous. He strode out to the kitchen, grabbed his keys from the bowl and left. So, he'd sit in the parking lot for forty-five minutes. At least he wouldn't be pacing the house.

"Are you fucking kidding me?" Jack had put the key in the ignition and it wouldn't turn over. Nothing. Not a moan or groan or death rattle. "It figures." He hit the steering wheel. "Son of a bitch." He thought about calling a tow truck to come get it, but didn't want to deal with it tonight; Parker, for a ride to the restaurant… oh, hell no. He looked at the sky. Clear, cool. Beautiful. He'd leave the car until tomorrow and walk. Why the hell not? It'd get rid of some nervous energy and the frustration over the car. He stuffed his hands in his pockets and started out.

It took about forty-five minutes, but Jack got to A Touch of Home with about ten minutes to spare. The parking lot was well lit and he didn't see Laurel around yet. He made a quick trip into the men's room to make sure he still looked neat and not too terribly windblown. All was well. He stepped back out into the restaurant and waited by the entrance.

Laurel walked up, right on time, in jeans and an attractive V-neck sweater. Purple. Always a good choice. Her hair was loose and brushed her shoulders as she walked. He gave the door a push open for her to step through. "Remember me?" He asked with a smile.

"Yes, yes I do," his smile was reciprocated, along with a quick hug. "Nice cologne."

"Thank you."

"Feels a little odd, waiting for the hostess to seat us."

"Did you want to go somewhere else? Really, it's okay."

She smiled. "No, it's fine. I do like it here."

Jack had the hostess take them to a booth, beside a window, on the far side of the restaurant. "Do you need one of these?" He handed her a menu.

"I usually work days," she offered. "The night menu is a little new." She unwrapped her silverware and put her napkin in her lap. Jack followed suit. "A few of the other waitresses say you're quite the regular on weekends."

"Oh, yeah," he said. "Bachelor life, I guess. It's nice to have something that tastes homemade. I usually live out of my freezer."

A waitress stopped by their table, turned over their glasses and poured cold water. Jack appreciated that and thanked her. His throat was dry.

"Well," Laurel began. "You know what I do for a living. What do you do?"

"By day or by night?"

"Oh, now that's intriguing. Are you Batman?" she smiled.

"Haha. Well, week days I drive a bus for Houghton."

"Ah."

"Yeah, I know. Exciting as paint drying, right?"

"No, I didn't mean…"

"No, it's true. No worries." They both laughed, nervously? Earnestly? It didn't matter. He was happy to be there, with her, regardless. "It wasn't what I went to school for, either. But… by night, I'm a paranormal investigator."

"Get out. Are you really?"

He nodded, sipping some water. It was icy cold, nearly making his teeth ache.

"That's so cool."

"Thanks. I enjoy it."

The waitress came back and took their orders. Jack didn't care what he had. He was hungry, but more interested in the woman sitting across from him. She was pretty and intelligent. She hadn't pursued a conversation about ghost hunting, and that was cool. Most people he ran into were suddenly wanting to know what had he found, anything negative? Had he been touched, heard his name called, and more. She was interested in HIM.

He wanted to know, why waitressing? She had started when she was in college. Her major was wonderful, English. But unless you went into teaching or writing, it was tough finding a job you were qualified for. She had made the mistake of going for her passion and not for something that would become a career. He could totally understand that. She loved this area, so didn't want to move to some big city where there were more jobs. She was taking more classes and enjoyed the people at the restaurant.

"When I figure out my 'life's direction,' I'll change jobs," another beautiful smile from her. "Any pets?"

"A three year old Russian blue cat named Caesar. You?"

"Oh, he sounds pretty. Love the name."

"Yeah, he rules," Jack grinned. He loved bad puns. The worse, the better. It seemed that Laurel liked it, too, although she almost lost a mouthful of coffee.

"They don't allow pets where I rent. Would love some someday, though. A cat, a dog."

A few minutes later, the waitress was back with their meals; roast beef for him, with mashed potatoes and gravy, and chicken parmesan for her. Coffees. People in the restaurant came and went, but there was no people-watching for him. He was fully focused on his date. They hit every "first date" subject they could think of, siblings, parents, college days, favorite foods... he learned she had three sisters, loved pizza, hated liver, her parents lived in Maine. She had been married, once. Young. It lasted about a year and they were both better off. He volunteered a brother in Missouri, a love of anything home cooked and that his parents, unfortunately, had passed. And, he was divorced. They continued chatting over more coffee and apple pie. Split, though. Two forks. She didn't think she'd have room after the chicken parm. He didn't mind at all.

The waitress stopped by one more time, leaving the check face down on the table. Jack picked it up and Laurel asked, "Dutch?"

"Nope." He pulled out his wallet. "I've got it, Doll."

A small, sweet smile and she said, "Then I've got the tip."

"Fair enough." They walked slowly to the cashier counter, making some small talk. Jack paid and they stepped outside together. "Well."

"Well." Laurel looked around. "I'm parked about three rows over. Where're you?"

"Funny story…"

"Oh?"

"I was going to get here early and, so, of course, my car was dead when I got in."

"Oh, no! What'd you do, a taxi?"

He laughed. "I walked."

"Walked?!"

"Seemed like a nice night for it. Was only about forty-ish minutes."

"Jack, would you like a ride home?" She looked up at him. He figured she was about 5'4" or so to his 5'11".

"I don't want to take you out of your way."

"I don't mind. Really."

"Okay, then. That'd be great. Thanks!"

Jack directed her the few streets, lefts and rights, and to his dead end. She pulled into the carport. "That your poor dead Subaru?"

"Yeah… gonna have to get on that tomorrow. What a pain."

They paused that awkward pause. He turned to her, "Thanks for a great evening. I really enjoyed it."

"Me, too."

He leaned in for a quick kiss on her cheek.

"You have a roommate?"

"What? No. I live alone, why?"

"I thought I saw someone at the window."

"Maybe I left the TV on when I left. The delivery guy thought he saw someone the other night, too. But, it's just me."

"No, I really think I saw someone."

Jack got out of her Corolla and quickly checked his doors. All locked. He walked over to her side of the car and she rolled down the window. "Seems fine. No worries."

"Jack?"

"Yeah?" he bent down and she gave him a kiss.

"Call me." She put the car in reverse and backed out of his driveway.

"Be careful what you wish for!" He waved as she drove off. Jack was beaming and took his steps in one leap. Unlocking the door and dropping the keys into the bowl, he was on top of the world. He saw that a drawer was open in the kitchen and shut it absently. His mind was on his date and how happy he felt. It was only 9:00, but it could've been midnight or two in the afternoon, he was ecstatic. Wide eyed, heart pounding, happy.

He scooped Caesar out of the recliner and sat down, holding him close and telling him about the night. He grabbed his phone to call Parker, but... put it down. Men don't call men. Not like that. It'd be, "Did you do her? How far'd you get?" All the usual guy talk. He thought he'd keep this to himself for now. Maybe tell Parker tomorrow. Ah, he couldn't sit. "Sorry, Cees." He picked up the dishes on the coffee table and deposited them in the sink, getting out the dish soap from underneath and started the water running. Not his favorite job, but necessary, and he was too antsy to sit right now. Better to get a few things done before bed. He rinsed the cups and plates, putting them into the dishwasher. Yeah, a single guy with enough dishes to fill a dishwasher. Kinda pathetic, but, it worked. He'd run it later and have enough plates and things for almost two weeks.

He thought about Laurel. He already wanted to call her under the guise of asking if she got home safely. Just really wanting to hear her voice again and talk some more. He'd wait to call, though. Perhaps tomorrow night after work. No one wanted to be THAT guy. The needy guy. The "he got so clingy, I couldn't stand it" guy. Damn. Life was too complicated. If he wanted to call, he should be able to pick up the phone. But, not yet. The last dish went into the dishwasher and next, laundry. He had a pile sitting in the corner, waiting until there was enough to make a load. If he put them in now, they'd hit the dryer before he went to bed. Fresh clothes in the morning. Nice. He scooped up the clothes, fought with the doorknob on the door to the basement, and then was down the stairs.

It was cool and dark in the basement; a little musty. Definitely not fresh, but not unpleasant. Jack struggled to pull the string for the light, but when your arms are wrapped around jeans, socks and shirts, not easy. He piled them on the washer and turned to get the light. A cool breeze whipped past his face, toward the stairs. He recoiled. How odd was that? He checked both of the small basement windows, but they were latched pretty tightly. Eh, he shrugged it off and went back to shoving the laundry into the front loading machine. Jeans, tees, work shirts… he never sorted. It went in the pile, the pile got cleaned. That was that. Jack pushed the start button and went back up the stairs to the kitchen, kicking the door shut behind him. He grabbed a bag of dry cat food and walked around the corner into the living room. He'd stopped feeding Caesar in the kitchen; the bizarre animal wouldn't eat there. So, now, the food and water were next to his recliner. Not optimal, but Cees had to eat.

He looked around and sighed. He didn't want to put clothes away, or work on "house things" at all. A book until he got tired might hit the spot a little better. He meowed for Cees and got undressed. Slipping under the covers, he suddenly had a cat on his pillow, nosing his cheek. He leaned into Caesar, rubbing the cat's ears, forehead to forehead. All he could hear was a satisfied purrrrrrrrrr. He fluffed his pillow a bit behind his back, pulled up the comforter and opened his book.

It had to have been about half an hour later when Jack heard a doorknob turn, a latch click. He glanced up from his book as Caesar growled in the direction of his doorway. "Hello?" he called, knowing they were alone. He left the book on the bed and went out to the kitchen. Somehow, the door to the basement had opened. He examined the latch. It seemed to be working perfectly. He swung it shut three or four times and tried pulling it open. Each time, it stayed tightly shut with a satisfying thud, having to turn the knob to unlatch it. Another head shaker, but perhaps it hadn't fully latched when he kicked it with his foot. He pushed it shut, tested it, and went back to bed. He tucked the book away on his night stand, turned off the overhead light, and went to sleep.

It was a restless night, filled with dreams. Not great dreams or nightmares. Just dreams. When you wake up and know that you're brain has made up stories all night, but you were too tired to remember them. Especially at 5:30 a.m. Damn alarm. He tried to remember one as he got under the steam of the shower. He lathered up and bits and pieces of the last dream came to him. He and Laurel were together. They were out, having a good time, at...a concert? An amusement park? He couldn't put his finger on it. At the high point of the dream, suddenly, Laurel was seized from behind. She was pulled away from him and into the darkness by something he couldn't see as he watched helplessly. Something maniacal laughed in the background. He had woken at that moment to the noise, BEEEEP BEEEEEP BEEEEEP. A little perplexing, but probably his own psyche at work. It'd been a long time since he had dated or let a woman get close to him. Probably part of him was afraid she'd disappear. Huh. Armchair psychologist to the stars.

Wrapped in a towel, he went into the kitchen. The basement door was open. Damn it! Well, no time now to mess with that latch. He quickly went down the steps, barefoot, to grab the clean clothes from the dryer. Then he realized, he had never gone back downstairs to move his things from the washer. Fuck! He threw them into the dryer and ran back up, dropping the towel on the bed, and dug through what was still in the clean basket. Luckily, there was a pair of jeans and a work shirt in the pile. He finished getting ready, gave Caesar a quick pet, and was out the door, grabbing his keys from the bowl on his way. He was in the car and turning the key when he remembered that the car was dead. Shit. But it turned over. It was running. He didn't have time to question it now; he put it in reverse, backed down the driveway and got his ass to work.

At least it was Friday and he was on time, even with stopping at DD. He hated to feel rushed and was rarely ever late. It just wasn't him. Anywhere he went, he needed to be on time or early. His mother had instilled it in him when he was young: You never made anyone else wait. He had an intense concept of right, wrong and how the world worked. Had to be his German side. Thanks, Mom. He chuckled. He loved that in her and clung to the ideals within himself, as well.

The office was already buzzing and he had his paperwork in hand when Bill walked in the door. "Like two ships that pass in the night, eh, Bill?" he nodded at his friend as he went right out to his vehicle. He sat for a moment to inhale the steam from his coffee. Damn, it smelled good. A fast sip and he burned his tongue. Unreal. And, it would be another day without breakfast. He hoped this wasn't becoming the norm. He got the bus warmed up and hit the route.

"Hey, Mabel. How's it going?"

"Oh, I'm going, I guess." She paused by the fare box and gave him the hint of a smile before moving down the aisle to her seat. Senior citizens rode free on Fridays. Sometimes he thought she only got on to ride around because of that. It was a "secret" that she had over the other riders. Ah, he did like that little lady.

"Where you going today, Mabel?" He pulled the doors shut.

"Oh, you just drive. Don't you worry about me." He smiled to himself. She was something else.

He drove his route, with all the familiar hellos and the unfamiliar nods, watching the traffic and stop signs, traffic lights and pedestrians. Even the dull creak of the brakes and the smell of the exhaust was ordinary; the quiet thud as the doors came together before he gave the bus gas to move on. Today felt entirely routine, with a more than just "It's Friday" need for the day to wrap up. He wanted to get home and call Park. And Laurel. In that order? Hahaha. Maybe not. He was hoping for another date with her, and to set up some review time with Park. He was giving in to not doing this review alone. He needed Park there to bounce things off, to chat it up and to make sure he didn't lose it. Laurel, well, she was Laurel.

He turned in his paper work and got to his car. He pulled out his phone and dialed, sitting in the parking lot. Voicemail. Damn. "Hey, Laurel. It's Jack. I had a great time the other night and was wondering if you'd like to do something over the weekend? Give me a call. Bye, Doll." Damn. Well, Park could wait until he got home. He turned the key in his ignition and it shook to life. "Good girl," he whispered, and guided her out of the lot.

Jack went up his side steps in a bound. He was ready to start the weekend. He unlocked the door and held out his hand to drop his keys in the bowl as he went by. Chink. They hit the counter. WTF? The bowl that was always right beside the door was at the other end of the opposite counter. He stared. He didn't move it and Cees might have knocked it down, but he never would've gotten it back up on the other side of the room. Something was definitely not right. He left the bowl where it was and turned, noticing that the door to the basement was unlatched. Again. His cell was out of his pocket and he was speed dialing Parker before he even tried processing what was going on.

It rang three times. Park, come on, man. Be there. Four. Voicemail. Fuck. "Park, call me. As soon as you get this, call me. Something's up, man." He stood in his kitchen, looking from the bowl to the door and back. No wonder Cees wasn't himself. This just wasn't right.

His phone went off. Jack jumped, he had been so focused on his kitchen. "Park, drop what you're doing and get over here."

"Um, Jack?" He looked at his phone. Shit, it was Laurel.

"Oh, hey, Doll. Sorry. Thought it was my buddy calling back."

"Did I get you at a bad time?"

"Oh, hey, no. It's a great time." Truly, he was happy to hear her voice, but he needed to talk to Park. "I was hoping you'd call."

She laughed. "I was hoping you were telling me to come right over."

He smiled. "You're always welcome." He could almost see her blush. He could settle into this phone call without a thought.

"What were you thinking of over the weekend?"

"Now that, I hadn't figured out yet. I thought that whatever it was, it'd be more fun with you."

"How about I cook you dinner and then we can figure it out? We can stay in and watch a movie, or go out?"

"Oh, that sounds nice. How's Sunday? Park and I will probably be working on some evidence review tomorrow and I can't guarantee what time we'll get done."

"Sounds great. I'll text you my address. Be there... 6:00 ish?"

"Perfect. See you then, Doll."

Jack was startled out of his thoughts by a pounding at the door. Parker walked in. "What's up? I got your message on my way home."

"I've got something here, Park. It must've followed me home."

"What? Wh-"

Jack pointed at the bowl. "It was over there when I got home and the basement door keeps opening, no matter how securely I close it."

Parker would've questioned anyone else. Did they move the bowl and forget, is the latch broken on the door, etc., but he knew Jack. Better than he knew almost anyone. Jack wouldn't have called if he wasn't sure.

"And Cees' been acting strange for days. Won't eat in the kitchen, hides under the sofa. I thought he was being weird. But now I know."

"Okay. What do you want to do?"

"I want information. I want to know who or what is here. And why."

"Then let's set up some equipment and see what we catch."

Jack smiled. He knew he could count on Park. "A couple video cameras should be good, and we can do some EVP sessions. I had been thinking we'd finish up the review tomorrow, but maybe we'll work on some of that tonight."

"You got it. Hey, did you eat? I'm starved."

"You're paying this time. Order us whatever. I'm hungry, too."

"Sheesh. Do a friend a favor and buy dinner, too?

"Yes. Do it well enough and maybe we'll grab drinks later. My treat." Jack opened the case closest to his side of the kitchen table.

"Now you're talking!" It didn't take long for the two of them to decide on a camera angle for each video feed. One in the doorway between the living room and the kitchen, facing the basement door, and the other at the far end of the kitchen, so it would see both where the bowl should be and the basement door. If either moved, they'd have it from two angles. They taped the wires up high and ran them to the DVR so that Caesar wouldn't trip them. Jack switched out the batteries in his voice recorder.

"Any ideas as to who it is?" Parker asked.

"None. Maybe Carla? She seemed to be a little active that night. James? I have what appears to be his ring… no idea. But I want whoever it is, out."

"Have you noticed anything else unusual lately?"

Jack had to think for a minute. "A cold breeze went past me in the basement, but that could be anything." Park nodded. Yeah, that's the old Jack starting to surface. "Oh! Yeah. The delivery guy thought he saw someone standing in the kitchen. Laurel saw the same thing."

"Really? A shadow? A full out apparition?"

"I'm thinking silhouette. They thought someone was there besides me."

"Cool. Can't wait to see what we get. Hopefully you only brought a curious spirit back."

Jack went silent. He hadn't considered anything else.

3

Dinner arrived about thirty minutes later. Parker paid the delivery driver. "I got us subs, Jack. Ham, provolone, oil and vinegar." He found some plates in the cabinet and started opening the wraps. He handed Jack a plate.

"Sounds good to me. I'm starved." Caesar sat in the bedroom doorway, eyeing Jack and Park, and the ham. Jack meowed, but his cat was having none of it. He finally had to get up and bring Caesar a few strips of ham. Caesar purred like a motor that just wouldn't quit and then curled up on the bed to sleep.

"Okay, Park. What say we get started?"

Parker wiped his face on a napkin, then wadded up the wax paper wrap the sandwiches came in. He threw it into the garbage pail and smiled. "2 points. Let's do it, man. Where do you want to start?"

"How about right here? The basement had the cold breeze, but everything seems to be centered here."

"Break out with that voice recorder. Let's get some EVP's!"

Jack loved Parker's enthusiasm. He turned on the recorder. They sat silently for a few minutes and Jack asked, "Is there anyone here with us tonight? Carla? James? Did you come back with me?"

"If so, you need to go back," added Parker. "You don't belong here, and you're bothering the cat." Jack rolled his eyes. "Well, if it's them, they used to be human. They can relate. Sheesh." Jack laughed. They continued on, lighthearted. It felt better having Park around. Didn't seem as serious. He knew they'd figure it out, send it on its way. He had always debunked and documented. Never had any occasion to try to move someone, or something, on, or back where it came from. This was new territory. Rather intriguing. He was getting his "investigative excitement" on. His "ghost groove." He chuckled.

"I think it's getting colder in here," Park said, after a few quiet minutes. Jack pulled the Mel-Meter out of his case and turned it on. It registered at a steady 67 degrees. "Thermostat's set at 68 day and night, so probably not a dip. I'll watch it, though."

"Is that you, making it colder?" Parker asked. He waited. "Can you move the bowl for us?"

"Did you open the basement door?" He was no longer as uncomfortable with the thought of the door unlatching. They stared at the door, tense and waiting for any type of movement. Any indication. Caesar meowed. Jack turned quickly in his direction. Nothing. "He probably wants more of that ham."

"Well, Caesar," Parker said, hunching forward to look into the bedroom doorway, "You are SOL."

"Focus, Park," and then, to the room, "Why are you here? Why did you move the bowl?"

"Have you been bothering the cat?" Parker shrugged.

"What year did you die?"

"Can you give us a sign of your presence? Let us know that you're here?"

"You know, I could get down the –"

"Oh, no, you won't!"

"Just saying. It might make it easier for them? Isn't that the idea?"

"No, the idea is you'll be opening a portal that you won't know how to close…and who knows if it's already been done, before you? Bad idea, Jack."

"Fine, fine. Ya pussy," Jack teased his buddy.

"I'll be keeping my pussy alive and well, thanks," Parker said without batting an eye. "If I had one."

They sat a little longer. "Maybe this would be easier after it gets dark," suggested Parker.

"You know, as well as I do, time of day doesn't matter when it comes to this stuff. That's all what they build up on TV."

"Yeah, yeah, I know," Parker rubbed his chin. "But the energy is different at night. What time of day did the others see the shadows… the delivery guy and Laurel?"

"It was later. Laurel saw it after dark."

"See?"

"So, you're tired of sitting here already and want to do something else until its dark?" Jack asked. "And you call yourself a ghost hunter."

"No, I call myself an educated paranormal enthusiast. I'm friends with a ghost hunter, and yeah, this is pretty fucking boring." He smiled at Jack.

"Okay. Let's do this a little longer and then we'll hit a bar for some drinks. We can leave everything running while we're out."

"Yes! A little motivation!"

Jack laughed, shaking his head. "You're such an asshole." He set the voice recorder on the kitchen table.

"So, how was the date with Laurel?"

"What date?"

"Now who's the asshole? You forget how well I know you," Parker leaned back in his chair, arms folded across his chest.

"Aren't you supposed to be asking the ghost questions?"

"Hey, Ghost! How'd he do on his date?"

"You're like a freaking five year old, you know that?"

"Yup."

"It was great," Jack sighed.

Parker slapped his leg. "I KNEW it! I knew you went out with her."

"Okay, okay! Let's go. I fucking need a drink."

"Yea!" Parker got up, checked his wallet.

"Leave everything set up and we'll check it all out when we get back."

"Drunk evidence review? Is that a thing?"

"It may become one! Get your jacket."

Jack strode into the bedroom, grabbing a sweatshirt. He put his wallet into his back pocket and gave Caesar a quick pet. His cat shifted in his sleep, giving a short stretch and relaxing back into position. As they went out the door, Jack took his keys out of the bowl.

"You know, it was dead in there," Parker ran. Jack chased him around the cars. "Old and slow, man. You're getting old and slow."

They laughed and strolled up the street, heading into town. The night was cool and crisp, a typical October evening, with damp leaves clinging to the sides of the road. It was twilight and the street lamps were coming on. They crossed Jones Street, passed the park and walked into the center of town.

"Where do you want to go?" Jack asked.

"O'Malley's, O'Riley's, O'something. The Irish have the best bars."

Jack laughed. "O'Malley's it is!" It wasn't far from where they were, either. He found himself in need of a drink and some unwinding. O'Malley's never disappointed. It was a great little pub. Well lit, with a huge selection of beers and ales, bottles and cans lining the walls, a really friendly establishment. Great music in the background, too. None of the top 40 crap. Parker opened the door and walked in in front of Jack. A number of hellos were called out, a few Park's. Jack looked at his friend. "Does everyone know you?"

"Just about. Yeah," he smiled.

They took a seat at the bar itself. A few of Park's friends stopped by, patting him on the back and introducing themselves to Jack. They were mostly work friends, glad to chill with a beer on a Friday night. But, who wouldn't be? The bartender approached them, quite neat in a red vest, putting napkins on the bar for each. "What can I get you tonight?" The guy put on a pretty good, but fake, Irish accent. All in good fun.

"Well, Park? What are you buying me?"

"Tonight was your treat, my friend, and you're having shots of Jagermeister, with a beer chaser."

"I hate Jager."

"Deal." Parker tapped the bar and the bartender got them the shots. He put a beer on the table in front of each of them.

Jack sighed, picked up the shot and downed it, grabbing the beer to try to get rid of the taste. He made an awful face at Parker who nearly choked on his shot.

"That stuff is God awful."

"Yeah, but it gets the job done."

"Amen to that," Jack took another long drink from his bottle. "Let's get a table."

"And two more shots," he motioned to the bartender to let him know where they'd be. The bartender nodded and was immediately at their table with two more shots and two beers. That shot went down a little more easily. A little. Jack was starting to relax. Ending a long work week felt great. He eased back in his seat, cradling his beer on his leg.

"You haven't told me yet. The date? Laurel?"

"We had dinner, talked. It was great."

"That's it? 'It was great'?"

"It was really great," Jack laughed.

Parker smiled and shook his head. "You're such a shit."

"I really enjoyed it. We spent about two hours at A Touch of Home."

"No wonder you loved it."

"Ha! We kept talking. Like we knew each other forever, but getting to know each other. Hard to describe."

"Seeing her again?"

"She's cooking me dinner Sunday night."

"You dog. At her place or yours?"

"Her's."

"Niiiiiice."

The music got a little louder and a younger crowd was filing in. The just turned twenty-somethings. The ones who wouldn't know a Cheers moment if it bit them in the ass. Ah, well. He looked at his beer. He wasn't old, but he was feeling a generation separated from the ones around him. He looked at Parker.

"Yeah, man. I get you."

They finished their beers and left the bartender a generous tip. He deserved it. Who wanted to work at a bar on a Friday night instead of being in one? Jack chuckled. They left O'Malley's and stood on the sidewalk for a few minutes, watching the traffic go by.

"It's too early to go home."

"We could bar hop, but you'll probably find the same thing on this drag. Movies?" Parker asked.

"Nah. I don't feel like a movie."

"Get a bottle of something and go see if your ghosties had anything to say?"

Jack smiled. That was just what he was thinking.

They got back to his house, vodka in hand, and went inside. Jack started pawing through the refrigerator to see what he might have to mix it with. "Orange juice," he called out, moving things around. "Root beer."

"Man, you're sick. Bring out the juice, we'll have screwdrivers. Geez, root beer?"

"Was just saying."

"Don't say."

Jack took two mugs out of the cabinet, while Parker watched. "Mugs? You're full of class, aren't you?"

"You want a drink or not?"

"Oh, yeah. Pour...pour."

He made the drinks, a little heavy on the vodka, but neither of them cared. It had been a pretty good night so far. Why not keep it rolling? And what was wrong with mugs? They stood at the counter for a few minutes, killing their drinks and chatting. Jack poured the next set, emptying the bottle.

"Well, that didn't last."

"Did you expect it to?" Parker asked.

"Not with you around," Jack laughed. "Let's go play back that audio. See if anything visited."

They sat at the table, Parker slightly spilling his mug as he sat down. "Careful, Park. That's expensive equipment. I don't want any of it to go out with a spark and a sizzle."

"Is that what you call your sex life? Spark and sizzle?" He erupted into laughter. Yeah, this wasn't going to work well.

"Leave it," Jack said. "We'll check it out tomorrow."

Into the living room they went, mugs in hand. Jack clicked on the television and sat on the sofa. Parker followed suit, kicking his feet up onto the coffee table. "Find me some boobs, Jack!" he commanded.

"Boobs, it is!" Jack searched out one of the porn channels. He held out his arm toward the television. "Boobs!"

"Damn, do you know how long it's been?"

"Yeah, you aren't alone there. But those... they're so fake."

"At this point, I'd take 'em. I'd take nipples painted on balloons."

"You're a sick fuck."

"I'm a horny fuck." They laughed, chatting and watching porn till Parker fell asleep. Jack got up and joined Caesar in bed, falling asleep with his clothes on and the blanket half pulled up. He hadn't shut off the television and the flickering light from the living room would catch his attention every so often, out of the corner of an eye. Neither one of them heard the basement door unlatch and open. Caesar did, and hid behind the sofa, crouched, back to the wall and in attack position. He was the only one who heard the footsteps, followed them with his eyes in the only place he felt somewhat safe, until they disappeared. He stayed under the sofa until morning, pressed against the wall.

"Jack? Jack!" Parker called him from the kitchen.

Jack woke up, wiped the sleep from his eyes and sat on the edge of the bed. "What?"

"Jack!"

He got up and wandered into the living room, picking up the remote and shutting off the television. He stood in the doorway to the kitchen, looking at Parker. "What?"

Parker pointed to the basement door. It sat ajar. "I think we had a visitor last night."

"Kill the cameras and cue up last night's footage," Jack said, suddenly awake. "I've gotta pee." He left the room as Parker rewound the DVR recordings. The monitor displayed both camera feeds, both angles they had set the night before. He ran through it at triple speed, from the time they got back from the bar until everything quieted. There was the bouncing light from the television in the next room, and both cameras had a full focus on the basement door and kitchen area.

"Hurry up! How long's it take to drain that thing?" Parker yelled. He was excited to find the time, the exact moment that the door opened. Leaving the DVR paused, he walked over and tried the latch. He tested the door, open, closed, pulling on it, shoving it to see if it would pop open. He even opened and closed the side door to see if the change in air pressure would help it unlatch. Nothing. It was solid. Jack returned.

"About fucking time," Parker hit play. They watched, glued to the screen, and at 3:11 a.m., the basement door clicked and slowly swung about a foot open. Jack sat back, Parker looked at him and they broke out into big smiles. "High five!"

"Loop it!" Over and over, they watched the latch click and the door open. On two cameras. "You got it, you got it, man!"

The excitement was palpable. Jack was jazzed. Parker could barely contain himself. "This is amazing!"

"Okay, kill the loop. Let's see if there's anything else." Just as Caesar had, they could hear the footsteps. Slowly, steady. Like a boot across a wooden floor. And then it was gone. "You know what's next?"

"Gimme the voice recorder. I'll get it downloaded."

Jack handed over the recorder, then went to the fridge. "Breakfast? I think I've got some eggs in here."

"You? Cook? Taking my life in my hands, but…sure." He had connected the cable from the recorder to the laptop and was watching the green bar on the screen show its progress. "Loading."

Jack put the egg carton on the counter and pulled a frying pan from underneath the stove. He opened the refrigerator door and brought out a stick of butter. Holding the knife over it, he slid the knife along, trying to figure how much he'd need for about six eggs. He lopped off a chunk and dropped it into the pan. The butter sizzled.

"Better turn it down a bit before it burns," Parker called out over his shoulder.

"Yeah, yeah. You'll eat it and you'll like it." He broke the first egg and dumped it into the pan. "Shit!"

"Eggshell?"

"Yeah."

"Get it out, Jack. I don't like my eggs crunchy."

"Fuck you. Adds character." Jack fished the chip out of the pan with his finger and cracked the next egg. "Shit!"

Parker laughed. "You suck."

The next few eggs went into the pan without an issue. Jack started whisking them around and then remembered the milk. "Damn it!" He sloshed in some milk and attempted to turn it all into scrambled eggs, throwing in some pepper and salt. Then, some frozen green pepper chunks that he'd microwaved for a minute to get the ice off, and some cheese. It all went into the pan. Call it a scrambled omelet. Or an egg mess. It'd taste good. Just looked like hell. Once it was crispy on the edges and mostly dry in the middle, he put half of the…mixture…on a plate and gave it to Parker.

"You know, I love you, man. Why you trying to kill me?" he smirked.

Jack handed him a fork. "Shut up and eat." He sat down with his own plate and dug in.

"Any juice left?"

"Nope."

"Coffee?"

"Instant, if you want it."

"You need a woman. This place sucks." Parker microwaved a cup of water and put a teaspoonful of instant coffee granules into it. He watched them dissolve, making brown ribbons through the hot water. "You want?"

Jack debated it, but really did need some coffee. "Yeah. Thanks."

Parker made him a cup and sat at the table. The download was done and they turned it on, volume high, while they ate. Jack noted everything in his journal, in between bites of egg.

"There!" Parker almost dumped his plate into his lap. "Did you hear it?"

"Sounded like a sigh. Go back."

They rewound the audio, looking at the soundwave with Jack's audio editor. They blew it up and expanded it on the screen to narrow down the spot they needed. Parker hit play. They had to listen a few times, and Jack grabbed his headphones. "Not a sigh."

He handed the headphones to Parker. It was a fairly clear catch. Long, drawn out, but definitely a voice. A whisper. Jack's name.

"Wow," was Parker's only reaction.

"Yeah."

Jack marked down the time and recorder details in his journal, and saved the clip to his desktop. "Let's see if there's anything else."

They sat and listened, adjusting volume and speed off and on, checking and rechecking the audio, working across their empty plates. Nothing. Just "Jack."

"Maybe it was a breath. Maybe it was Cees."

"Caesar doesn't say 'Jaaack.'" Parker offered. "You know what you heard. Besides that cat isn't coming anywhere near the kitchen anymore. The recorder was on the table."

"True."

"So, what's our next move?"

Jack sat and thumbed through his journal. He started adding things. Little things. Like the stuff with Caesar, the cool breeze downstairs. Normally, he'd chalk them up to coincidence or the work of an overactive mind, but they were adding up to a bit more now.

"I want to find a way to communicate with whoever it is. I want more information. Maybe the ghost box."

"You can't stand the ghost box. Too much static and the findings are too debatable."

"Well, we could try the…"

Parker cut him off. "You are NOT using the Ouija board. Everything I've ever read says two things: don't investigate in your own house and don't use a Ouija board."

Jack smiled. "And I break all the rules."

"I'm in for the ghost box, man. Anything you want to try, I'm good with. Not the board. It's already got some off vibe about it."

"Oh, please," Jack looked disbelievingly at his friend.

"Just listen to me for once."

"For now."

Parker looked at Jack and knew he was fighting a losing battle. "When do you want to set up the ghost box?"

"Tonight. Late. Like midnight or so."

"Okay. I'm gonna go get a shower and get a few things done for myself. I'll be back tonight. Don't start without me." He slapped Jack on the back.

"Sounds good. I'm gonna start researching how to get rid of whatever I've got." He picked up his laptop and headed in to the living room. "See you tonight." Parker gave a quick wave and disappeared out the side door.

It was time to get serious with some google searches. He thought for a few minutes, then got his journal out of the kitchen and a pen out of the cup on the end table. Brainstorming key words to search, he noted each word on its own line. How to get rid of a ghost. Spirit. Entity. Attachment. Negativity. Shadow. He paused and added demon to the list. Not that he had one, but it was good to be thorough. He hadn't even believed in them until a week ago. Well, he didn't know if he believed in them now, but he knew something bad was out there. Something mean. He hesitated to say evil. That remained to be seen. It could have even just been a force, passing through, that didn't know he was there. He snorted at that thought. Whatever it was knew what it was doing. That attack was planned and there were no two ways about it.

"Okay, Ghostie, it's time to figure out how to send you packing." He typed in the first search and then stopped to pick up his pen. He added "Ouija board" to his list. He'd see what he could find on that, too.

His searches brought up the usual: dictionary definitions, some history, a slew of paranormal teams offering up their views and expertise. Yeah, he didn't need help. Just information. Everyone, it seemed, had their own take on things, but most generally agreed on how to get something unwanted out. Fairly simple, tell it to go. Command it. Take control, it's your space, and so on. From there, if it still hung around, a cleansing. He didn't know how much stock he put into that, but if there could be a ghost in his house, he guessed something a little unconventional might be the way to proceed. He wrote it all down; printed some out. There appeared to be volumes written about demons and negative entities, ghosts versus spirits. He had to laugh when Slimer, the little green ghost from the movies, popped up. He loved Ghostbusters.

Caesar jumped up and laid across his keyboard, looking for some attention. "Okay, okay. I guess I've been at this long enough." He slid his cat to the side and shut down. They both stood and stretched. "Can't sit here all day, huh, Cees?" Jack looked around and sighed. He'd neglected things around the house lately. That sucked. He liked it neat, but damn, he hated cleaning.

Caesar wound his way through Jack's legs, rubbing and purring, while Jack picked up mugs, plates and made his way into and through the kitchen. He turned on the water in the sink, letting it run to warm up a bit. He turned. The little hairs on the back of his neck stood up and he stared at the basement door and through the archway into the living room. He cut the stream on the water, gave a squirt of liquid soap and started scrubbing the plates. Again. He turned. He could swear that someone was watching him, peering at him. That feeling you get when someone is standing right behind you and not saying a word. That uncomfortable sense of someone leaning in, almost breathing on your neck.

"Back off. Whoever you are, get the hell out of my personal space," he said to the empty room. Well, if you could tell a ghost to get out, perhaps he could get one to back off. Was worth a try. And damned if it didn't dissipate. He returned to washing the dishes that had piled up and felt quite satisfied with himself. He could do this. He smiled. Not that he ever doubted that.

He left the dishes in the drainer to dry and wandered the house, room to room, picking up clothes, putting things away. There were still clothes in the dryer from the other night. He got them and folded them. Eh, it was time. Once in a while it felt good to have everything done. Caesar was following him, everywhere except the kitchen and basement. Silly cat. "Don't worry, Cees. It'll all be sorted out soon. I'll get rid of the big, bad ghost." He rubbed Caesar's ears. "I'll even clean your cat box."

With the house fairly well set, and his stomach growling, he checked his watch. 3:30. Damn, no wonder he was hungry. He didn't feel like it, but guessed he needed to go to the store. Get some food in the house; especially with Park coming back later. Hell. He'd go broke feeding that man. "I'll be back soon, Cees. I'll bring you back some tuna or something."

Jack pulled on a hoodie, snagged his keys from the bowl and left. He parked at Walmart and switched off his car. It rumbled for a few extra seconds, then quit. Yeah, that was next on his list when he could afford it. He walked inside the super store and made a beeline to the frozen food section. He didn't want to spend any longer there than he had to. A bag of fries, chicken strips, a box of lasagna. Staples of the bachelor life. He juggled the tower of food he was building and headed to the snack aisle. Some nacho chips, a jar of cheese sauce. Shit. Coffee. This was ridiculous. Why did he never grab a cart when he shopped? One last stop in the coffee aisle and he was ready to go. Express lane.

Standing in front of him was a little old lady. Her pink wool coat and small box hat were a dead giveaway. She turned and said, "Oh, you shop here, too? Did you bring the bus?" She winked at him.

"Hello, Mabel. No. Brought my car." He winked back, shifting uncomfortably, trying not to drop anything.

"You've got a lot there."

"I do. How'd you get here?"

"Oh, I have friends," she paused.

"I'm sure you do." The line advanced to Mabel's turn. She put her things onto the conveyor belt one by one, eyeing each, checking them against the coupons in her hands.

"Damn it!"

She glanced at him. "What did you forget?"

"I was going to bring my cat a treat. A can of… something."

"Here." She shoved a can onto his tower.

"What? Oh, thanks, but I can't take your tuna."

She smiled. "You can. You will. Mine has plenty."

"Thanks, Mabel. You're a doll."

"I know." She blushed a bit, nearly as pink as her coat, and went back to placing her items on the belt.

When she was done and bagged, he put his things onto the belt. He watched a man, probably in his thirties, take her bags and her arm to walk out of the store. "Bye, Mabel! See you Monday!" She gave a little wave.

"Any coupons?" The voice brought him back to his own groceries.

"Uh, no."

The cashier rang him through in under a minute. "$35.17."

"Wow. Racks up fast." She gave a bored nod, holding out her hand as he dug the money out of his wallet. Not very talkative. Whatever. He took his bags and left, tossing them onto the passenger seat of the car. He hoped it would start and held his breath, just a little, as he turned the key. It rattled to life. His exhaust might be going. Ah, well. Something else to think about fixing. As long as he didn't get a ticket for the noise, he'd be happy.

With the oven preheating, he sat for a few minutes in the living room, jotting down in his journal the feeling he had had earlier in the day. Once the lasagna went in, he'd see what was on the news. Maybe there was a movie he could watch until Park decided to show up. He reached for the remote, which should have been on the coffee table, but it wasn't there. "Okay, Cees. Were you messing around again?" It wasn't on the floor or under the sofa. "Geez, cat. Were you feeling playful or what?" He looked, but Caesar wasn't around. Odd. He felt between the cushions of the sofa and searched the recliner, sure he had left the damn thing on the table. His frustration was building and he decided to turn the television on at the source, when he noticed the remote. It was balanced on the top of the television. On top of a 46 inch flat screen, mounted onto the wall. What the fuck? He didn't do it. Caesar didn't do it. No one had been in his house...and who would put a remote on top of a television? That's why you have a remote. To sit across the room and control it. He snatched it down. "Not funny, Mr. Ghost. Leave my things alone."

Jack turned the television on and thumbed through the menu. "Nope, nope, nope...." He was reminded of Pink Floyd's The Wall. "13 channels of shit on the TV to choose from." Only he had 150 channels. Same same. While he tried to decide, he grabbed the pen and made a few notes in his journal. He stood up, clicked on a news channel, and walked into the kitchen to check the oven. Cold. The dial was set to off. Had he forgotten to turn it on? No way. He rolled his eyes in frustration. "Come on!" He flipped it on. By now he was starving. He ripped open the bag of chips and stood in the archway snacking as he listened to world news. The oven finally beeped and he slid the lasagna in on a cookie sheet.

He sat on the sofa, bored and hungry. Picking up his phone, he shot Laurel a text. *Looking forward to tomorrow night.* It only took a minute for her to respond. *Me, too.* Aargh. Face palm. He should have picked up a bottle of wine while he was out. He guessed he'd have to stop on the way to her place tomorrow. *Still need directions.* He waited, staring at his phone, turning it over in his hand. *137 Summit Ave.* Ah, the other side of town, about twenty minutes from him. Not bad. He'd pass a liquor store on the way. Fingers crossed it was open on Sunday.

Caesar came out of hiding and rubbed on Jack's leg. "Should've named you Garfield," he picked up the cat, snuggling him. "Lasagna's not done yet." Caesar curled up beside him and began a bath, licking his hind legs, tail. Jack flipped channels. There had to be something more interesting than old news repeated. Someone knocked at the side door. "Park, just come in," he called, leaning to peer around the corner. He couldn't see anyone at the door. He tossed the remote onto the coffee table and got up. "Hello?" He opened the door and looked outside. No one was anywhere near his door. Odd. Maybe he had misheard. Maybe it was something on the television and he hadn't been paying attention. He touched the oven's glass window. Nice and hot. Still thirty minutes on the timer, though. Ugh. His stomach growled and he went back to his spot beside Caesar. He was done with television for now. There was nothing new or interesting. He reached for the remote. It was gone. Again. "This is getting old. Fast. I want the remote and I want it now," he said forcefully. He heard something hit the floor in the kitchen. He jumped up and ran in. There, in the middle of the floor, was the remote. "Fuck." Things were getting a little nuts. A little bold. "After tonight's session, you're out." He looked around, trying to pin point whatever might be around. "Got it? You don't belong here." He snatched up the remote and strode into the living room, tossing it onto the coffee table beside his journal. It was already time to update it, more with annoyance than fascination. He knew he had something that he couldn't debunk and he was ready for some real house cleaning.

4

Parker arrived around 9:45 p.m. The first thing he noticed was the half gone lasagna in a pan on top of the stove. "For me?" he called out.

"Yeah. Figured you be hungry." Jack came into the kitchen. He had a pot of coffee going on the counter and two mugs waiting.

"Nice! Thanks, man." He dug through the silverware drawer for a fork, took the pan and sat at the table. "I know you don't like to wash dishes, so I thought I'd skip the plate."

Jack laughed. He poured two mugs of coffee, his with milk and sugar, and handed the other, black, to Parker. "More stuff's been happening, Park."

"Oh?" Parker's eyes were wide over the brim of the coffee mug. "Like what?"

"Knocking, with nothing there. And it keeps hiding my things. Twice the remote has disappeared. Found it once on top of the television and the other…it was dropped onto the floor out here. I heard it hit."

"That's crazy. Not good."

"Yeah. I think after we do the ghost box session tonight I need to get rid of it. I've been going over how all afternoon."

"Maybe that's why the activity is kicking up. It doesn't want to go."

"Well, it's going. I just have to figure out where to get some sage. Seems to be the most popular way of cleansing an area."

"There's a new age shop over on…tenth, I believe. Nice little place with incense and crystals. They probably sell sage, or know where you can get some."

"Great. Hopefully they'll be open tomorrow. I've got to hit a liquor store before I go to Laurel's anyway. Might as well kill two birds with one stone."

"Ahh, bringing wine? What's she making?" Parker asked between bites of the lasagna.

"No idea. Thought I'd see if they had something generic…something that would go with anything."

"Red with meat, white with fish."

"So, I'll get rose, right?"

"No idea, man. That's it for my knowledge of wines." He shoved the empty lasagna pan into the garbage and grabbed a paper towel to wipe his mouth. "So, is that all? Dinner at her place?"

"Gonna figure that out then. We might go out. We might stay in."

"Ooooh! Nice. See how well she cooks and then see if you can get cooking!" Park ducked as Jack fake swung at him. "You know I'm right."

"Jerk."

"Yeah, maybe. But you know I'm right. So what else is there to eat?" Jack rolled his eyes and pointed to the bag of nachos. "Cheese sauce? You know I like my cheese sauce." He pointed to the jar on the counter. Parker opened it and popped it into the microwave.

"Do you ever eat at home?"

"Are you kidding me? Never!" They both laughed. The microwave dinged and Parker looked for a potholder. "Nothing to take it out with?"

Jack pulled his arm inside the sleeve of his sweatshirt and used the end of the sleeve to wrap around the jar. He nearly dropped it and shook his fingers after getting it to the counter.

"You're an idiot, you know that?"

Jack smiled. "Yeah."

They snacked on the nachos and cheese sauce, standing over the kitchen counter. Caesar meowed at them from the living room, as if to say, "Come on, guys."

"Just a minute, Cees," Jack called back. "You don't like jalapenos anyway." Caesar disappeared into the bedroom.

They finished the nachos and got two more mugs of coffee. "You sure you want to wait until midnight to get started? If you're having that much obvious activity, it probably doesn't matter what time you start."

"When you're right, you're right. Let's do it." He squatted beside his cases and pulled out the ghost box. He was still surprised that someone had ever come up with it for ghost communication. An AM-FM radio scanning, with the station pause disabled. Simple. He should have come up with it. Could've made millions off all the armchair ghost hunters across the globe. He shook his head. He'd gotten some interesting results using it in the past, but the jury was out. For a lot of things the jury was out for him. He didn't want to be gullible or run in blind. It was worth a try. He set it on the fastest scan, so they'd get the fewest and shortest blips and beeps from radio stations. The static came up loudly and the ch-ch-ch-ch of the stations as it scanned.

"Damn, I hate that noise."

"If we get any voices going across multiple stations, that's supposedly our ghost communication."

"You know, I've done this before, right?" Parker smiled.

"Just wanted to be sure."

Parker shook his head. Jack handed him the ghost box and turned on his voice recorder. "Everything takes place either in the living room or kitchen, it seems."

"Let's do it."

Jack nodded. "We already know you're here. Who are you? What's your name?"

The ch-ch-ch-ch of the ghost box's static churned on.

"Why are you here?"

"Do you know what year it is?"

"Why are you messing with my things?"

Jaaaack.

Jack and Parker looked at each other. "Yeah, that's my name. Tell me your name."

Ch-ch-ch-ch and static.

"What can you tell us?"

"Can you say my name again?"

"Is it just you, or are there more than one spirit in this house?"

Nothing. Barely even a blip of a radio station. The waiting was getting boring and the sound of the stations going by monotonous.

"Are you the one that scratched Jack?" Jack shot Parker a glance.

"I know you're here. What the hell do you want?"

A low growl erupted, but whether from the ghost box or around them, they couldn't tell.

"Turn it off. Turn it off, man!"

Jack almost dropped the radio, but managed to hit the power button, cutting it off. They sat, silent. Parker was rattled and Jack, well, he didn't really know. "Fuck."

"If it wasn't you, Jack, I'd be out that door right now. The scratches, that growl. This is bad."

"I'll pick up sage tomorrow."

"I don't know if that'll do it."

"I'm sure it will," Jack said. He wasn't entirely sure, but power of positive thinking, right?

"I don't think you should stay here tonight."

"Come on, Park."

"I'm fucking serious and you need to listen to me. Grab a few things and stay out tonight." Parker's tone was urgent. Jack had never heard him sound like this.

"And, because it's YOU is the only reason I will."

"Bring Caesar."

Jack almost protested, but the look on Parker's face shut him up. "Okay." He dug through the closet until he found Cees' cat carrier and packed him up. He threw a few things into a gym bag he had and headed out. As he got to the side door, he dipped into the bowl for his keys and glanced at the Ouija board. It was a little crooked. He reached over, righted it, and left.

They drove both cars to Parker's apartment building. He lived in the third one back, third floor. It always seemed like a chess move to Jack. He pulled into a parking place beside Parker's reserved spot and sighed. The lot was well lit, surrounded on three sides by four story red brick buildings. He didn't like apartments. Felt weird having people under and above you and, not that he was loud by any means, he always felt like he had to tiptoe around. It also bugged him to open his front door and be in a hallway with other people. Guess he was a loner at heart. He really only had Parker as a good friend. Everyone else was an acquaintance.

"Hey, you ever getting outta there?" Parker tapped on his driver's window.

"Whoa, sorry. Was lost in thought."

"Yeah, I saw. Come on. It's not often I get to have a sleepover."

Jack rolled his eyes and smirked. "It's going to be a long night, Cees," he poked a finger through the bars of the carrier. Caesar yawned.

Inside, Jack stopped at the elevator while Parker went for the stairs. The lobby had that hard tile floor that was easy to clean in winters where everyone tracked in muddy slush. Well lit, but not overly friendly. A cork board with community happenings that no one ever went to hung on the wall opposite the elevator. "Come on! Good for the calf muscles."

"Nothing wrong with my calf muscles."

"Lazy ass." Parker started up the stairs, two by two. Jack sighed and followed, cat carrier in one hand and gym bag slung over his shoulder.

"You're not carrying a suitcase and a fifty pound cat."

"Oh, what a catastrophe!" Parker offered.

Jack shook his head. "Just shut up and open the door." He put Caesar's carrier on the floor of the hallway while Parker fumbled with his keys.

A woman was walking by with her young son. He looked about eight years old, rather sullen. Park nodded to the woman. She gave a slight smile, a nod, and kept walking, the little boy keeping closer to her. The boy kept his eyes on Parker and went into his apartment with his mother. The metal thud of the door shutting echoed down the hallway. It was an empty, lonely sound. The management had tried for elegance with a hotel-esque red and gold swirled carpet, nearly threadbare now. Dim as forty-watt bulbs, the lights were sealed in yellowed plastic shades giving an eerie odd glow to the walkway.

Parker got the door open. Jack walked inside, sliding Caesar's carrier along the floor with his foot. Parker rented a two bedroom. The second room still had boxes of books and things from when he moved in two years ago. A computer on some inverted crates, a stereo on the floor. At least there was a futon on the one wall. He could drop some boxes and sleep there. Cluttered, but clean. The living room was immaculate. A tan suede couch, glass coffee table. No magazines or takeout containers littered the place. He dropped his bag at the end of the couch. Parker was already in the kitchen.

"Want a beer?"

"Sure."

Parker brought back two beers and a can opener. He handed one to Jack after he had opened it.

"Okay. We need to plan."

"Plan? Plan what?"

"How to get rid of this thing."

"Sage. I'm going to the new age place tomorrow." Jack motioned to Caesar's carrier, asking if he could be set free.

Park nodded. "Jack, you don't get it. Scratches, the growl we heard, all the activity ramping up…"

"I've got some things going on, sure, but I wouldn't call it 'ramping up.'"

"Really? You wouldn't?"

"It's not like I'm calling in some priest to do an exorcism, come on, Park." He sat on the sofa, two hands around his beer.

"Look. I'm asking you to have an open mind about this."

"Yeah, I'm trying. I said I was buying sage. How closed is that?"

Parker looked at his friend, taking stock of the conversation. He knew what Jack had was not going to leave after a smudging. It was too strong. And negative.

"Human spirits don't growl."

"And you know this because…?"

"I read. I watch. This isn't Carla or James or somebody's dearly departed great grandma, Jack. I swear."

"Then what would you suggest?"

"To start, get rid of that damn spirit board."

"Park. It's a toy. A tool."

"It's thought and desire focused. Even if it's only the want to communicate. It opens a portal. Anything can come through. You don't know what you could be dealing with. We've been through this all before."

"Look. I haven't used it since I brought it back. It's been on the wall the entire time."

"But suppose something was opened before you got it. Before you used it the first time. Whatever those kids summoned, well, it could be attached to the board. Or to you now. Having it in the house could be what's kicking up the activity."

Jack paused, tracing the label on his beer with his finger. He wiped the condensation off on his pants leg. "I read up on Ouija boards, too. Most people think they're harmless."

"Most people are idiots."

Jack chuckled. "Well, that's true. I just don't want to jump on the 'gullible train.' Some people call them evil, some say they've used them forever and nothing bad has happened. I don't see it as a problem."

"Well, if it's not, do it to humor me. Get rid of it. See what happens. If nothing changes, fine. I'll buy you dinner. If things get better, great. It's win-win for you."

"Damn. You MUST be serious to bet food on it."

"You know I am."

"Fine. I'll get rid of it." He set the beer on the coffee table and leaned back, arms behind his head. Parker relaxed a bit.

"Good."

"And then you can cleanse the house."

"Yeah. I will." Jack started quietly laughing. "This is crazy, you know. All the years I've spent debunking. Here and there some great EVP's, a few pictures I can't explain. But this…"

Parker smiled. "Yeah. You'll have to write a book someday. Call it 'I was a Fucking Doubting Thomas until Park showed me the Light.'"

Jack laughed a little harder and threw a pillow at his friend. Park caught it and put it on the floor beside him. Caesar cautiously sniffed, then curled up on it.

They talked into the night, drinking beer and looking up details on how to cleanse a house. Sitting on upended crates in the second bedroom wasn't half bad. Hopefully he wouldn't get a splinter in his ass. It'd be a bitch having Parker go at it with a tweezer. He'd have to change his Facebook status to "it's complicated." Jack chuckled. At least the saging looked pretty damn straightforward. Jack took notes anyway. He'd be sure to get it right the first time. Always a detail man, he prided himself on his tech and investigative skills. This was just expanding his repertoire.

Park stood and stretched around 2:30 a.m. He slapped Jack on the back and said with a wink, "Night, man. Try to get some sleep. Gotta recoup your strength for Laurel."

"She'll be in good hands, Park. No worries."

Jack sat back as Parker left the room. He rubbed his eyes. Might as well turn in. He'd definitely want to be well rested for Laurel. "Come on, Cees. Time for bed." The cat came from down the hallway and jumped onto Jack's lap. He rubbed Caesar's ears and snuggled him close. Then, the two cuddled up on the futon, pulling a blanket from a big box beside him. He shook his head. Park would never unpack. Caesar purred into Jack's ear as he drifted off.

The sun shone brightly into the second bedroom, right onto Jack's face. He checked his watch. 7:20 a.m. Fuck. He looked over his shoulder. Parker had no shades on his windows, let alone curtains or anything that would shut out the freaking early morning light. Jack rolled over, jamming his face into the back of the futon. Caesar crawled up and sat on his ribs. He gave the cat a gentle shove. "Go away, Cees. It's not time to be up yet." The cat purred and made a nest at the back of Jack's knees.

He dozed on and off until 9:00 a.m. when he heard Parker rummaging through the kitchen. Pots, pans were banging around and was Parker...whistling? He picked up Caesar and set him in a ball in the blanket. "At least you can sleep in, lazy cat," he sighed. After peeing, he wandered into the kitchen. "What the hell is wrong with you? Why are you up so early?"

"Early? You're sleeping the day away. Here." He shoved a plate of eggs and bacon into Jack's hands and grabbed one for himself. "There's juice in the fridge and coffee is brewing. Get with it."

Jack stared at the plate in his hands. "You can cook? How the fuck have you hid that from me for so many years?"

"It's a knack. Bite me."

"I'd rather bite these eggs, believe me."

Jack sat across from Parker at the dining room table. Nothing fancy, but a nice oak. The guy had great taste. "So what are you doing today?"

"Not sure yet. Go for a run, read a book. Oh, and remind you to get rid of that fucking board."

"I said I'd do it."

"Yup. Just making sure."

"Fuck you."

"And the horse you rode in on." They laughed.

"These eggs kick ass."

After breakfast, Jack stuffed his things into his gym bag, packed up Caesar, and left. Parker stopped him at the door. "Call me later, man. Let me know how it all goes."

"The saging or Laurel?"

"Both."

Jack smiled. "Yeah, yeah," and let the door shut with its echoing metal thud.

The new age store was easy to find. It was right on the main street of town and the most colorful store front he'd seen. Everything Ecclectic. The door bells chimed as he walked in and a woman in a long, flowing patchwork dress and sandals smiled from the back of the store. Hair down to her... "Good morning! If there's anything I can help you with, let me know." She was the quintessential new age shop owner if he'd ever seen one. Stereotypical and unique at the same time. Someone who just gave you a good feeling.

Jack nodded and thanked her. He looked around on his own for a bit. The store was small, no more than maybe a 15' x 20' space, but was filled floor to ceiling with all sorts of products. Incense, figurines, jewelry, soaps, tarot cards, clothing, books, crystals...he walked around, taking it all in. Even if he had gone out and come back in again, he never would have seen it all. He breathed in. It had that aroma of pleasantness, of too many scents to be able to name one. Peaceful. He finally walked up to the woman in the dress. "Um, excuse me?"

She smiled brightly. "Yes? What can I get for you?"

"Sage. I was looking for sage."

"Ah! Yes, of course." He followed her to a spot near the register. "Would you like loose or a sage stick?"

"Hm. I don't know. Which would be better for cleansing a house?"

She eyed him almost knowingly. "I'd use a stick. It's easier. These are white sage and should do what you want them to."

"Okay, a stick then. Thank you," he smiled and handed her a ten dollar bill. After she counted out his change, she handed him the bag with the sage stick. Then, she took his other hand and pressed into it a small, opaque...stick?

"Selenite," she said. "It aids in protection and can help dispel negativity. Take it."

"Thank you." He took the stick and the sage and walked out of the store.

This was getting to be a bit much, but he appreciated the thought. He guessed. He may be giving in to some of this stuff, and would get rid of the Ouija board, but...crystal magic now? He turned the selenite around in his hand and popped it into the cup holder in the Subaru. His next stop was the liquor store. Quicker and easier than the Eclectic shop, he grabbed a semi-expensive bottle of rose and was done. Fewer options and he'd been there before. It all worked.

Home by noon, he brought Caesar's cat carrier into the living room and opened its metal door. Caesar strolled out as if he owned the place, and, quite frankly, he did. After putting the carrier away and emptying his gym bag, Jack stopped for a moment in the kitchen. He looked up at the Ouija board and sighed. He did like it on the wall, but had promised Park he'd get rid of it. He took it off the wall, leaving the planchette attached, and put it into a dark green garbage bag. He quickly ran it out to the garbage can, dropping it in and putting the grey metal top back on tightly. Done. It was time for the next job.

He took out the bag from the new age store and let the sage stick roll into his hand. Jack examined it. He had to dig around in the junk drawer in the kitchen for a lighter, and then found a small plate to catch the ashes. That was essential. He didn't want to burn the place down. Most people online, it seemed, used some sort of seashell. He wasn't that fancy and didn't think it would matter what he caught the ashes in. He was ready to get this done.

Jack set the plate on his coffee table and lit the sage. He held it in the flame of the lighter until it was smoldering. Dropping the lighter onto the table, he picked up the plate. "Only positive energy is allowed in this space. Negativity of any kind is not welcome here." He walked through each room, clockwise, making sure to wave the smoke into the corners of each room. The closets, the bathroom, his bedroom. Repetition, focus. "Only positive energy is allowed in this space. Negativity of any kind is not welcome here." He let the smoke waft through each room before he moved to the next.

He hesitated at the basement door for a moment, then proceeded downstairs. He found himself a little bolder, a little more confident, as he went. "Only positive energy is allowed in this space…" He was almost surprised that nothing happened as he made his way through the house. It was calm. He stopped at the washing machine and blew across the smudge stick so the smoke would flow inside. Why not? Might as well get every spot. He finished the basement quickly and returned upstairs into the kitchen, continuing clockwise until he was back where he began. He sat down to extinguish the stick, pausing, trying to sense if anything was different. Had it changed? The house was quiet and…lighter? Had it worked? He couldn't be sure. He felt good, though. It was time for a nap.

When he woke at 4:00 p.m., he was refreshed. The scent of sage was still fairly strong in the room and he liked it. A shower and an evening out with a beautiful woman. Ah, this was going to be a great day. Caesar sat on the edge of the bed, watching him get ready. He settled on a forest green button down shirt and jeans. Dark boots. A brown herringbone sport coat in case they ended up going out. Casual, but presentable. He admired his choices in the mirror. Yes, this worked.

Jack pulled into Laurel's driveway about twenty minutes early. He let the motor run for a bit, trying to be inconspicuous. The bottle of wine sat in the passenger seat. He wondered if she knew he was outside; if he was making her uncomfortable by being early. Damn his eagerness. Well, he couldn't sit there, rumbling car and all. He turned the key and let it slowly die. Rattle, rattle, wheeze. He took a deep breath, grabbed the wine and stepped out of the car.

"I was wondering if you were going to come in," Laurel called out from her doorway. "I've been watching you the last five minutes." She was also in jeans and a sweet V necked black tee, with her hair swept up in a ponytail.

"Oh, sorry," he said, walking up her steps, "I was early and didn't want to come in if you weren't ready yet." She had a jack-o-lantern on her front stoop. "Nice pumpkin."

She smiled. "Come in." He handed her the wine and stepped inside.

Laurel's home was small, sitting on a quarter of an acre, with no basement or attic. She had decorated it quite prettily, with a few tapestries on the walls. The flat screen television sat catty cornered at one end, with a couch angled in front of it. At the other end of the room, a recliner, some bookshelves. Very homey. And it smelled wonderfully. He laid his sport coat across the back of the couch.

"Meat loaf?"

"Meat loaf."

"It smells amazing."

"I hope you like it," he followed her into the kitchen. "It's my grandmother's recipe."

"Well, then it's got to be good." He smiled. The kitchen was warm, inviting. Yellows and beiges, some faded wallpaper that ran around the edges. Her table was one of the old style Formica tables with the metal legs. "Very retro."

She laughed. "Very cheap. It came with the house."

"I didn't know what type of wine would be good. I don't know wine...so..."

"It'll be great. Thanks. You didn't have to bring anything, though."

"No problem, Doll." Her eyes sparkled whenever he said that. He noticed that right away. The slight glance away, the barely noticeable blush on her cheeks, damn, she was gorgeous.

They chatted, small talk and pleasantries, while she got the meat loaf out of the oven. The weather, their families, the holidays coming. He sat at the table and she brought over mashed potatoes and gravy, broccoli. "I hope you like it."

"It's delicious." He knew it would be, even before he tasted it. He hadn't had a home cooked meal like this in, he didn't know how long.

"So," she said, "You don't like Halloween?"

"Not especially. I don't get any kids where I live, and I can't see getting all decked out for nothing."

"Ah...but would you if you were somewhere else?"

"Probably not," he chuckled. "I'm more of a Thanksgiving and Christmas guy." He paused. "Must be the food. No one cooks a big meal for Halloween."

She laughed. "I might."

"Then I might have to come eat it." He already loved her laugh. It spoke to something deep inside him.

"So, a paranormal investigator who doesn't like Halloween. You're quite unique."

"As are you." He reached over and squeezed her hand. "Did you want some wine?"

"Oh! You'll think I'm terrible, but I totally forgot." Laurel went to the cabinet over her stove and retrieved two wine glasses. Jack got up and she gave him the corkscrew.

"It's a twist off," he mentioned sheepishly. "You probably think I'm terrible."

"Haha, never." She handed him the bottle to open. Jack poured both glasses and handed her the first.

"Cheers, Doll." They both sipped and, Jack decided, it wasn't bad. A little sweet, a little not. It definitely wouldn't replace a good cold beer, but it would do. "Did you want to stay in or go out?"

"Truthfully, I'd love to stay in, watch a movie and relax. It's hard to go out when you've got to get up early for work on Monday."

"Yeah, it sucks. But a night in would be nice."

Laurel took her wine and went into the living room. "A movie?" She started thumbing through a rack with DVD's.

"Sure. You pick."

"If you're sure. I'm always up for a comedy."

"Anything is great. Really," Jack sat on the couch, gently placing his drink on the coffee table.

She set a handful next to the DVD player and hit the power button. The tray ejected and she put a disc in. "Have you seen Ghostbusters?" she bit her lip, her eyes smiling.

"Once or twice."

Laurel hit play. She turned around and Jack had his arm across the back of the couch. She cozied up next to him, knees bent, feet on the cushion beside her. It was comfortable. The couch, the evening, being with Laurel. It all just fit for him. Having her under his arm he could smell her hair. It was a fresh, apple like scent. Here and there they chatted through the movie. She finished her wine and he was up to pour her another glass. When he sat back down, he pulled her closer, arm around her once more.

The movie ended and Laurel clicked around from channel to channel, looking for something they could watch together for a bit longer. She landed on a ghost documentary. With raised eyebrows, she asked, "This?"

"Sure. If you're good with it."

She leaned in against him, taking the afghan off the back of the couch and covering them both. "I keep the thermostat turned low at night. It gets a little cool sometimes."

"Not with you around." He watched the documentary on some castles in Scotland and the hauntings they've experienced. Soon, he felt Laurel go a little limp and felt her breathing change. Asleep. The clock on the wall showed 12:30. Shoot…getting pretty late if he was going to be up at 5:30 a.m. and he really didn't want to leave. He sighed. Quietly, he turned off the television and maneuvered around her to pick her up and gently carried her to her bedroom. Laying her on her bed, he pulled the comforter up around her shoulders. He had gotten to the doorway when she called in a sleepy voice, "Jack?"

"Yeah, Doll?"

"You don't have to leave."

She didn't have to tell him twice. He was back at the side of the bed in a heartbeat and took off his belt. Stripping down to his boxers, he let his pants and shirt drop to the floor beside the bed. Jack lifted the comforter and slid in beside her, wrapping her in his arms and kissing her neck. She pulled him closer and returned his kisses. Slowly and gently, at first. He let his right hand drift to the small of her back, putting his leg over hers. He took his time and explored her body over her clothes. She ran her hands along his back.

Jack wrapped his fingers in hers and moved her arms above her head, nuzzling her neck. He let go of her hands to pull her shirt up and off, and unhooked her bra. He buried his face in her breasts, his tongue finding her nipples, one at a time. Laurel arched her back as he did, pressing against his mouth.

Jack found her mouth again, more passionately now. He pushed a stray piece of hair out of her face and looked into her eyes. He fumbled with the button on her jeans. She put her hand on his, then undid them herself, sliding them down and kicking them off the bed. With just the thin cotton of her bikinis and his boxers separating them, he rolled back over her. A soft moan escaped her lips as she felt how hard he was, pressing against her. Fuck. He was all feeling now. No thought. He was lost in a sea of skin against skin. All he wanted was to make her feel as amazing as he knew he would be feeling. Bring her to the edge and go over the cliff together. God, he wanted her so badly.

He hooked a finger into her bikinis and removed them, slowly. The boxers came off more quickly. Rock hard with need, he balanced on his knees before her. Laurel spread her legs, just a bit, and that was it for Jack. He grabbed her ankles to pull her farther down on the bed and took her. With every thrust, her gasps drove him further. Harder. The passion overwhelmed him. When she came, he couldn't hold off any longer. It couldn't have been more perfect, laying together, breathing hard and so damn satisfied. She snuggled into him, her head resting on his arm. Jack stole a few kisses before they both curled up and fell asleep.

Jack's phone was ringing, and for a moment he didn't know where it was, or where he was, for that matter. He looked around and it clicked. Laurel's. He was at Laurel's. He smiled, then realized. Shit! Work! Grabbing his pile of clothes, he found his phone in his pants pocket.

"Yeah? Hello?"

"Where the hell are you? Are you coming in or what?" It was his boss. The clock on the nightstand read 6:20 a.m.

"Damn it. Yeah, I'm on my way. I'll be there soon, no worries." He hung up the phone and looked at Laurel. Fuck, she was stunning. She even slept beautifully. Her hair draped across the pillow, the blanket across her breasts, showing just enough cleavage to tease him. He smiled, remembering last night, getting hard at the thought. She opened an eye to look at him as he searched the floor for his boxers.

"Late for work?"

"Yeah."

"Trouble?"

"Nah. May catch a little hell for it, but nothing I can't handle." His pants were on, shirt half tucked.

"You're cute."

He chuckled, and gave her a quick kiss. "And you're beautiful. Call me tonight." Keys in hand, he left her house, even not hating at the jack-o-lantern on her porch.

"Please start," he whispered as he turned the key. The Subaru came to life, almost flawlessly. "Thank you," Jack mouthed, backing out of Laurel's driveway. He made his way to the station, California rolling stops at all the stop signs. He hated to be late.

"Hey, I'm really sorry," Jack greeted his boss. His paperwork was sitting on the counter.

"Grab yourself one of the promotional tees, since you seem to have forgotten your uniform," the boss looked at him over the top of his glasses. "Late night?"

He took a tee off the pile they kept to hand out to customers and clients. "Yeah. Pretty late. Sorry." It wasn't his norm to come into work like this and it was embarrassing and great at the same time. He could take the look and be the alley cat for once. Jack slipped into the bathroom. The tee looked good. He wondered for a second if Laurel would like it. Hell, he wished he was back in bed with her instead of walking out to the bus. When all was said and done, he started his run about fifteen minutes late. Fuck. He'd be bitched at all day long for that.

"You're late."

"Yes, Mabel. I'm sorry."

"I didn't think you were coming." She gingerly climbed the steps, making sure she had a good hold on the railing for each. He silently wished she could walk up them like the rest of his fares. Would've carried her up them if he could have. Damn. He needed to make up that time.

"It won't happen again."

"I hope not. It's getting colder, you know."

Jack would make sure it didn't happen again. Next time he'd have the alarm set on his phone. Next time. Ah. He slipped into the memory of last night once more. Laurel was amazing. The way she bit her lip when he slid her shirt up... Shit! Almost missed a stop sign. He was off his game. Wonderfully, incredibly, off his game. And late. Damn it.

The rest of the day was a series of stops, annoyed riders and complaints. Apologies. Sorry, I was doing the woman I hope is now mine and mine alone. Sorry. I was too exhausted after cumming in her that I held her in my arms and slept the most restful sleep I've had in ages. Sorry, not sorry. He chuckled.

Rush and wait, hurry up and watch the minutes tick. Rush to make up time, wait for people to get on and off. Nothing sped up, everything dragged. He just wanted to be home and done. The leaves were off the trees now, the wind and rain had seen to that. Everything looked dead and cold, but, inside, he was on fire. It was a great feeling and something that had eluded him for a long time.

Jack pulled up to the senior center at 4:47 p.m. Mabel had rejoined him at the pharmacy stop and was inching her way to the front of the bus. "You'll be on time tomorrow?"

"Yes, I will."

"I hope so. I have a doctor's appointment and don't want to be late." She adjusted her hat, making sure the plastic daisy was along the right side. She checked it and settled her hand on the metal railing. She leaned in close to him and whispered, "And I don't really like this shirt. Your other one is more professional."

Jack smiled. "I'll wear the other one tomorrow, Mabel. Thanks for the advice." He waited, mostly patiently, for her to traverse the steps to the curb, and then to the sidewalk. She was a good old bird. He closed the bus doors. By 5:03 he had handed in his paperwork. Finally, he was on his way home.

Although he didn't live far from the station, it still seemed to take forever. It was overcast and the Subaru was now having an issue with the heat. Well, there wasn't an issue, there was just no heat. One more thing. At least it still started. Barely. He supposed he'd have to give in soon and either spend his savings to fix the thing or get another car.

He drove into the driveway and waited for the engine to die, which seemed to be his usual now, and noticed something leaning beside his steps. A package? He hadn't ordered anything. Jack got out of the car and walked over, curious. "What the fuck?" he said, under his breath. Someone had taken the Ouija board out of the garbage, out of the plastic bag, and left it next to the house. Who would've done that? Odd, but he guessed the garbage men might have dropped the bin; maybe it fell out of the bag? And they thought he didn't mean to throw it away? It didn't add up, but must be what had happened. The planchette was next to it in the dirt, too. He picked them both up and looked them over. Not a scratch or dent. Someone had to have set them there. He walked them over to the bin and dropped them in. It was a shame. He really did like the way they looked on the wall.

Jack unlocked the house, dropped his keys in the bowl and walked into the bedroom. Caesar was waiting for him on the bed as if he had been gone for weeks. "Did you miss me, Cees?" He took off his boots, his clothes, and went in to the shower. As it steamed, he shaved. He could almost smell Laurel still on his skin and it made him hard. Grabbing a new bar of soap, he climbed into the shower.

Caesar was meowing and his phone ringing when he got out of the water. He ran out, skipping the towel and dripping on the floor as he grabbed the phone. Unknown caller. He tossed it onto the bed and went back into the warmth of the bathroom. "You'll have to wait a minute, Cees. I'll feed you when I'm done." His phone rang again. At least this time he had a towel. He snatched it up and it said unknown caller. Damn. He set it down on his dresser. Call again, buddy, and you're going to get an earful. He pulled on a pair of sweats and a sweatshirt. The house was cooler now. He kept it set at 68 degrees, not bad for sleeping, but a little cool when you just got out of a steamy shower.

He put his phone on the coffee table and went into the kitchen to turn on the oven. Fries and chicken strips. The life of the bachelor. It had its drawbacks some nights. Back in the living room, he sat, deciding what he would do next. Again, the phone went off. Again, unknown caller. He grabbed it and swiped the call. "How many times are you going to call, asshole?!"

"Uh…Jack?"

Oh, fuck. He sat upright. "Laurel. Hey…sorry. It, I kept getting calls, and all it said was 'unknown' instead of your name. Hey, Doll, sorry."

"No problem. I just didn't expect that kind of greeting."

"If I had known it was you, you wouldn't have," his tone was lower, calmer. He settled back into the sofa. "What's doing?"

"I was thinking, if it's not too soon…" she gave a little nervous laugh, "that you might want to get together on the weekend?"

"I'd love it," he paused and laughed. "Did I say that too fast?"

"Great. I was hoping Saturday night?"

"Whatever you want, I'll be there. You've been on my mind all day." Could he hear her blush? He chuckled.

"Aww. It's a date then. Saturday night. Now, don't back out..."

"Why would I? Ever?"

Laurel laughed. "It's Halloween. We'll be giving out candy to the little ghouls."

Jack moaned. "Oooookaaaaay."

"Still with me?"

"You know it. I wouldn't miss it." What he really meant was he wouldn't miss her. The rest, eh, he'd deal with it.

They talked for the next half hour. He managed to use one hand to get the French fries and chicken sticks onto a cookie sheet and into the oven. Setting the time was a little difficult, but he finally got it set, holding the phone with his shoulder. He loved the lilt of her voice and didn't want to miss a second of it. God, he was like a kid. If he had been a teen girl, he'd have been twirling his hair around a finger, doodling their names and little hearts. He had it bad.

"I've got to go, hon," she was saying, "but will see you Saturday. 6:00, again?"

"Works for me, Doll. I can't wait." They ended the call and he hit the red button, cutting the connection. He was jazzed about spending another evening with Laurel, even if it was giving out Halloween candy. Sheesh. Park would have a field day with that when he found out. If he found out. He chuckled. Yeah, Park would know. After the fact.

"Where are you, Cees?" he had forgotten the poor cat when the phone rang. "Chicken strips tonight?" He heard a meow coming from the bedroom. "Come on, kitty kitty. I saged the place. You can come into the kitchen now." Caesar wasn't having it, though. Odd cat. Maybe it was like a Pavlovian response. He had gotten used to not being in the kitchen, so avoided it still. Perhaps it would just take him a little time.

The timer went off and Jack opened the oven door to check on his dinner. He had set the temperature a little higher than what the packages had called for, figuring it would cook a little faster. They looked okay. He picked up a fry, trying to not burn himself, tossing it from hand to hand before he bit into it. Crunchy on the outside, a little undone on the inside. Doable. He switched off the oven and pulled out the tray. He had to use the spatula, with some force, to get them off. Damn. Should've put down some tin foil. Ah, well. He'd let it soak later. Inside the refrigerator were some little packets of duck sauce, hot mustard and ketchup that he saved from nights of takeout meals. He put a handful on his plate, with the chicken and fries, and sat down. He half expected Park to be at the door.

Jack flipped open his laptop and turned it on. It was time to coordinate the evidence he had gotten on the investigation at New Castle. He needed to get his equipment broken down and put away until he planned out his next investigation. Every so often he bit off a small piece of chicken and tossed it into the living room for Caesar. Hopefully soon his cat would ease up and have the run of the house again. He pulled his journal to the edge of the table and started thumbing through, page after page. After confirming that all the pics, video and audio were safely saved in his laptop, he started deleting off his camera, voice recorder and DVR. He washed off his hands and began putting his equipment into their respective cases. Cords, lenses, motion detector...and then the cases into his bedroom closet. Next, it was time to cut the audio and video into clips. The KII sliding across the laundry room floor, even though you couldn't see it, should be noted and saved. The EVP's, the attack. He paused, a slight hesitation, but small. It was holding more fascination for him and less intimidation now. More confidence. Hey, he lived through a paranormal attack. Stronger, smarter. What doesn't kill you makes you stronger, right? It could only add to his veracity as an investigator. Things were going his way.

He clipped each notable section and saved it, separately, to his laptop and then to the external drive. Then, he burned them to a CD, which would go into his library of investigative evidence. Not that it was a big library, it mostly held everything he'd debunked, but there were some unexplainable moments. This was the tops, though. The pinnacle. So far.

It took him a few hours to get all the clips sectioned off, saved and burned to the CD, but now he actually felt he was back to his old self again. He labeled the CD and put it in a case in his bedroom closet. Safe. He went back to the kitchen table and cleared everything pertaining to the New Castle Investigation off his laptop. Methodical. Where he was a messy bachelor in his home life, his paranormal life was incredibly neat, orderly and precise. He smiled. He was an internal Felix and Oscar. An odd couple under the skin. A psychological dichotomy. And now he had Laurel in the mix. He yawned, stretched. 10:15 p.m. Time to get some sleep.

He woke and looked at the clock. 3:10 a.m. Aargh. He felt as if he had tossed and turned all night and he still had a few hours to go. Nights like this were hell. They didn't happen to him often, but they killed the next day, always. It was almost as if he was having nightmares but couldn't remember them. That vague dread dogged him. He flipped his pillow, punched it a few times, and moved to a cooler spot on the bed. He waited for sleep to overtake him, for that thick, heavy feeling to settle in. At 5:30 a.m. the alarm went off and startled him awake.

Jack sighed. Even the shower didn't bring him back to the world of the living. He moved slowly, getting his clothes from the basket and somehow getting out of the house on time. When he stopped at the drive up, he ordered two large coffees and a bagel. He was going to need that caffeine if he was going to survive until 4:30.

It was another dreary October day. Chilly, with snow flurries predicted. Snow! He wasn't ready for that shit. Way too early. As he went through the motions, stopping at his usual stops, hitting the usual pleasantries…Good morning, Fine, you? Yeah, the weather's looking iffy, have a nice day…he noted how the shop owners were adding bits of Christmas and taking down some of their Halloween displays. Already? Halloween wasn't for another few days. He shook his head. Commercialism driving the holidays. Disheartening.

He sighed and swung the bus into the next stop. A number of people were waiting to get on and he looked over his paperwork while they filed in. "No hello?" He glanced up. Laurel! His heart skipped a beat. Fuck, he had it bad.

"Hello, Doll! What brings you here?"

She slid into the seat directly behind him, pulled her scarf off and leaned onto the railing behind his seat. "I was hoping I'd catch your bus." Mabel was behind her on the steps and watched their interaction. She moved into the seat beside Laurel.

He pulled the handle to close the bus doors and eased back into traffic. "How'd I get so lucky?" he caught a quick glimpse of her in his rear view mirror. Beautiful. Windblown hair suited her. No makeup.

"My day off. Thought I'd surprise you."

"Ah, the best surprise! Where are you going?"

"Where are you taking me?" She smiled and squeezed his shoulder. He smiled.

"You know him?" Mabel asked Laurel.

"Yes, a bit," she leaned closer to Mabel and whispered, "We're dating."

"Oh!" Mabel pursed her lips and gave her a knowing look. "He's a good man," she whispered. "Likes cats."

Laurel nodded. She and Mabel chatted, with Jack keeping track of things in his mirror. He liked her on his bus. Loved her this close, although closer would be better. Much closer. Skin to skin… Okay, mind on the road. Sweet, though, that she thought of him and took the opportunity to be there. She rode with him until he came back through town to the stop closest to her house. Another squeeze of his shoulder as she got up to leave.

"Have a great day," she said, over her shoulder.

"Doll, you made my day." And she had. The rest of the afternoon was lighter, brighter. Easier. He drank his second coffee, and didn't care that it was cold. Mabel stood up for her stop.

"I'm not going to squeeze your shoulder," she said, quietly. "But treat her right. She's a keeper."

He winked at her as she adjusted today's hat, keeping the peony straight. "I will, Mabel. I will."

Energized, despite his crappy night and not due to the caffeine in his less than lukewarm coffee, the rest of the afternoon smoothly sped along. He was stopped at the red light before his last stop and he saw there was one person waiting ahead. He'd have to tell them that this was his last drop off before heading back to the station and they'd have to wait about twenty minutes before the other driver would come along. His light flipped to green and he pulled in at the stop. The last two passengers got off, and he turned to greet the person waiting to get on, with a "Sorry, this isn't a..." but there was no one standing in the shelter. He moved so he could see to the sides and behind it, but no one was there. Strange. Maybe it was the sun, or lack of sun, that had played tricks with his eyes. But he swore he had seen a man standing there. He shrugged it off and drove on. It was time to park the bus for the night and head for home.

Caesar was waiting for him, half in the archway to the kitchen, half in the living room. It was closer, anyway. Jack picked him up, scratching him under the chin and ears. Caesar snuggled him back. He unbuttoned his shirt and tossed it on the back of the couch, then got the mail from the slot in his front door. Odd that that was the only use he had for that door. Never unlocked, the only things that ever passed through the space were bills, flyers and supermarket circulars. He chuckled and wondered if it was that way for other people. Somewhere, someone must use their front door as an actual entranceway. He dropped the mail onto the coffee table. "Bills, Cees. All bills," he looked at the lovable ball of fur. "You might want to start picking up some slack." Caesar licked a paw and began washing his face. "Lazy bum."

Jack went into the bathroom and turned on the shower. He stepped under the water and stood there, letting it wash over his chest and arms. The heat felt so good, warming him from the outside in. He turned to let it flow over his back and thought of Laurel. Her hair, her face. Her breasts. And she was into him. HIM. How the fuck did that happen? Didn't matter. It happened. He lathered up, rinsed off and reached for a towel. No towel. "Oh, come on," he said to no one. They were probably all still in the clothes basket. Damn it. He stepped out onto the bath mat, dripping. Figures. Air drying was not an option. He was already getting cold, so he ran to the basket, digging through the pile of clothes until he found a towel. He got himself dry and threw on a pair of pajama bottoms and a tee shirt. Marvel superheroes pajama pants. Yeah, that was more like it.

He scooped up his phone and hit the speed dial for Luigi's. Tonight there was a large supreme pizza with his name on it. And Parker's, although he didn't know it yet. That would be his next call. He got Parker's voicemail. Again. Did that man ever answer his phone?

"Park. Pizza. My house." In fifteen minutes, Parker was at his door. "How the fuck do you DO that?" Jack asked.

Parker winked, walking in. "It's my super power. Where's the pizza?"

Jack had to laugh out loud. "You beat the delivery guy. Did you at least bring some beer?"

From behind him, Parker held up a twelve pack.

"You're a good man, Park. A genuinely good man."

They each cracked open a bottle and sat down in the kitchen to wait. Headlights flashed into Jack's carport and he handed Parker the money. "Go. Use your superpower. I need to pee."

When he got back from the bathroom, Parker had the pizza box open on the table and half a slice was gone. "Damn."

"Hey," Parker said. "I thought you were going to get rid of it."

"What?" Jack looked up from the pizza, a slice in his hand.

"The spirit board. You left it outside. That's not the same as getting rid of it, you know."

"What the fuck are you talking about?" Jack took a bite, looking confused. "I put it in the garbage a couple of days ago. In fact," he said. "I put it there twice."

"Okay, what?"

"I put it there twice. The first time, someone must've grabbed it back out and left it next to the house. The second time, I threw it back in the bin. That was that. What are you talking about?"

"That's weird. When I paid the delivery guy, I saw it on the far side of the steps. Figured you left it there and forgot to throw it out."

"Are you kidding me? What the hell?" Jack got up and went outside to the top of his steps. There, on the ground to his right, was the Ouija board. He came back in and sat down. "Somebody's got to be screwing with me. Or they think I want it."

"Or, it's the entity attached to the board, Jack."

"Look, I saged the house and have had no issues in days."

"You've read about these things just like I have. It wants back in."

"I'm still not 100% on that. Could be some kid messing around."

"Or not. Most likely not. After all you've been through recently, how can you discount that?"

Jack thought about it. Had another beer. "Suppose you're right. Suppose it wants back in, whatever it is. I'm good, then, because it's out, right? I'm not inviting it back in."

Parker laughed. "You asshole. It's not a vampire movie." He shook his head. "How can you be so good at what you do and so unknowledgeable about what's out there? I don't get it."

"Bite me," Jack countered. "I've never dealt with anything like this before. Everything I've encountered has been a flashlight turning on here, or a chair sliding two inches there. Nothing like this. And I'm still not convinced it's anything more than a spirit that followed me home."

"Okay. That may be so, but what about the Ouija board hanging around outside? Who do you think is taking it out of the garbage and leaving it at the door? And why?"

"I don't know."

"Right. No one would, if you think about it. Maybe once, I don't know. Maybe someone thought you didn't mean to throw it away. But not twice. Come on, Jack. Think."

"Maybe it's Carla. Or James, wanting to talk through the board."

Parker shook his head. "From all I've seen and read, a human spirit doesn't have that kind of energy to be carrying a sign back and forth. I definitely think it's something bigger."

"And what am I supposed to do if you're right? If something is trying to get back in?"

"Obviously the board wasn't closed when whoever used it opened it. I've seen different opinions on how to get rid of a board when there's a problem. Some say to break it into seven pieces and bury them in separate places. Holy water. Some say only the person who originally opened it can close it and get rid of the problem."

"Sort of like killing the head vampire..." Jack chuckled. A pause. "So, you're saying I'm screwed? I'll have something opening my basement door, drawers and moving a bowl for all of eternity?"

"Maybe. Maybe not. That growl we heard really bothers me. And the scratches. That all points to something inhuman."

Jack rubbed his eyes, tired of the whole conversation. The pizza was getting cold and the beer, warm. "The growl could've been something on the radio, or a malfunction. You know, we didn't look into it."

Parker started at him incredulously.

"You know, Park, I really don't feel like discussing it tonight. The house is quiet; the board is outside. I'm good. I can research it, figure things out. But not tonight." He pulled another beer out of the box.

"Fine. Just don't put it off, okay? I'll help, if you want. I'll see if there's anything I can find out for you tomorrow."

"Fine."

Parker cracked another beer for himself. "So…how's Laurel?"

Jack smiled. "Now there's a subject I'm into." He tipped his chair onto the back two legs and balanced there for a moment.

"Doing a lot of…research?"

They both laughed, the atmosphere lighter. Caesar even cautiously joined them in the kitchen, jumping onto Jack's lap. "Trying to. Seeing her again Saturday night."

"Saturday? Halloween?" Parker whistled. "You are gone. Hook, line and sinker. In a costume?"

"No fucking way. Just gonna hang. Watch her give out candy."

Parker gave Jack's chair a knock with his foot and watched him scramble not to fall. "Right around her little finger, aren't you?"

"Hell, yeah. And loving it."

Parker left around 10:30 p.m. They both needed to get up early for work and they'd learned long ago that late nights killed the next day. Jack locked the door behind him, cut all the lights and went to bed.

The next few days, and nights, went quickly. The house stayed calm, with no activity except for Caesar occasionally playing with his tail. Jack left the Ouija board outside; he'd do something with it over the weekend. Ah, the weekend. He was looking forward to seeing her again, even if it was for Halloween. Maybe the kids would quit fairly early and they could go out. Or stay in. He smiled. Add to that the fact that daylight savings time ended on Sunday and getting that hour back was going to be heaven. Short lived, but heaven none the less. It'd be so wonderful if he got to spend that hour with Laurel. A little extra sleep and a little extra skin? Hmm. He was daydreaming while he drove; half expecting to see Laurel at his bus stops, even though he knew she wouldn't be. She had her work to do, as well. But he hoped she'd surprise him again. Soon.

Saturday morning and Jack was up and out of bed earlier than he had anticipated. Usually, he'd sleep in on Saturday, eat a leisurely breakfast…he chuckled…at A Touch of Home. Today, he wanted to get a jump on things. He threw on some sweats and walked into the kitchen, getting a bowl, some milk and a spoon. He sniffed the milk. Still okay, though not the freshest. After he poured some on his cornflakes, he dumped the rest down the sink. While he stood, taking mouthfuls and looking out the kitchen window, he thought he'd put on a pot of coffee. He set down the bowl and started looking through the cabinets for filters. Aargh, out. Well, paper towels worked. He ripped one off the roll and shoved it into the basket. Shortly, the pot was bubbling and the aroma was fabulous. The beverage of kings. A good way to start the day.

With the chilly fall weather he didn't need to work on the grass, but some outdoor clean up felt like a good idea. Get a few things done, some fresh air. Win win. "Too bad you're not a dog, Cees," he said as he walked out the door, "or I'd take you with me." Caesar jumped into the window above the sink and licked the condensation off the glass. Jack tapped on the window from outside. Caesar was definitely unimpressed. Ah, well.

There was a bite in the air this morning; Jack could see his breath linger before disappearing. He raked for a while, then brought his yard furniture into the house, carrying each piece down into the basement, leaning them on his side wall. He only had two folding chairs, a lounge and a small table, but he didn't want them to get ruined over the winter. They suited him. Comfortable enough for a beer in the shade on a nice day, but quite unpretentious. He chuckled. Woven plastic seats. Classy. He turned to go back upstairs when the light flickered a few times and went out. Damn. He'd have to see if he had any lightbulbs to switch it out. There might be some upstairs in his closet. One more trip.

He stood at his closet, staring at the junk he had stuffed onto the shelf above his clothes. Boxes upon boxes, old sneakers and even a sewing kit his mother had given him once, years ago. He might use it. Someday. He reached up for a small red and white box. Bingo. There were even two bulbs still inside. He took the one out and shook it next to his ear. Double bingo. Jack went back into his basement, pulled over a stepstool and changed it, the light coming on bright in his face. Satisfied, he tucked the stool back beside the washer and headed up to get the last piece of lawn furniture. As he reached the top of the stairs, the new bulb went bright and then out with a pop. Shit. He should have brought them both down with him. Caesar's feet slid as he tried to get traction and run out of the kitchen, startled. "Really, Cat? Really? It's just me," although for a half second, he felt as if he were being watched. He turned, but, of course, nothing was there. "Thanks, Cees, for giving me the creeps." Jack grabbed the other lightbulb and switched the one in the basement. He tried it a few times, pulling the string on, off, on, off. All fixed. He refused to be paranoid.

Jack brought in the folded chaise lounge and left it in the basement with the others. He gave a quick look around. He'd need to pick up down there one day. It wasn't a very large basement and, aside from the washer and dryer, his storage was taking over the place. Maybe he'd get a shed, he certainly had enough room to put one in. A nice little pre-fab at the end of his carport would help. That'd definitely be on his list for spring.

It was too nice a day to sit inside and he decided to take a walk. Dishes and laundry could wait, and making a bed was only something that happened in movies. He smiled to himself. The sun was peeking out from behind a few clouds. White, fluffy ones. Not the dark, sky-covering clouds that had been hanging around the last few days. The air held the usual October dampness and scent of wet leaves that was vaguely pleasant. He walked with no particular destination in mind, just enjoying the cool breeze on his face. He looked back at his house and thought he saw a man, the shadow of a man, standing on his side steps, but then the clouds continued moving and uncovered the sun. It was gone. He crossed the street and went through the park.

Children were on the playground equipment while parents watched from the side, or from benches around the perimeter of the grounds. Some of the kids were dressed for Halloween already, little ghosts, a Spiderman, a princess, a mermaid. The usual. Young moms sitting together, chatting and comparing Little Johnny with Little Suzie, proud dads with cameras trying to capture the exceptional cuteness of Baby Mary. It was all rather Norman Rockwell to him. Americana. Something he had never been able to attain, but could appreciate.

Jack emerged on the other side of the park and looked both ways. Where should he go? An easy decision, DD was to his left about a quarter of a mile. Coffee was always in order.

He pushed the door open and heard the familiar ding of the door bells. Standing on line, he read the menu on the wall behind the cashiers. "A hot coffee, milk and sugar, please. Oh, and a blueberry muffin. Thanks." The girl behind the counter handed him his order and deducted the amount due from his DD card. He sat at a window seat so he could watch the passersby while he ate.

"Hey, you're that guy. That Ghost Guy, am I right?" a tall man with a crew cut stood by his table. Jack nodded. "Yeah, of course you are. I caught your talk last June."

"Oh, great," Jack said, swallowing his bite of muffin. "Hope you liked it."

"I did! Fascinating stuff you do. Oh, I'm Joe. Joe Paine," he held out his hand.

They shook hands. "Nice to meet you," Jack offered up.

"You, too. Really nice. I'm in town, working some construction. Well, I don't want to bother you. Just had to say hi. Keep up the good work!"

The guy walked off. "That ghost guy." Too cool. It appeared he had a bit of a reputation. He liked that. Every once in a while someone would recognize him after a talk, but it usually wore off pretty quickly. His phone went off. A text from Laurel. Cool. He leaned back to read it.

Hey, Jack. One of the girls called out, so I'm working a little later than I thought. Can you grab something for us for dinner? Anything is fine. Sorry for the late notice… ;-)

He texted a quick, "No problem, Doll." For a split second he considered grabbing some things at the market and cooking her dinner. He almost broke out laughing. Yeah, no. Bad idea. But then he wondered, what could he bring? What did she like? Damn. In all their talks, they hadn't touched much on food. Pizza? Boring. Chinese? He had no idea. Subs. He could get a few different kinds, some chips, cheese. Wine. Beer? It'd be eclectic. He crumpled his napkin and stuffed it into his empty coffee cup.

He walked home, enjoying, well, everything. Even the rug rats playing in the park and their yuppie parents. If he had been with the right woman, he might have had kids. Maybe not. Kids and then the divorce would've been complicated…and kids after it? He laughed. More complicated. He had to admit it. Kids just weren't his thing. He wondered what Laurel thought.

The walk back home seemed shorter than his way in to DD. Quicker. Laurel had a way about her that definitely took the edge off of things. As he approached his driveway, he could see the light on in his basement. Huh. "I thought I turned that off," he said under his breath. No matter, he was inside in a minute and quickly went down the stairs to pull the string. His washing machine was running. He knew he hadn't started it this morning. He hit the power button and let it drain. Empty. How weird was that? Could he have hit the button when he was carrying the lawn chairs? That must be it, although somewhere in the back of his mind, he knew he hadn't.

He spent the rest of the afternoon on the sofa, flipping channels and relaxing. He dozed off to a documentary on Komodo dragons, came to on Naked and Afraid. Two people, deposited in some remote area, naked and having to find their way out after twenty-one days. Now THAT was a challenge he could get into. Unfortunately, they blurred all the best parts. He chuckled and stretched. 4:30. He could get a shower in, pick up dinner and be at Laurel's in an hour. Perfect.

Jack stood and stretched again. The nap had been wonderful and he was totally refreshed. He went into the bedroom and dug through the clean clothes for a towel. The overhead light got bright and then popped. Caesar growled and crawled under the bed. "Damn it! What's with my lightbulbs lately?" He pawed through the upper shelf of his closet, but that was it for extra bulbs. "Fine. I'll have to go to the store. It'll have to do for now." At least the bathroom light worked.

As he moved around the bedroom after his shower, Caesar remained under the bed. He tossed his towel onto the bed and the cat growled. "Come on, Cees. It was only a lightbulb. How'd you become such a scardey cat?" He looked through the basket of clothes. What do you wear on Halloween? Jeans, a midnight blue sweatshirt. Yeah, that would be good. He ran the comb through his hair, brushed his teeth and was ready to go. Before he left, he bent over to try to coax Caesar out of his hiding place, but he wasn't having it. "Fine, silly old cat. I'll be back la-" he cut himself off mid-word, "tomorrow morning, hopefully." He grabbed his cell phone and car keys from the bowl and left.

On the way to Laurel's house was a great little sub shop. They made the best heroes, or hoagies, or subs. Geez. Every town he'd ever been to, it seemed, had its own word for them. He grew up knowing them as subs. And soda. He chuckled. He didn't get the people who called it "pop." Ah, well. Tradition, he guessed. He ordered a few different kinds, turkey and provolone, roast beef and American, hot meatball. Figured he'd cover all bases, and threw in a couple of small bags of chips. Next, he stopped at the liquor store for another bottle of rose. Wine and subs? Not fancy, but he didn't need to be. Laurel was…comfortable. Or, more accurately, he was comfortable with her. He took the bag with the wine and was back out to his car in under five minutes, happy to be finally on his way to her house.

She had the front door opened before he could turn off the Subaru's engine. He waited a moment for it to rumble to a stop, as he always did. She called to him, "I didn't want you thinking you had to wait before coming in!" She laughed as he walked up the steps. He gave her a quick kiss on the lips and went inside.

"Are you ready for trick or treaters?"

"Not really," he smiled. "But we can make it work." Laurel got a couple of plates out and he spread the waxed paper rolled subs and the bottle of wine out on the coffee table. "Turkey, roast beef and hot meatball. I wasn't sure which you'd like best."

"A little of each?" She held up a knife from the kitchen.

"Awesome." This was going to be quite a good night. He sat on the sofa, legs out in front of him, ankles crossed. He stretched his arms above and behind his head. Laurel walked over with the knife. She unwrapped the subs while he took the knife and cut short sections of each. The doorbell rang. Their eyes locked as she was licking tomato sauce off her fingers from the meatball sub.

"No worries," she said to him, winking. "I've got it."

Jack grabbed a piece of the hot meatball sub and listened as Laurel answered the door. "Oh, what have we got here? A ghost, a witch, C3PO! You guys are great! Here…" He knew she was holding out a big plastic bowl filled with lollipops and mini chocolate bars that he had seen when he walked in. "Enjoy! Happy Halloween!" She closed the door and sat next to him. After a few bites, her eyes got wide. "Oh, the wine!"

"I can get glasses," he said, getting up.

"Thanks. Would you rather have a beer?" She looked up at him, questioningly. He paused. "It's fine. I picked some up."

"Yeah," he replied. "I really would. The wine is great, but…"

"But go get yourself a beer and bring me a glass for the wine."

Damn, she was wonderful. He chuckled. The little things. He walked into the kitchen like he owned the place and pulled a beer out of the refrigerator, then got a wine glass from the cabinet. He could hear little voices approaching outside and the doorbell rang. "Oh, hello!" Laurel was back in action. He poured her a glass of wine and sat back down to get another piece of sub.

The night wore on, with witches, ghouls and all sorts of Star Wars creatures begging for candy treats. 7:00, 8:00, 9:00. Jack didn't know there were this many children in the entire city, forget just coming down this road. It was taking a little longer between groups showing up now and things seemed to be winding down. Finally, Laurel closed the door and shut off the porch light, holding the bowl out toward Jack. "That's it for the candy."

"Good," he replied, taking the bowl from her and setting it down. He took her hand and pulled her down to him to kiss her. "I've been waiting to do that all night."

She laughed her sweet laugh and he let her go. They picked up the remnants from dinner, throwing out the garbage and putting the dishes into the sink. "That last little witch was so cute." She began rinsing off the plates and putting them into the dishwasher.

"Not as cute as you."

"Are you saying I'm a witch?" she smiled.

"Well, you've cast a spell on me," he said and kissed the back of her neck.

"Be careful what you wish for," she laughed. "They do say that on this night, the veil between the worlds is the thinnest."

He kissed her neck, again, softly. "Do they? Spooky."

She laughed and turned toward him, sliding her arms around him. "They do." Jack kissed her, more passionately, picked her up and carried her to the bedroom.

He eased her down onto her feet and began to gently take off her clothes. This would be different than the last time, he thought. That was need. This was desire. Gentle, sweet, teasing desire. He dropped her shirt to the floor, reaching around her to unhook her bra. She let it slide off her arms to the floor while he pulled off his shirt. An embrace. If he could've melted her inside of him, he would have at that moment. He breathed in, loving her scent and the feel of her breasts against his chest. His mouth found hers while his hands wandered. Breasts, back. Looking into her eyes, he asked, huskily, "Do you know how much I want you right now?" She kissed him harder and he squeezed her ass, pulling her in tightly against him. "The jeans gotta go, Doll."

She playfully asked, "Yours or mine?"

"Be careful, or the teaser will get teased."

"Oh, I might like that."

"I guarantee you would."

"Bring it."

She turned to run to the other side of the bed when he grabbed her from behind. He nibbled on her neck while he undid the button on her pants and unzipped them. His hand slid inside and deliciously gripped her pussy. Delicately, he slipped his fingers between her lips to reach her clit. She let out a soft, "Mmmm," as he rubbed and teased. She leaned against him, his left arm still wrapped around her, holding her. Soon, her hips were moving in time to his hand, slowly, deliberately.

"Not yet, Doll." He pulled his hand out from the slippery warmth between her legs and yanked down her jeans. She stepped out of them, taking his hand as he led her to the bed. He sat on the edge of the bed. She approached him and gasped when he started sucking on her nipples, one then the other. Straddling him, he guided his cock into her. They kissed and she started to move on him. He held her down. "Nope. Sit still." She did, kissing him passionately. He held her there as they kissed, as he fondled, until she couldn't take it anymore.

"Pleeeease," she begged him.

He scooped her up, swinging her to the bed, on her back, and pushed deeply into her. He took her hard and fast, grinding into her clit with every thrust. She moaned and gave a yell, grabbing his ass and exploding on his cock in a throbbing orgasm. She held onto him, her fingernails digging into his flesh while she rode it out, the contractions getting slower and less intense, when he started again. Slowly this time, in, out, in, out. He played and teased, just the tip, then plunged. He could feel it building in her again when he got lost in the amazing feeling of her. He grabbed her legs and eased her knees up under his arms, pounding her as deeply as he could. A thundering orgasm tore through him. They came together, again, and lay sweating and exhausted when it was over.

"Trick or treat?" he asked, holding her close.

She snuggled into his chest, smiling. After a few minutes, she said, "You know, it's too early to go to sleep."

"Hmmm," he lifted his head and looked at her with one eye open. "You sure about that?"

"Yup!" She climbed out of bed and grabbed a white, fluffy short robe out of the closet, tying it at the waist. "Come on," she took him by the hand and pulled him into a seated position.

"You got a man's robe in there?" He joked.

"Actually," she turned to the closet. "I do." She pulled out an old, worn blue flannel robe and handed it to him. Jack raised an eyebrow. "My dad left it the last time he visited." He stood and put it on. "Now, come on," she said. "I need a snack."

He followed her down the hallway to the kitchen. She took one of the sub ends from the refrigerator and got cozy on the sofa, sitting with her feet tucked under her. He cracked a beer and sat next to her. Sitting with his knees wide, he had to keep adjusting the robe. Laurel giggled. He sighed. "I'll be right back." He came back, still in the robe, but with his boxers on. "That's better," he sat comfortably next to her.

Jack reached over, picked up Laurel's wine glass and handed it to her.

"Trying to get me drunk?" she smiled.

"Yup. So I can have my way with you," he chuckled.

She laughed, almost losing a mouthful of sub. She took a sip of wine.

"Good girl," he said. "Should I get the bottle?" Laurel gave him a playful shove and put the glass on the coffee table. He hugged her and she leaned into his chest.

"See? Halloween can be nice."

"Hmmm, yeah," he whispered. "I think a new Halloween tradition has begun."

She turned toward him, sitting Indian style. She made sure the robe covered her, and smiled at Jack. "So, when do I get to meet this famous cat of yours? Caesar?"

"Whenever you want. You can make an appointment with his secretary."

"And that would be?"

"Me." He swallowed the last of his beer and got up to find another. "His calendar is pretty open. No worries."

"Well, pencil me in."

Jack opened a beer and stood in the doorway to the kitchen. "Yes, ma'am." He raised his drink in her direction. "Anything you desire." He hit the dimmer switch and turned down the lights, then turned on the radio, low. He sat beside her and pulled the afghan over them. They talked and snuggled until late in the night, then turned off the light and went to bed.

Half asleep, Jack reached out to find Laurel but her half of the bed was empty. He looked around, rubbing the sleep from his eyes and heard the shower running. 9:00 a.m. He piled up the pillows behind his back and waited for her to come out.

"Morning, you," she came out of the bathroom dressed for work, a beige colored dress, her name tag crooked, hair still in a towel.

"Morning, Doll. I forgot you had to work this morning."

"Yeah, it rots. I can dry my hair out here if you want the bathroom."

"That'd be great," he got up and gave her a kiss as he went into the bathroom. He turned on the water and heard his phone ringing in the next room.

"It says 'Jerk,'" Laurel called in to him. "With a picture of...Godzilla?"

Jack laughed. "It's my buddy, Park. Answer if you'd like, it'll twist his brain."

Laurel swiped it. "What's your code?"

"4785."

She typed it in and answered sweetly, "Hello?"

"Uh...um...Ja, is Jack there?"

"He's in the bathroom."

"Well, this is awkward," Park laughed.

"He said it'd make you crazy if I answered. So, I had to. It's Laurel."

"Well… yeah, hey, Laurel. Are you guys hanging out today, wait, it's early. Guess you had plans last night. Did you have fun?"

She laughed. "Yeah, it was great. You should have seen him with the trick or treaters."

"Oh, REALLY? That's right, he has this thing about Halloween."

"Not anymore," she laughed.

"I'll have to talk to him about that. Would you tell His Royal Highness to give me a call when he gets home? IS he going home today?"

"Yes, yes. He'll be home today. I have to get to work soon."

"Tell him I want to hear all about his research later," Park said, "And you have a good day, Laurel."

"You, too, Park." She hit the call end button and dropped Jack's phone on the bed. The toilet flushed and she called in to him, "He said he wants to hear about your research later." Jack opened the bathroom door. "Research?" she asked.

Jack smiled. He leaned through the doorway and kissed her. "You." She handed him his clothes from the floor and he tucked his phone into his pants pocket.

She folded her arms. "I'm RESEARCH?"

He pulled her close, wrapping his arms around her. "You are amazing."

"Never forget that."

"Never."

She glanced at the clock. "Oh, hell… I've gotta run."

"Okay, Doll," he finished putting on his shirt and they walked out of the house together. The morning was cold and he could see his breath. "Call me later and I'll set up a meeting between you and Caesar, the Great."

"You've got it, sweetie."

Jack got into the Subaru, turned the key and it shook to life. He turned on his blinker and turned right out of her driveway, watching in his rearview mirror as she turned left. Traffic was light. Sunday morning in a small town. If he had had fresh clothes with him, he might've gone over to A Touch of Home and let Laurel wait on him. Or not. It'd be good to get home, call Park, and just relax in the afterglow of last night. Maybe she'd want to come over later to see Caesar.

He pulled into his driveway and turned off the car. It took a little longer each time for it to decide to shut down. He grabbed his keys, went up his steps two at a time, and unlocked the door. Dropping his keys in the bowl, he walked into his kitchen. Caesar meowed from the bedroom. "Hey, Cees, I'm home!"

He turned. The Ouija board was on the kitchen table. He stared. The Ouija fucking board was on the fucking table. How was that even fucking possible? He paused, trying to wrap his head around it, then picked up his journal and started writing. This shit was getting real and it fascinated him.

He left the board on the table and went through each room. Nothing seemed upset or out of place. Even Caesar came out of the bedroom to meet him on the sofa. Rubbing and meowing for pets, he was his happy cat self. Perhaps it was just the board itself. A strong attachment, some bizarre paranormal phenomenon. Or, maybe Park had stopped by and brought it in? Kind of a kick in the ass for him, since he hadn't gotten rid of it yet. He knew that was unlikely, but it was the most plausible thing his mind could hang on to. He dialed his friend.

It rang. Once, twice. "Hey, Jack, you dog!"

"Yeah, yeah. Park, were you at my house earlier?"

"What? No. I've been here all morning."

"The Ouija board. It was on my kitchen table."

'What?"

"When I walked in, it was sitting on my kitchen table. Everything else was fine. Even Cees was happy."

Parker was silent for a minute. "That's fucked up, Jack. I didn't do it."

"Fucked up, but pretty cool."

"If you were reading about it in some book, sure. What did you do with it?"

"Nothing yet."

"You need to break it up into seven pieces and bury it. Keep the planchette separate. Sprinkle it all with holy water."

"Holy water."

"Yes, holy water."

"Where am I going to get holy water?"

"Really?"

"I am not walking into some church and asking the priest for holy water. 'Excuse me, father. I've got a demon in my Parker Bros. toy and could use some of your blessed water.'" Jack used his best Irish accent in his sarcasm.

"Fuck, you're an asshole. You know this is bigger than you, right?"

"I know it's got me off my game, at the moment. I know it's some sort of paranormal activity, an attachment of some kind. But, it's just annoying. Making itself known."

"You heard the growl, right? Spent the night at my place? Or did you forget? And if it doesn't want to leave? If it's masquerading as something knocking around and is really a darker entity? You've been attacked once already, for God's sake."

"That was at New Castle."

"And where the fuck do you think THIS came from?"

"Want me to take it the fuck back?"

"I don't think that would help. You've got to destroy the board or find a way to close it. IF those things would help at this point. I think there's a portal open and something's stepped through.

Maybe it came through at the asylum and came back with you, I don't know. But you need to take it more seriously."

Jack rubbed his hand across his eyes. All this shit after such a great night with Laurel. Yeah, he'd have to address it. He didn't want her to come over and have it look like the house out of Poltergeist or something. "Okay. I'll take care of it."

"Do it. Want help?"

Jack smiled. "Looking for lunch?"

Parker laughed. "Why the fuck not?"

"I'll take care of the board. You bring food. I haven't even had breakfast yet."

"You suck."

"Grab something good. I'm starved."

"Okay. Be there in an hour."

Jack dropped his phone onto the coffee table and rubbed Caesar's ears. The cat purred, closing its eyes and pressing against his leg. "Want a shower, kitty cat? I do." He stood, looking around the place another time, and walked into the kitchen. What to do with the board? Park could be right and that might be where the attachment was, but he really did like the thing. And he'd love to do some experiments with it. He ran his fingers across the lettering, and let his hand stop on "Yes." He would keep it. For now. When he was done, he'd get rid of the thing like Park had said. Done and done. He picked it up, walked into the bedroom and hit the light switch. Nothing. Should've asked Park to bring a lightbulb. He chuckled and tucked the board up high on the shelf in his closet. He slid the closet door closed and looked at Caesar. "Don't tell Park."

The steam felt soothing as he pulled off his clothes. Relaxing. He stepped under the water and let it flow over him, feeling for the shampoo bottle. He lathered his hair, and rinsed. The lather circled the drain while he soaped up and rinsed. He stood, letting the heat soak into his back, when the water went cold. Ice cold. He yelled, "Shit!" and jumped to the side. Damn it! He fumbled with the faucet, trying to get the hot water back. It slowly began to heat back up again. He'd have to have it looked at. Maybe there was a pipe issue. His house wasn't that old, but he guessed things went bad every so often.

He reached for the towel from the rack and dried off some before stepping out of the tub. The bathroom was still foggy with steam. He tossed the towel over the shower curtain rod and turned to the mirror. "What the fuck?" he muttered. In the middle of the mirror was a hand print. A large, man's hand print. He held his hand up to it for a second, just to see. To measure. It was larger than his. "What the fucking hell?" He threw open the bathroom door and ran to get his phone. He wanted a picture of this.

It was still on the mirror when he ran back in and he snapped pictures from different angles. Finally, he took the towel off the rod and wiped the mirror. Always the investigator, he shut the door, turned on the hot water and waited. Nothing. He waited longer, the mirror fully fogged, but nothing. He quit. It was probably explainable. Maybe at some point he had touched the mirror, put his hand flat on it. When he was cleaning or something. Cleaning. Him? Yeah, probably not the mirror. But perhaps he had and in the condensation it had expanded. He'd check out the pics once he was dressed. Yeah, odd happening, but probably explainable. Still, he wrote it down in his journal. Might as well.

He dressed. A pair of jeans and an old red flannel shirt. He didn't shave. It was Sunday and Parker was coming. Maybe they'd do some outside stuff. He didn't need to clean up. Laundry, though, had to be done for work tomorrow. Caesar followed him through the living room, to the archway to the kitchen and stopped. "Really, Cees? Are we back to that?"

He turned the doorknob of the basement door and tugged. Nothing. It didn't give. "Come on," Jack pulled harder. The lock wasn't engaged; the knob was turned, the damn thing should have opened. "Fucker." A shove might do it. Might loosen whatever was stuck. He gave it a push. It didn't even give. He stepped back to assess it for a moment and the door clicked open. Just an inch, but open. On its own.

"Not funny. Don't screw with me, whatever you are. I'm not playing." Frustrated, he went downstairs and threw the load into the washer. Maybe the damn thing wanted to be immortalized in his journal. He shook his head, trying to rid himself of the annoyance it had conjured up. The sun was out today and he could see the rays of sunlight coming through the little basement windows, lighting up the dust in the air. Parker would be there soon. He went back upstairs and gave the door a push closed. It latched. Like normal.

Parker was at the door with a bag. Subs. Okay, whatever. It was all good, even if he had had them last night. "Turkey, roast beef and meatball!" Parker had said excitedly.

"Yum," replied Jack.

Parker set the bag on the kitchen table. "What? What... not good enough for you?"

Jack laughed. "They're great, Park. Really. Thanks."

Parker eyed him and got plates from the cabinets. "Well, you could be more appreciative."

Jack bowed. "What are you, my wife? Thank you from the bottom of my heart, dear Park. You shall be knighted for this performance."

"About fucking time," Parker said.

They ate. Jack didn't mind that they were having subs again. Parker knew what he liked. The provolone with red wine vinegar was delicious. He could eat it anytime. He popped some of the shredded lettuce that had fallen out of the sandwich into his mouth. "Delicious."

"So...aside from the obvious Ouija board, demon attachment issue, how's Laurel?" Parker took another bite of his sub.

"Fuck, Park. She's amazing."

"And the...research?"

Jack laughed. "So fucking fine."

They both laughed and continued eating. "Kind of amazing, am I right?"

"What?" Jack asked.

"That she's into you!" Parker ducked as Jack made a swing for him.

"Asshole."

"Yeah..." Parker continued eating.

"Was hoping she might stop by tonight after work to meet Cees."

Parker rolled his eyes.

"What?"

"That's the oldest trick in the book. Come to my place...we'll pet my cat."

"Fuck off."

"You know it's true."

"Yeah, well, we've already been out a few times. Already...well..."

"Already hit that?"

Jack laughed. "Already slept over. More than once."

"Already hit that thang!" Parker got up and started twerking in Jack's kitchen.

"Quit it, quit it, God! Burn my eyes!!" They laughed, side splitting, rib hurting laughter, and it felt good.

Parker sat back down and picked up a piece of the turkey sub. After a bite and a long, thoughtful stare at Jack, he asked, "You get rid of it?"

Jack looked at his friend. He hated to lie. "I took care of it."

Parker's eyes narrowed a bit. He knew the semantics Jack could play if he wanted to. "You..."

"Took care of it. End of story." He wadded up the wax paper and threw it into the garbage. "Two points." He turned toward Parker. "What do you want to do today?"

Parker stared at him. He knew having the same conversation again would be futile. He sighed. Jack reached over and shoved his shoulder. "Come on. Let's go shoot some hoops or something. Get some energy out."

Parker eased up a little. "You'll probably have a heart attack, you old fart."

"Run circles around your sorry ass."

"You think so?"

"I know so."

Parker got up, sliding his chair to the table. "I'll get your wheelchair."

"I'd run you over in it."

They laughed, grabbed their things and headed out. Jack dipped his hand into the bowl to get his keys, half expecting them to be gone, but they were there. Cold metal in his fingers. He tossed them up, caught them, locked the door and they left.

There was always a game to join in the park on a Sunday afternoon, especially on cold fall days. It was as if no one wanted to let go of summer and were fighting off the dead days of winter ahead. Different guys from the neighborhood would hang out, talk some trash, and get out the week's frustrations on the basketball court. It was friendly and Jack was glad there were already a couple of guys he recognized playing some one on one. "Hey…can we join in?" The guy with the bandana, Jack thought his name was Paul, nodded and threw him the ball. They got into position for some man to man, with Parker covering him.

Jack dribbled the ball. Parker tried to block him. He bounced the ball to a guy on his team, who ran closer to the net and tried a layup. It rebounded off the rim, with Parker catching it. They went back and forth, hoop to hoop, for about half an hour. "24 to 17, we killed you," Parker said to Jack as they fist bumped the guys they played with and walked off. "Old fart."

Jack laughed. "You're not much younger, asshole."

They talked and laughed as they walked, trading jibes, sometimes silent. The sun was out, but it was cold. Most of the trees were bare and only the evergreens showed any life, although more dull than a month ago. The grass was faded, with brown crispy leaves and old pine needles piled up. Jack pushed his hands deeper into the kangaroo pocket of his sweatshirt. He'd never been a fan of winter. Spring always seemed so far away. He should've grabbed his jacket before they went out today; something that would've helped keep him warmer; keep his heat from pouring out. Being sweaty didn't help.

They circled around the bend of Ridley and could see Jack's house in the distance. His phone rang. Unknown Caller. Again. He answered. "Hello?" Static. Bizarre. Frustrating.

Parker looked at him questioningly.

"It keeps happening. Unknown fucking caller. And static. What the fuck?" He hung up. It rang again. He tossed it to Parker.

"Hello? Hey, Laurel!" Jack tried to grab the phone back, but Parker was quick and kept it pressed to his ear. "Yeah, this is Park. How's things?" Jack held out his hand. Parker ignored him. "Uh, huh...uh huh... Yeah, I know."

Jack was getting impatient. He hit Parker in the shoulder. "Please, I'm on the phone!" He ducked when Jack swung at him.

"So, Laurel, what do you think of my man, Jack?" Jack was chasing him around the cars now. "Oh? Oh, really?"

"You're like a fucking ten year old. Give me the damn phone," Jack lunged and Parker ducked.

"Nice talking to you, Laurel," Parker, a shit eating grin on his face, handed the phone to Jack.

"Asshole," Jack smirked. "Hey, Doll. Pay no attention to that jerk. What's up?"

She was laughing. "I've got a few minutes between my errands. Thought I'd stop by and meet Caesar."

"You're in luck. He's free all afternoon."

"Great. See you in about fifteen."

"Bye, Doll."

"Bye, Laurel!" Parker yelled.

"She already hung up, you jerk."

"Nice girl."

"Yup."

"Too good for you."

"Fuck off," Jack laughed. He went up the side steps and unlocked his door. "Coming in, asshole?"

"You asking for anal?" Parker walked in behind him. Jack rolled his eyes and dropped his keys into the bowl.

"You're a jerk, you know that? I don't know why I keep you around."

"Comic relief," Parker volunteered, sitting on the sofa, feet on the coffee table. "Is she coming?"

"Yeah."

"Great. She and I can have a little talk."

"You're going to behave."

"Yeah. I'll behave." He burst out laughing. Jack shook his head and watched out the window.

"You can sit down. I'm sure you'll hear her car pull up. Damn, you've got it bad. A little sex and your head's in the clouds."

"Bite me."

After about ten minutes Laurel drove up. Jack watched her get out of her Corolla, then stop at the passenger side to get a bag. She had on a dark blue wool jacket over her uniform. Damn, she made everything look good. He had the side door open before she could knock.

"Hey, there."

She smiled. "Hi." He let her in and she handed him the bag. "Dinner for later. I know how much you like to cook. Just a little something from the diner."

"Aw, thanks, Doll." He gave her a quick kiss, then sniffed the package. "Meat loaf?"

She winked.

Parker leaned from the sofa to look into the kitchen. "Hey, Laurel!"

"Hi, Park," she said. "There's enough for two."

Damn, she was thoughtful. He was so...smitten? Taken with her? Infatuated? In...he hesitated. Too soon, but damn. He did have it bad. Laurel followed him into the living room.

"I'm sorry if the grand tour isn't very grand," Jack smiled. "My living room." He held out his arm to show it off, as if selling her the furniture. "And, if you walk this way," he guided her through the next doorway, "my bedroom." He put his lips beside her ear and whispered, "And, God, I want to take you on that bed right now." She blushed. "There's my bathroom," he pointed. They walked back into the living room, where Parker still sat on the sofa. "I've got a basement, but...it's not so interesting."

"Charming," she said. "Where's the kitty?"

"Hmmm, I haven't seen him since we came in. Cees? Come here, you lazy cat," he called. Caesar emerged, sleepily, from under the sofa. Parker picked him up and brought him over to Laurel.

"Ooh, he's adorable." She rubbed his ears, giving him some long back pets as well.

"He agrees." Jack smiled.

She pet Caesar a moment longer. "So sorry to drop off food and run, but I do have to go."

"Glad you came, though. Even for a minute."

"Me, too," she smiled. "Nice seeing you, Park."

"You, too, Laurel," Parker called after her.

Jack walked her to the door, scooping her into his arms and kissing her long and hard. "Take that with you."

"I will."

He watched her back out of his driveway before he turned, almost bowling over Parker standing behind him. He gave him a shove. "Asshole."

"Yup. What's for dinner?" He clapped his hands together.

Jack rolled his eyes. "Meat loaf. But you can't be hungry yet."

Parker raised an eyebrow.

"Fine, fine. Warm it up."

Parker grabbed the bag and pulled out the two meat loaf meals. "Damn, she's so great! Jack, there's mashed potatoes…and carrots." He microwaved the dinners, got two forks out of the drawer and put them on the kitchen table. "So, tell me about those trick or treaters, you kinky fuck."

"You need a woman," Jack laughed.

"Yeah, but for now I can only live vicariously through you. So don't skimp on the details." He stabbed the meat loaf with his fork. Parker looked at Jack out of the corner of his eye. "Is she good?"

Jack stared back, with a smirk. "Do you really think I'm going to answer that?"

Parker waited, and motioned "go on" with his hand.

"She's fucking amazing."

Parker beamed at him and put his hand up for a high five. Jack paused, then high fived his friend. They laughed and finished the meat loaf. Jack threw the forks into the sink and dumped the rest into the garbage. "Want to catch the end of the Giants game?" He walked into the living room and picked up the remote.

"Who are they playing?"

"Saints."

"Oh, man. That could be a close one. Nah, thanks. I need to get some things ready before work tomorrow."

"You eat, talk sex and ghosts, and leave, you know that?"

"Yup. Let me know how your ghost goes," Parker said, heading to the side door. "And get rid of that damned board. I don't want to walk in and find you dead one day."

"Yeah, yeah. See ya."

"Not if I see you first," Parker laughed and gave Jack two finger guns.

Jack shook his head. He clicked the remote and the television came to life. It was already on the game. Caesar saw his opportunity. As soon as Jack sat down, he was on his lap, purring and kneading. Jack watched the game, some news, and part of the night game before he decided it was time to turn in. 5:30 am would come early. Way too early. "Come on, Cees. It's time we got some sleep." He walked into the bedroom and the Russian blue trotted along behind him, hopping up next to Jack's pillow. "Be right there, kitty." Jack changed into flannel pajamas. Keeping the house chilly at night was great for sleeping, and he liked the soft, cozy feel of the flannel. The comforter was nice and cool as he pulled it up around his neck. "Night, Cees." The cat purred and Jack thought of Laurel as he waited for sleep.

He was running. From who or what, he had no idea, but it was that fear driven run where you can't look back because if you do, it will be inches from your face. The sweat poured from him and his lungs were burning, his breath coming hard and raspy. The darkness was circling him, and his hands were cut from brambles on the branches he shoved from his path. He paused, hand resting on a tree as he tried to pull more air into his lungs. The bark was cool and damp under his palm, but he barely noticed. There was a faint bite of ozone as more black clouds rolled in. He couldn't stop here for long. Even the trees had that creepy vibe, like their branches were rubbing together, like hands wringing... anticipating. Glancing around, he took his next step. His socks were almost as damp as the tree bark, but from sweat or rain, he didn't know. Or care. Few things mattered now. He wiped his hand distractedly across his shirt and stumbled on.

As he half tripped into the road, he looked back, almost expecting to see something, large and unwavering, bearing down on him. Braced for another attack, he only saw the house he had run from. Its flickering light almost a beacon in the darkness. But not. Not life preserving in a sea of darkness, but soul drowning. He rubbed his eyes and ran his hands through his wet hair. No, not drowning. Damning was more like it.

A car's headlights appeared through the rain, which was heavier now. He started waving, arms flailing with desperation. He had to calm himself, slow down, or no one would stop. Pinning his arms to his sides as the car rolled to a stop, he hoped it was a stranger. Please, don't let it be a neighbor, someone who would ask questions, or, worse yet, want to take him home. The window opened and terror gripped his heart. He scrambled backwards, half running, half sprinting into the woods.

The trees opened into a clearing and he stumbled to a stop. Behind him was the forest; the trees were a black-green now and more tightly grown. Ahead of him, a cliff. How was this possible? He could almost hear the steady footsteps of what was behind him…but that was impossible… it didn't walk. It FELT. It willed itself. Bore down on him as its evil spread like the night across the landscape. Faster, though. So much faster. He slow jogged to the edge of the cliff and peered over. An empty abyss. And now, he could feel the breath of it on the back of his neck. Cold. He was tense, terrified, and waiting for the next attack. It came with a ferocity he hadn't anticipated and he fell into the pit. The darkness echoed with its laughter.

Jack woke. Panting. 3:00 a.m. He was covered in sweat and cold. So cold. He took off his pajamas, there'd be no sleeping in them, and pulled on a pair of sweats. And socks. What was the fucking temperature? 58 degrees. Damn it. The boiler was probably on the fritz. He'd have to call someone in the morning. He got back into bed and pulled the comforter up around his neck. He was shaking, but not from the lack of heat. There was no more sleep that night.

His alarm went off at 5:30 a.m. on the dot. He had watched the countdown from 5:27, 5:28, 5:29, and still jumped when it went off. It was an awful feeling, being up most of the night. And from a god damned nightmare. What the fuck? He had a headache now, but at least he wasn't so cold anymore. He checked the thermostat. 68. That didn't make any sense. He'd definitely have to have a guy out. Hopefully his water would be hot.

He showered without a problem, the water warm and inviting, but he was too tired for it to be invigorating. It was going to be a long day. The steam cleared from his mirror while he shaved; no hand print, no nothing. At this moment, though, he wouldn't have cared if all the doors and drawers in the house were wide open. He'd just zone out, grab his keys and head to his bus. Not good being this tired. Caesar was lucky he got fed. Jack chuckled. Tiredly.

The day moved at the steady pace of molasses. He hated having to drive when he was so sleepy. He fought to keep his eyes open and his head from nodding. Torture. During a lull, he picked up a coffee, black, with some espresso added. Something. Even if the caffeine made him sick, he needed to be alert. He barely even spoke to his passengers, probably adding to the "surly bus driver" image some drivers had. It couldn't be helped. He felt like shit.

His shift ended. Finally. He pulled the bus into its usual spot, slightly crooked, but he couldn't care less at the moment, handed in his paperwork and left. Not even a "have a good night" on his lips or a nod. Just a bit of a "Mm" and he was out to get his car. All he wanted was to get home and go to bed. A nap. Hell, he didn't care if he slept till tomorrow. He got into the Subaru and turned the key. Nothing. Not even its usual moans and groans and complaints. Dead silence. He tried again. The lights didn't even flicker. Nothing attempted to come on. "Fuck me!" He must've left the lights on or something. Fucking battery. Tonight of all nights.

He got out of his car, slamming the door. He would've kicked the damn thing, if it wouldn't have killed it more. Pulling open the glass door to the station, he called in, "Hey, anybody got some jumper cables?"

His boss looked at him from across the counter. "Yeah, in my car. You need?"

Jack nodded. Too frustrated to provide more of an explanation; too tired to chat about it.

"Gimmie a minute."

By the time his boss was out of the station and had gotten the cables from his car, it was after 5:00 p.m. Fucking hell, he was beat. Come on, come on…they got his car charging and finally, finally, the engine turned over. He disconnected the battery. "Thanks," Jack mumbled. His boss waved and left. "Finally. Fucking finally." He got into the car once more, and started the drive home, carefully watching every stop sign, every red light. If he had had toothpicks, he would've propped open his eyes.

The phone rang on his drive home. He didn't pick up. It didn't matter who it was, he didn't feel like talking. He pulled into his carport and sighed, turning off the key. The car sputtered and quit. He fought the urge to turn it back on to test it. He dragged his tired body up the steps, unlocked the door and dropped the keys into the… chink. Counter. "Fucker," he whispered. The bowl was about three feet away on the counter. Well, it could have been Cees. This time. Since it was at least on the same counter. Who knew? Who cared? He picked up the keys and tossed them in the bowl, leaving it where it sat. Why fight city hall? He walked into the bedroom, took off his shoes, and went to bed, leaving his phone on the night stand and giving Caesar a quick pet before dozing off.

He slept. Restlessly. He knew it was his imagination, but it felt like something kept slowly tugging his comforter off him toward the end of the bed. It was almost like when you'd fall asleep and feel like you're falling and grab the bed…he kept grabbing the comforter. It'd start to move, or so he thought, and he'd grab it. Still there. Damn, what was fucking wrong with him? Maybe he was coming down with something. The flu. Who knew what? He wrapped himself up more tightly and dozed off again. Somewhere in the back of his foggy mind, he could hear his phone ringing, but it didn't register. He was out till morning.

Jack woke. It was still dark outside, but he couldn't sleep any longer. 4:15 a.m. Damn. Well, he had time to put on a pot of coffee, if he wanted to. Nah. He'd definitely get out and get a breakfast on the way to work, though. He rubbed Caesar's belly until the cat was awake and annoyed. "Start your day, lazy bones." Caesar moved about two feet over on the bed and curled back up. "I don't blame you. Enjoy, Cees." Jack went into the bathroom.

After a satisfying pee, he showered, dressed and went through his phone messages. There were two from Park. He had hoped one would be from Laurel, but maybe they weren't on the "call every day" part of their relationship yet. Or maybe she was just plain busy. He'd call Park after work. It was too early anyway, and now, he was ready to head out for a hot breakfast. Nothing fancy, but actually sitting in a fast food restaurant while he ate instead of eating out of his lap as he drove. "I'll see you tonight, Cees," he called over his shoulder. He dipped his hand into the bowl for his keys and came up empty. "Damn it." He looked over the counter, the floor. Nothing. "All right," he said, looking around the kitchen, "Wherever you put them, I want them back. Now." Nothing. No clink, nothing. He checked in drawers, under the table, everywhere, and then started on the living room. Finally, after going through the sofa cushions, he found them back behind the sofa, next to the wall. "Not funny." All the searching ate up his extra time. He'd have to grab a breakfast sandwich and eat as he drove. It figured.

He got into the Subaru and begged the universe for his car to start. It did. "Thank fuck," he muttered. When he got to McDonald's, he ordered a sausage, egg and cheese biscuit. Small and tasty, he could've used more but there was no time. He grabbed a coffee from DD's and drove on one handed, avoiding potholes and trying to not spill coffee in his lap.

He made it on time to work, but felt rushed all day. Frantically searching for his keys in the morning had set the tone for the day. Hurry, hurry, hurry to be on time. It was the opposite of yesterday when he dragged his ass all day, but just as frustrating. Damned ghost. He wondered what it could possibly want from him. Why hide keys? To be noticed? To be fucking mischievous? Maybe he'd have to pull out that board and see if he could get any answers. It must be Carla or James. Playful as hell and not understanding how annoying they were being.

Jack pulled the bus into position at his second stop and Mabel gently stepped on. "Morning, Mabel. Cold today."

"Morning, Jack." She slowly worked her way up the steps, taking care to hold onto the railing. "Quite cold."

"How are you today?"

"Fine, fine," she said as she walked past him and took her seat. Next to the window, so she could watch the people and shops go by.

"Mabel," Jack said, closing the bus door. "Do you believe in ghosts?" He didn't know why he asked. He sort of blurted it out. But, if anyone had an opinion, it was her.

Mabel adjusted her hat, pink today with some baby's breath sprigs tucked in the side. She looked at him out of the corner of her eye. "There are more things in heaven and earth, Horatio, than are dreamt of in your philosophy." She glanced back out the window.

Jack smiled. "Mabel, that's Shakespeare!"

"Why, yes. It is. Hamlet, to be exact. Don't sound so surprised," she chided him.

"Forgive me, my dear."

"Of course," she adjusted her hat yet again. "And yes. I do. Just be careful what you deal with, Mr. Jack. Not everything out there is friendly."

He nodded. She went back to staring out the window, done with the conversation. She had given her bit of advice and that was that. He drove on, continuing to ponder what he should ask the board when he got the chance. Get it all planned out, the information he needed, what to ask. That was his next step. In control again, he felt that confidence flood in, like when he had debunked something huge. He'd get to the bottom of this ghost and get back to his life again. Just had to put his mind to it and he would have the upper hand.

Jack drove on. The stops were secondary to the planning he had going on in his head. He'd get home, eat, maybe get the board going after that. Or tomorrow. Tonight he might plan it all out. Who it was, why it was there. What the fuck it thought it was doing. He'd get his answers, do some more research, and send them packing. Back to New Castle, to the light, wherever. He knew where he wanted his life to go, and it didn't include having a ghost in the house. Laurel. Yeah, that was where he wanted his life to go. Anything that included her was fine with him.

As Jack approached Mabel's stop, she paused beside him. "I know who you are, Mr. Jack. I've heard your talks."

"Oh?" Jack was surprised. He didn't remember ever seeing her at one of his events. But it wasn't hard for him to miss someone in a room full of people.

"Yes." She adjusted her hat, making sure the baby's breath were in place. "Not everything can be explained. Not everything wants to be explained." She touched his arm and looked directly into his eyes. For some reason it made him deeply uncomfortable. "Be careful."

"I will."

"You won't," she squeezed his arm. "But I wish you would."

He watched her move slowly down the steps. "See you tomorrow, Mabel."

She waved at him without turning around, heading straight to the senior housing. Slowly, but surely. He closed the bus doors and pulled back out into traffic, pondering what she meant. By the time he reached the station, though, he had shaken it off and was back to planning. He climbed into the Subaru eager to start his evening; his mind racing.

His phone ringing brought him out of his daze. He hadn't even seen that he was halfway home already. It was Parker. He hit the answer button. "Yeah, Park. What's up?"

"Hey, Man. What's doing tonight? Want to grab some beers?"

"Oh, hey. Sorry, not tonight. I'm really beat."

"Beat? You don't sound it."

"I'm shot, Park. Just want to get to bed early."

"Okay, Man. If you're sure. Maybe tomorrow then."

"Yeah, sounds like a plan. Catch me after work."

"You got it."

They hung up as Jack hit his driveway. He hated putting Parker off, but he knew his friend would have a ton of issues with what he was planning. He shut off the car and almost didn't wait for it to die down before heading into the house. All the drawers were open in the kitchen. "Well, you've been busy, I see," he muttered. Ignoring the drawers, he walked into the living room and opened his laptop. "I have, too."

Jack opened his journal to the page he had started when he was researching Ouija boards. It looked pretty simple. Get started, chat with the spirits, hit goodbye when you're done. He could do it. Parker thought the board had already opened a portal, or that it was cursed, he guessed. Not that he really bought that. Focus, intent...opening up a convo was all it could possibly be. Sort of like an app for ghosts. He chuckled. Twitter for your spirit friends. Whatsapp for the deceased. Instaghost. He laughed. Come on, gotta get serious now.

He took some notes...use around midnight, not that he thought it mattered, but he wanted it to work and he'd follow the "rules" out there. If it's on the internet, it must be true, right? He smirked. He'd follow some of the rules, anyway. Most of this stuff was up to interpretation, it seemed. Low light, white candles. He wasn't sure if he had any candles in the house. He'd have to check the junk drawer later. Simple questions, ones that would get direct answers. Close the board. Pretty damned simplistic, if you asked him. He'd record the session. Audio and video, he figured. If things went well, he could add it to his talks. Debunking and now Ghost Chat and Removal. Yeah, this would be very cool.

He read and wrote until his stomach was grumbling and he realized he hadn't eaten yet. He thumbed through his phone and landed on one of the Chinese restaurants in town. Yes. Delivery was the device of the Gods. He placed a quick order and then continued through his contacts. Laurel. Yeah. He hit her number and waited as it rang. Voicemail. Damn.

"Hey. Wanted to say hello. Hope you had a great day. Will chat tomorrow. Going to get an early night tonight. Bye, Doll." He hated leaving messages. They always sounded so fake to him. Hey, just wanted to blah blah blah. Whatever. He went back to reading through ghost sites on the internet. Gullible city. So many were "bump in the night OMG a ghost" sites. Bugged the shit out of him.

Caesar strolled out of the bedroom and jumped on the coffee table. "Hey, Cees buddy." He gave Caesar some long, to the tail, pets and the cat sprawled across his keyboard. Purring. "Come on, you. I was working there." He scooped up his attention starved cat and snuggled him, putting him on the sofa beside his thigh. "Stay there." Never to be told what to do, Caesar jumped back up in front of the laptop. Jack tried to see around him for a minute or two, but couldn't work that way. "Think you own the place, don't you?" Jack smiled. He loved that animal.

A knock at the door and he jumped up. "Dinner's here." Caesar followed him into the kitchen, part way, and then halted. Jack paid the delivery guy at the door, tipping him well, and took the cartons. He spread them out on the counter, opening each one and smelling it. Delicious. He grabbed a plate and piled it with pork fried rice, sweet and sour chicken, shrimp with lobster sauce, an egg roll. Ahh. Always too much, but then there was Caesar. And leftovers. He loved leftovers. A fork, a beer that he found in the refrigerator, and back to the coffee table. Caesar weaved his way through and around Jack's legs, making sure he wasn't forgotten. "As if I'd ever forget you, you silly thing," Jack said. He cut up some of the chicken and dropped it into Caesar's bowl. "There. Don't say I never gave you anything."

He shut his laptop, fairly confident in his newfound "Ouija abilities." He had this. Time for some dinner and a little television. He found a paranormal "reality" show. Didn't people know these shows played for ratings? It's called "acting," and most of the time it shouldn't be. He watched, critical of every bump, movement, and yell. In all his years of investigating, it just didn't happen like that. You might get the stray EVP, perhaps a shadow or something that resembled an apparition, but pleeeeease. He rolled his eyes as the supposed "investigator" screamed and ran out of a room. Because of a…heating pipe expanding and banging the pipe next to it? Yeah. He should have a show. The "What's Paranormal and What's Reality Show." He finally got too annoyed and had to change the channel.

He watched some mindless sitcoms until about 11:30 p.m. Then, he slapped his knees, causing Caesar to startle. "Sorry, kitty. It's time to get this show on the road." He went into the kitchen to search for some candles. Rooting around in the junk drawer, in among batteries, scotch tape and screws, he found two small, round white candles. Now what would he put them on? A plate, he guessed. One more thing to clean later. He pulled a lighter out of the back of the drawer and rested it on the plate. Well, that didn't take long to put together. Not very scientific. He was better versed in the technological, but perhaps the spirits weren't.

Caesar followed him into the bedroom, jumping onto the bed and watching him pull out his equipment cases. One camera, set up next to the television, facing the coffee table should do the trick. He took out the DVR and a voice recorder. Two devices recording was always better than one. Next, he got the Ouija board from the closet shelf. The planchette slid off the board and hit Jack in the shoulder before falling to the floor. He picked it up, turning it over in his hand. "Time to do this thing," he said under his breath as he walked into the living room.

He set up the camera first, plugging it and the DVR in, then lit the candles before turning out the lights in the living room. The Ouija board was in front of him on the coffee table and Caesar had jumped up beside him on the sofa. He hit the record button on the voice recorder. "I ask that only positive spirits talk with me tonight," he said out loud. He shrugged. "Not sure if it matters what I say, but we do what the rules say, eh, Cees?" He gave the cat an extra scratch behind the ears and then put both hands on the planchette.

He waited, trying to sense the atmosphere in the room, seeing if he could discern any subtle changes around him. Shadows? None but the usual. He took a deep breath and began.

"Is there anyone here with me tonight?" Nothing.

"Is there any spirit who wants to communicate tonight?" Nothing.

He started to circle the planchette around the board, slow circle after circle. He asked, again, "Is there any spirit who wants to communicate tonight?" The planchette slid to **Yes**. Could it have been him? Wishful thinking? No. He had felt the planchette pull his fingers along.

"Well, now maybe we're getting somewhere. What is your name?" The planchette started circling, not driven by his fingers, and landed on the letter J. Caesar growled and ran into the bedroom.

"J. James?" He watched as it slid to No.

"What is your name?" J. "Yeah, I got that." A C K

"Yeah, that's me. What's your name?" No.

"Okay. Did you come from New Castle?" The planchette spun, a little faster this time, to the Yes.

"Did you die at the institution?" No.

"No? Where did you die?" Nothing.

"Why did you come here?" U.

"U? U?" he sighed. "Is this bad text speak or what?" The candles flickered a bit and it gave the room an odd, creepy look. The shadows they cast seemed larger or closer than he felt they should have been. It had to be his imagination, but he didn't usually give in to that sort of thing.

"Did you leave the handprint on my mirror?" Yes.

"Was it you messing with my basement door and drawers? Hiding my keys?" Yes.

"Are you attached to something in the house?" Yes.

"What are you attached to?" Nothing.

"Why are you here?" D O N O T L I K E

"Do not like. There's something you don't like. What?" U He could feel the temperature change in the room. It was noticeably colder.

"Me?" The planchette slid to Yes.

He paused for a moment. "Is that why you're doing all this random shit in my house?" Yes.

"Well, you can cut it the hell out and leave." No.

"I've got news for you. You're leaving. You're out. I'm going to close this board, close your access to this house. You don't need to be here." No.

"Oh, yeah. You can go to the light or back to New Castle, I don't give a fuck. But you're not staying here." D I E.

He felt a rushing in his ears and the shadows in the room seemed to be coalescing in front of him, coming together into one, larger amorphous shape. He thought for a split second he felt something touch his shoulder, and a faint odor of decay. "I am done here," he said. "I am closing this board, this portal, this communication." He forcibly pushed the planchette to GOODBYE, but it was pushed back to the No. With every shove he made, it was pushed back. No No No No No. The planchette started spinning under his fingers and flew off the board, hitting the television. Jack sat for a minute in the darkness, with only the small candles as light. He didn't know if the board was closed or not, or if he had a real problem or not. An annoying spirit? For sure. Something dangerous? The jury was out.

He blew out the candles and walked over to the light switch. The shadows seemed normal again. He exhaled and turned on the lights, then went through the process of shutting down the DVR setup. He found the planchette on the floor next to the front door and dropped it onto the coffee table. Lastly, he sat down, rewound the voice recorder and hit play. It was going to be a short night's sleep before work, but he had to see if he had gotten any EVP's during his time on the board.

"Is there anyone here with me tonight?"

"Is there any spirit who wants to communicate tonight?"

Jack sat, listening, for any change, any whisper, any anything that might point to more communication from whatever it was. Nothing.

"I've got news for you. You're leaving. You're out. I'm going to close this board, close your access to this house. You don't need to be here. Oh, yeah. You can go to the light or back to New Castle, I don't give a fuck. But you're not staying here."

What was that? He could swear there was something behind his words. The faintest whisper, a low, male voice. He swiftly found his headphones and plugged them in. He almost couldn't wait the seconds it took to upload the recording. Bringing up the audio review program, he dragged and dropped the recording and hit play. He fast forwarded until nearly the end of the recording, giving it a first listen while watching the sound wave on the screen. "There!" He isolated the few seconds he needed and expanded the wave. There was another smaller sound behind his words. He played the clip. Over and over, slowing it down and upping the volume.

"Bastard," he whispered. "Son of a bitch." There, behind his words, he could hear a man's voice, almost a growl, deep and unnerving.

"You're fucked."

"We'll see about that," he slapped his laptop shut. He stared at it for a few minutes, considering his options. Get rid of the board, cleanse the house. Bring in a paranormal team? That's a joke. He already knew he was dealing with something he hadn't ever run in to before. He could get all the EVP's and video footage that they could, and that didn't mean they'd be able to offer up a solution. Bring in a priest? That seemed extreme. He wasn't a religious guy, who knew if a priest would even believe him. Or if that would help. He had a bitch of an attachment going and he'd have to figure out how to detach it. But for now, it was late and morning would come crazy early. He'd have to try to get some sleep.

He climbed into bed in his clothes, pulling up the comforter. Caesar was nowhere to be seen, but he assumed the cat was under the bed. When everything felt calm, he'd be out again.

The next thing he knew, the alarm was going off. Damn. He had slept, but restlessly. He had dreamed, but couldn't quite place them. Fuck all, he was exhausted. Grabbing a towel from the clean clothes basket, he walked into the bathroom. How was he going to get through the day? For a half second, he considered calling out. He had plenty of sick time, but unfortunately he was too responsible for that. He did this to himself and he'd have to deal. Kind of like having a hangover. If it was his own fault, how could he leave the company shorthanded? Sometimes it didn't pay to be rational.

He stood under the hot water, soaking it in, letting the steam fill the room. It felt great, but his distrust was heightened. He waited, prepared to jump out of the stream if it suddenly went cold. He lathered and rinsed, no change. When he turned off the water, he paused again. The house was quiet. No handprint on the mirror, no demonic entity waiting to stab him through the shower curtain. Well, he guessed there'd be no blood circling his drain today. He smirked and toweled off.

"Cees?" The Russian blue sat at the end of his bed, waiting for him to come out of the bathroom, purring like a motorboat. "Now that's a good kitty." A quick ear rub and Jack was pawing through the clothes basket for jeans and a work shirt. He dressed on his way into the kitchen. Partly because he was nearly ready to leave, but mainly because he had to see for himself if anything "out of the normal" had gone on during the night. The drawers were all closed and the bowl was right where it should have been, with his keys resting comfortably at the bottom. He wasn't gullible enough to believe the ghost was gone, but it did feed his confidence a bit. Perhaps he had made it think, made it back off a bit. And if that was true, he could absolutely get rid of it. He just needed to do a little more research. And figure out what to do with that damned board. For now, it was time to get to work.

He swung himself into the seat of his bus with less than his usual enthusiasm. At least his car had started. The morning had that damp haze of impending bad weather, where you felt the mist in the air more than saw it. The radio said they were expecting freezing drizzle throughout the day. Great. Just what he fucking needed. He sat for a moment and watched a town plow head down Main Street. You knew it was coming if they already had the sanders out. Luckily, there were only a few areas on his route that could be trouble spots. He started the engine, letting the windshield wipers run. They had that familiar scraping sound as they moved across the edges of the window where the mist had already frozen. "Here we go," he said quietly, and got his morning rolling.

It was hard to gauge days like these. You either had a ton more passengers, people who left their personal cars home so they wouldn't have to drive in this shit, or you had next to nobody. Not that it mattered to him. He had to drive the same route regardless. Sometimes it was nice to have a quiet bus. Tired as he was, he would prefer it quiet. He wasn't up for the parade of people, slushy shoes and complaints. Mabel wouldn't be out today. She was always very cautious about the weather. "You can't break a hip at 87," she told him once. Last year, was it? She was about the only one he'd miss today.

The universe was against him this morning. Groups of people were huddled under the overhangs at every bus stop. They climbed his steps holding newspapers over their heads and complaints on their lips. They thought he'd be there sooner, why weren't there more buses running, crappy weather today. Some shook off, some stomped their feet as they went down the aisle to find seats. Each and every person added to his growing headache and aggravation. A whoosh of cold, damp air accompanied his riders when he opened the door and he was getting pretty tired of that, too. Fuck, what a day.

The temps warmed up slightly enough that the roads were fine, but the rain still had everyone rushing the bus instead of walking anywhere. He just wanted to be done and home. He was sick of it all today. Maybe he was overtired. Maybe he was actually getting sick. Damn, he hoped not, but as the day wore on, he had an ache running through his skin. Fuck.

He just about closed the door on the last person getting off, he was so glad to see them go. All he wanted, all he needed, was to turn in his damn paperwork and get home and out of the damp air. It made his skin crawl when the breeze hit him.

"You look like hell," his boss said, taking Jack's paperwork. "Get into bed when you get home. Don't be calling out sick on me tomorrow."

Jack nodded, feeling too shitty to answer, and went out the door to the parking lot. The wind was whipping now, and the rain pelted his face. He jogged to the Subaru and climbed in. Wiping his face off, he turned the key in the ignition. It roared to life. "Thank God," he said. The car actually sounded better than it had in months. He had to put the wipers nearly on full to be able to see. The street lights were blurs of rain spatter. He hated this weather. Hopefully he wouldn't feel like death tomorrow, but if this kept up, he'd be staying home.

A car cut him off right before his turn and Jack hit the brakes. He hydroplaned a few feet and cursed. Not what he needed at this moment. At least he'd be home in two minutes, away from the jerks and out of the weather. He pulled into the carport, jumped out of the car and ran for the side door. Maybe he'd invest in a raincoat. Or umbrella. Or something to keep the shitting rain off his head. Damn it. It took him a minute to fumble with the lock, more out of frustration than anything. It gave and he was in.

Caesar meowed and Jack ignored him, making a beeline for the bedroom. He stripped out of his wet clothes, leaving them in a pile on the floor. He didn't care. He needed to be warm and dry. Flannel pajamas and thick socks were just what the doctor ordered. Next, he took the comforter off his bed and went to the sofa. He felt his forehead. Shit. Really getting hot. Thirsty, too. He left the comforter and his phone and went to the fridge. Nothing. Well, nothing he wanted. Fuck. Delivery? He couldn't be bothered right now. He ousted Caesar from the nest he was making in the comforter and climbed under it. He grabbed the remote and clicked the television on. Whatever was on, he didn't care. Just some background noise. He settled in, pulling the comforter up to his chin.

About an hour later, his phone rang. He had been dozing, uncomfortably, off and on. When he saw it was Laurel, he picked up.

"Hey, Doll," his voice was slightly raspy now.

"Hey, Jack. What's doing?"

"Nothing." His throat hurt; his breath felt hot.

"It's great weather to stay in with a movie and some popcorn. How about it?" She sounded hopeful.

"I can't, Doll. Am sick. Burning up and think I just need to stay in tonight."

"Oh, I'm sorry. That sucks."

"Yeah."

"Did you have dinner?"

"No. Have just been sleeping a bit."

"Leave your door unlocked. I'm bringing you some things."

"Oh, Doll. You don't have to do that."

"Yeah, I do. I know you and your refrigerator is probably empty. Or stocked with beer and frozen crap that you know you're not going to cook the way you're feeling."

He half chuckled and coughed. "Yeah. Thanks, sweetie. But I don't want to get you sick."

"Leave the door unlocked. Go back to sleep. I'll take care of the rest."

"Okay. Will do. Thanks, Doll."

She hung up the phone and he closed his eyes.

He woke to some rustling in the kitchen and at first didn't know if it might be Caesar, but the cat was lying across his feet. "Lau…" he tried to get out her name, but started coughing. She peeked around the corner.

"Hey, hon. Stay there." She went back into the kitchen and he could hear her moving things around, doing something with the refrigerator, the microwave. She returned a few minutes later with a mug of hot tea. She pulled the coffee table closer to the sofa so he wouldn't have to sit up for it.

"Wow. Thanks," he whispered.

"Lemon tea. With honey." She kissed his forehead. "You definitely have a fever. Hold on." Back out to the kitchen for a minute. He closed his eyes and laid back. "Ginger ale with ice and a bowl of chicken soup." She put everything onto the coffee table for him. "There's more chicken soup in a container in the refrigerator, along with two liters of ginger ale. Can I get you anything else? Do you have some Tylenol or anything for the fever?"

He shook his head. There was probably something in the medicine cabinet, but he could get it later. She leaned over and gave him a long kiss on the forehead. "You rest. I'll be over tomorrow with whatever you need."

She stood to leave and he grabbed her wrist. "You're all I need," he whispered between coughs.

She smiled and squeezed his hand. "Now, fluids and rest." He nodded as she left. Sick as a dog, he felt like the luckiest man alive.

While it was still hot, he tried a little of the soup. Not bad, but he wasn't hungry. The ginger ale went down a little easier, in periodic sips. The tea, well, he'd dump it later. For now, he rolled back into the sofa.

The night wore on, in and out of sweats and chills. There were shadows moving along the wall, crossing in and out of his dreams. He knew it was the television, still on, but it gave him an odd, less than comfortable feeling. Like being watched, but not. As if he were on the sofa in someone else's living room, an intruder in his own house.

At 4 a.m. he came to enough to realize he had to call his boss. At least it'd reach the answering machine and he wouldn't have to talk to the man. Fuck all, he hated to call out. "Hey, Earl, it's Jack Barnes. I'm sick as hell and won't be in today. Will try for tomorrow. Thanks." He didn't know why he felt guilty. They gave him sick days and he rarely ever used any. But, he was the guy they could always count on. And being sick sucked.

He made himself get up to pee at some point. His head throbbed. Everything ached. He popped a couple of Tylenol and washed them down with the old ginger ale sitting on the coffee table. Flat, warm and kind of gross, but it worked. He rolled up in the comforter again, on his other side, and tried to watch television for a bit. It didn't work. He closed his eyes and listened, dozing mostly. He hadn't been hit this hard in a long time.

Caesar's meowing pulled him out of his sleep, and he heard the shake of the cat crunchies. Someone was there and they were feeding the cat. Feeding the...? It didn't quite register in his sick, sleepy daze. He always fed Caesar. He started to sit up when Laurel stuck her head around the corner. "Don't get up, Jack. I've got it." She ducked back into the kitchen and he could hear the drawers, packages, something going on. When she returned to him, she brought another tea and bowl of soup. And crackers. She even took away the old cups and things. Damn.

He could hear her washing dishes and called out, "Doll," cough cough. "You don't have to do those."

"Yeah, I know. Don't worry about it."

He leaned into the sofa. His head was still hot and he felt like absolute shit. "What time is it?"

"5:30."

"In the morning?"

Laurel laughed. "At night. You poor thing." She came back in from the kitchen and sat at the foot of the sofa, sliding his feet aside.

"Must've slept all day. Damn."

"How are you feeling?"

"Like fucking hell."

She gave his foot a squeeze. "Is there anything else that I can get for you before I go?"

"Thanks, Doll, but I think I'm good. You've done so much already." She smiled that amazing smile that made him want to grab her and... "Wish I felt better. I'd keep you here all night."

"Wish you did, too. But you need your rest. I'll be back tomorrow to check on you."

"Sweetie, you are amazing."

She leaned in and kissed his forehead. "Oh," she remembered, "there's an odor in your kitchen. By the basement door. Nasty. I hope you don't mind, but I went downstairs to make sure an animal hadn't crawled in and died. I didn't find anything, but you might need to get your septic pumped or something. Sorry."

He rubbed a hand over his eyes. "Great. Ugh. No worries, Doll. I'll figure it out in a couple of days."

"Call me if you need anything," she said as she walked out. He heard the side door close and her car drive off. Slowly getting up, he left the comforter on the sofa. He needed to know what she was talking about and shuffled out to the kitchen.

Before he got to the basement door, he smelled it. Decay. Death. Septic. Fuck, it was foul. What the hell was it?! It made him gag a second and he put his hand on the doorknob. Out of nowhere, out of fucking nowhere, he was sucker punched. All the air went out of his lungs and he dropped to the floor. He lay there, arms wrapped around his stomach, gasping for breath and reeling in the ache and pain of it all. Closing his eyes tightly shut, he tried to get control of his breathing and make sense of what happened. The room started spinning and, just before he passed out, he swore he saw the shadow of a face, inches in front of his own. The eyes. The eyes were red. And it was smiling.

Jack woke, unsure for a moment of where he was. His mind wasn't taking in the cool tile against his cheek and the moonlight coming in the window over his…sink? He moved, and winced. Now, he fucking remembered. That son of a bitch wraith ghost demon shit of a thing had punched him. Took him right the fuck out. He sat up slowly, still holding one arm across his stomach. The smell was gone from the room and he knew he was alone. For now. He used one of the kitchen chairs to help him stand and made his way back to the sofa. His fever had broken while he was out, so at least that was good, but he felt like shit. He sat on the sofa and dialed the boss' number. "Hey, it's Jack Barnes. Still sick and will be out, but should be back in on Monday." He hit the off button and slid the phone onto the coffee table. Sleep wasn't far off, but wasn't coming too soon, either. He cozied up and tried to watch some television, if he could get his mind off the fucker who had decked him. Fear was a great cure for a restful night.

He watched early morning television; news, cartoons, ridiculous things he hadn't seen in the last twenty years, but somehow seemed comforting as he waited for the sun to come up. He got some ginger ale from the refrigerator and sat down on the sofa. He pulled up his shirt. There, on his stomach, was a bruise, in the shape of a fist. It hadn't been some bizarre dream, a sleepwalking sensation, a mistake. No, it had happened and he had the broken capillaries to prove it. Hurt like a bitch, too.

He needed to recuperate for a day or two and then he'd have to figure out how to get rid of this... thing. Parker would be pissed that he hadn't gotten rid of the spirit board; that he actually USED it. Fuck. He held his ribs. Hopefully that asshole spirit, negative entity, whatever, hadn't broken any ribs. He was in awe. What the fuck had followed him home? He couldn't have something in the house that would attack him out of the blue like that. He pondered, slept, pondered slept.

At length, Jack woke, with no idea the time of day. October was like that. Overcast days that were a blended gray; mornings slid into afternoons with no delineation of time. He grabbed his phone from the coffee table. 11:00 a.m. Not too bad. He sat up and his head didn't pound. Always a good sign. Taking stock of his options, he decided that some coffee sounded great. He might even be hungry. He stood, the ache in his side reminding him of the night before. Pausing to get his bearings, and his confidence, he took as deep a breath as he could muster in the doorway to the kitchen. Everything looked quiet, calm. That son of a bitch thing had no right to make him hesitant. It was his house. His fucking house.

He walked into the kitchen and opened the refrigerator. Damn. Soup and ginger ale. He wanted something more substantial. Well, maybe the soup was the smarter choice and he could ask Laurel or Parker to drop by with something more later. Getting a bowl out of the cabinet, he warmed up the soup in the microwave. While he waited for it to ding, he noted how clean his kitchen was. The sink was empty and scrubbed, the counters spotless. Laurel. So sweet. He smiled.

When his soup was ready, he took it and some crackers into the living room. He shoved the comforter to the side. His throat was still raspy, but he was definitely on the mend. Muscle tired, but his brain was less foggy. The soup wouldn't hold him for long. He really needed to shop and have more things in the house for days like this. His refrigerator was the ultimate, stereotypical bachelor fridge. It sucked.

He switched off the television. Now he knew he was starting to feel more like himself again. It was time to figure out a plan of attack for that shit spirit in his house. This thing had a bitch on and it had to go. He'd need to refine his search, try to zero in on what it could possibly be before he could find a way to kick it out. Or send it back to whatever hell it crawled out of. He opened his laptop and, while waiting for it to come up, Caesar sprinted through the room. Jack jumped, his heart pounding, and almost knocked the coffee table over. "Damn, Cees!" he yelled. Still half sick and nerves on edge, yeah. He had to get to work on this.

He thumbed through the list he had originally made in his journal. This one would be a little darker. Stronger. Negative entity. Dark shadow. Demon. Possession. He had pretty much disregarded the information on the internet regarding demons, but now? The jury was on its way back into the courtroom, but the verdict was still unsure. After the shit he'd been experiencing, he had to give credence to the fact that there was much heavier stuff out there than he had ever acknowledged. Or experienced. When something unseen can lay you out on your own kitchen floor, it kind of twists your head. Sets on edge everything you'd ever thought was possible. This was worse than being slammed at the asylum. He might have eventually written that off as something similar to an animal protecting its cave; he was treading where he shouldn't have. But this. This was intelligent. It was after his sanity. Toying with him.

He read for most of the afternoon. Cleansing, clearing, release. Exorcism, signs of demonic possession. He had the makings for a horror movie here. Grounding, centering, prayers of protection. Priests and shaman, mediums and paranormal teams offering to take on whatever the fuck might be haunting you. Do this, don't do that, and fucking never touch this or go near that. Signs, symbols. If you believed everything you read, he was fucked. Seems he hadn't done anything right in the field in the last ten years. He chuckled. None of this was truly helping. He was getting an education in the gullibility of world around him. Everyone had their own idea of how to get rid of whatever was stomping around your house. Unreal. He typed into the search bar, "how to get rid of a mean as fuck ghost." He'd had it. Everything that came up either wanted him to cleanse and bless the house or bring in an exorcist. There was no happy medium. Well, his head wasn't spinning and he hadn't spit out any of his soup. He didn't need a fucking exorcist.

He leaned back, pulled his comforter around his shoulders and rubbed his eyes. A nap wouldn't be half bad right about now. In his own bed. He pulled the end of the comforter gently out from under Caesar and walked into the bedroom. It'd be good to be in his bed again. Much more comfortable than the sofa. He laid down on his side. The sheets were cool and comfortable and he was out in minutes.

He woke to footsteps. He smiled and called out, "That you, Doll?" No response. "Laurel?" He listened more intently. Footsteps. Still there, slowly walking, but where? His eyes went to the ceiling above him. Step. Step. Step. They were coming from above him. The attic? He shook his head. There was only a crawlspace up there, and the only access was through an opening in his closet. No one could be up there, let alone walking.

"Cut it the fuck out!" he yelled. The steps paused, as if considering his demand, then continued on. Step. Step. Step. When they seemed to reach the end of the room, they stopped. Fucker. He heard the side door open and yelled, "What the fuck now?!" He ran through the living room like a mad man bent on killing whatever he found, but came to a halt quickly when he saw Laurel with a bag of groceries in her hands.

"Jack?" she said hesitantly. Her hair fall across her face as she tried to maneuver the paper bag in her arms and the door. He stepped forward and took it, shutting the door behind her.

"Hey, yeah, Doll. Sorry I yelled. I was… sleeping…must've been a bad dream."

"A hell of one. You okay?"

He shook it off, let it go. "Yeah…yeah, I am." He ran his fingers through his hair. He must look like hell. "Not really making a fashion statement here, am I?"

"All the sexiest men are wearing three day old flannel pajamas before dinner," she joked. He smiled. "I brought you a few things to get you by." She took the bag back from him and set it on the counter. She opened his refrigerator and started putting things in, arranging them. "Orange juice, a couple of dinners from the diner," she snickered, "you know, in case Park stops by. Bread, deli meat," she took her head out of the fridge to look at him. "Veggies."

"Ahh, solid food!"

"Feeling better, I see."

"Yeah, hungry as a bear and clawing my way back to the living."

"I'm glad. Now, you've got some supplies to keep you going."

"Thanks, Doll. I don't know what I would have done without you."

"You'd have told Park to get delivery," They both laughed. She was probably right. He pulled her close and held her, looking into her eyes. He kissed her, gently, then a little more passionately.

"You are feeling better."

He grinned. "I am."

"Too bad I'm on the dinner shift tonight."

"Damn. Really?"

"Yeah. One of the other waitresses called out. I'll probably be covering the next day or two."

"That sucks. I'd love to thank you…properly…for all you've been doing." He hugged her tightly, lifting her onto her toes for a moment.

"Hmmm. I think I deserve that thank you, too…but, I have to go." She tiptoed and gave him a quick kiss. "Call me."

"I so will."

She smiled and was back out the door and gone.

Damn, he wished she could've stayed. Even for an hour or two. He reigned in his libido. He was still sick, after all. Damn. He thought about going back on the internet to see what information he could find on nasty spirits, but he had pretty much exhausted every search he could think of. What did he find? How to bless, cleanse, purify, yadda yadda yadda. He probably needed something like Getting Rid of Ghosts for Dummies. Fuck yeah. Maybe he really had to take the Ouija board back to New Castle. Or break the fucking thing. It all sounded so ridiculous to him. He understood ghosts…people who hadn't crossed over. He also got it that bastards in life would be bastards in death. Fine. But demons? He wasn't a religious guy, but the whole demon thing crossed the line. Dark, evil entities bent on destruction and soul stealing. Come on, that's what the movies were made of. What he had had to be some schmuck, focusing all his afterlife energy on fucking with a guy who disturbed his happy little life at New Castle. That schmuck packed a hell of a punch, though.

Then he remembered. Everything Eclectic. Maybe they'd have some information, or a book, or even a pamphlet that would tell him how to get rid of the thing. Like the manual from the movie Beetlejuice. The Handbook for the Recently Deceased, or whatever it had been. He checked his watch. 4:35 p.m. Damn. He was sure they closed at 5:00 on Friday nights. No time for a shower, he pulled on a pair of jeans, tucked in his pajama top and ran a hand through his hair. It'd have to do and wasn't sick and unshaven the new sexy? He grabbed an old leather jacket from the closet and shoved his feet into a pair of loafers. Taking his keys from the bowl, he was out the door by 4:41. He hoped he'd make it.

He drove like his life depended on it, or nearly, anyway, and luckily there was a parking spot right in front of the place. He threw the car into park, not waiting for it to rumble into silence before jumping out and heading to the door. The owner, in a long forest green dress, was turning the key in the glass door as he strode up. He gave her his best, pleading eyes and an "I'm so sorry I'm late please forgive me I'll never do this again for the rest of my life" half smile. She smiled back and opened the door for him. Once through, she locked it behind him and turned the sign in the window to "closed."

"Thank you so much. I so appreciate it. I'll try to be quick," he began, grateful she had even considered letting him in.

She shook her head. "No worries. Take your time, there's no rush here." She walked behind the counter and started unpacking some small items. Jack went straight to the books. They had everything that he didn't want, as he looked through the titles. Crystals, healing, increasing your psychic awareness… well, he'd had enough of that already, it seemed. He stood, looking book by book, hoping for something that even remotely pertained to his situation. Intent, he didn't hear the shop owner walk up beside him. "Not seeing what you want?"

"No, not really." He sighed. The topic was rather embarrassing. "Do you have anything on getting rid of…?"

"Spirits?"

"Yes?"

"The sage didn't help?"

The tightness went out of his shoulders and he relaxed a little. "For a short time."

"Ah, a stubborn spirit. It happens," she smiled. "Footsteps, cabinet doors banging, things that go bump in the night?"

"Something like that, yeah. Any suggestions?"

"Well," she paused. "There are quite a few different remedies. It all depends on your personal beliefs."

Jack shrugged. "I really have no idea."

"The first thing I always suggest is sage. You can use it again and again and it helps with the feeling of the area, but...if that didn't work for you, there's blessed water..."

"Holy water?"

"Yes. It can be blessed by a priest or even the head of a Wiccan coven. It's the intent, not the robes or tradition of the person blessing it. You would put some on your fingertips and wipe it across the tops of your doorways. Windows, too. All entryways."

Jack nodded. He guessed that made sense, although he could feel the jury backing out of the courtroom, unsure.

"There's also salt, which can be blessed and used across doorways and window sills."

"Okay..."

"A skeptic, I see."

"Yes, and no. This is all new to me. I don't know what to believe."

"Totally understandable."

"Do you have any holy water or blessed salt?"

She smiled. "I don't sell blessed items. It wouldn't feel right, you know?"

"Ah, um, yeah. I guess you're right," he laughed nervously.

"I do have some blessed sea salt in the back room that I'll let you have. It may just do the trick." She walked toward the back wall, which had '60's style beads hanging down to cover the doorway. "A little black tourmaline couldn't hurt, either," she called.

"Is that a drink?"

She gave a short burst of laughter. "It's a gemstone."

"Ah!" he laughed, too. "Do you have any?"

"I do," she returned from the back and stepped behind the counter with a Ziploc baggie of sea salt and placed it on the counter, then put a small box of little black rocks in front of him. "Tourmaline. It aids in protection. Pick the one that speaks to you."

Now THAT was uncomfortable. "Umm…" He held his hand over the box and looked at her sheepishly. "Speaks to me?"

"Just look. Which one would be your first choice to pick up?"

There was a piece of rock in the corner of the box that was smooth and fairly large. He held it in his hand, turning it around and around. He liked the weight of it. "This one, I guess."

"Good choice. Always take the one that catches your eye that feels right in your hand. That's how you know you have the right one."

"Okay…"

She smiled softly. "Everything has its own properties, energy. If you're quiet, calm, and go with your gut, you can find the one that resonates with you and will work the best for you and your energy."

"Thanks. Like I said, all this is new to me."

"How'd you come across your spirit?"

"Hm? What? Oh… I guess he chose me after my last investigation."

"Ghost hunter?"

"Kinda."

"I see that more and more."

"Excuse me?"

"People who get attachments after investigating, pick up something negative. You've got to be careful out in the field."

"Oh, yeah. For sure, I guess."

"Please tell me you use a protection prayer before you go in anywhere."

"Of course!" Jack lied. Check off another thing wrong on the Big List of I'm an Idiot.

"Good. There're some nasty things in the world. Best to keep yourself safe."

"Absolutely!" He smiled again, paid for the tourmaline, and left.

The shop owner watched him leave through the glass door and couldn't shake the feeling that he was in something deep. And it wasn't good.

Jack dropped the tourmaline into the cup holder where the selenite stick from the last visit to the shop still sat, and put the bag of sea salt on the passenger seat. His car rumbled to life and he slowly pulled into traffic. He drove, lost in thought about how he had gotten to this point. Even a few months ago he would have laughed anyone out of the room if they had suggested he'd be using blessed salt and gemstones to get rid of a ghost in his house. Even a few weeks ago. Was he crazy? Did this shit work? He was rooted in the scientific, in figuring out why things weren't what they seemed. This wasn't the way his mind worked. He was trying to wrap his head around it all and wasn't having much success.

He sat in the Subaru for a few minutes, holding the selenite and tourmaline in his hand, turning them over and over. He liked the weight of them, the texture. It was hard to imagine these having any effect on a spirit. Or the salt, for that matter. But, he guessed an unusual situation called for an unusual solution. Some people swore by these things. He sighed. Maybe he'd have to take the Ouija board back to New Castle. Maybe that was the entire issue. Well, he'd start with the salt and see what happened. He tucked the selenite and tourmaline into his pocket, grabbed the bag of salt and went inside.

Everything inside seemed calm and quiet, just the way he had left it. He dropped his keys into the bowl with a chink and placed the bag of sea salt on the kitchen table. There was no other sound in the house. "Cees?" He heard the cat jump down from the bed, that soft little thud that he recognized as Caesar heading out for some pets. "Hey, you." He picked up his cat and snuggled for a moment, then let him gently slide to the floor. Caesar rubbed on Jack's ankles for a minute, then left for the living room recliner.

Jack debated for a minute. Start the cleansing or grab some dinner? Would it work better on a full stomach? Almost everything did. He checked the refrigerator to see what Laurel had dropped off, pulling out one of the containers. Before he could get it open, his phone rang. He chuckled. Without having to check, he knew it was Park. He swiped it and said, "Hey, Park."

"Hey! What's doing? Haven't heard from you in a few days."

"Been sick as shit. Just feeling like myself again."

"That sucks."

"Yeah. Missed a couple of days at work. What's up?"

"Wanted to see if you wanted to get dinner."

"I was just pulling out some containers that Laurel dropped off."

"Oh?"

Jack started laughing. "She brought enough for you, too."

"Did she really?" Parker laughed. "That's so cool."

"You coming? Not afraid of my germs?"

"I'll be there in five. Just don't kiss me on the lips!"

Jack smiled and rolled his eyes. "No worries there." He hung up and put his phone on the counter while he grabbed a second container out of the refrigerator. Roast chicken, baked potatoes, green beans. Wonderful. He stuck them both into his microwave and started them warming. It didn't spin very well with two containers on the turntable, but it'd do. They'd get hot well enough.

Parker walked in after about ten minutes. He hid his face in the crook of his arm, with only his eyes peeking out. "You sure you're feeling better?"

Jack nodded, putting a couple of forks on the table.

"Good," Parker put his arm down and swung a six pack of beer onto the kitchen table. "Didn't know if you'd be up for it, but I sure am!"

"I'm good for one or two," Jack smiled. The microwave dinged and he took the containers out, trying not to burn his hands on the hot trays. "Roast chicken dinners."

"Nice!" Parker sat at the table and he and Jack dug in. "I love that restaurant. Damn. And you better hold onto Laurel. She's amazing."

"You'd love any woman who fed you."

"I love you, don't I?" Parker ducked.

Jack almost lost his mouthful of food. "You're such a jerk."

Parker smirked. "Yup."

They ate their dinners, cracking a beer here and there, chatting about the weather, work, nothing much. Then, Parker noticed the bag on the table. He poked it. "What's this?" Another bite of chicken.

Jack picked up the bag and tossed it over to the counter. "Just some salt."

Parker eyed him. It wasn't usual to have a bag, of salt, sitting around. "A bag of salt."

"Yup."

"Gonna do some major baking?"

Jack eyed him back. "Maybe."

"Kill some giant slugs?"

"They can be a problem. Especially with the zombie apocalypse coming. Gotta be prepared.

"Everything Eclectic doesn't generally sell grocery items or slug-i-cide."

"Noted." Jack kept eating. Parker had him there. He hadn't realized that the store name was on the bag, but he hadn't needed to care, either. "You think she brought dessert, too?" He slid his chair back a foot.

"I'm in if she did!" He took the last beer, popping the top off while Jack checked the refrigerator.

"Oh, my God. There's an apple pie she didn't tell me about."

"Marry her!" Parker held up his fork.

"Plates?"

"Just bring the container."

The two sat at the table, the pie plate between them, diving in with their forks. Jack reached behind him for his phone, but his hand hit nothing. He turned in his chair and looked at the counter. Empty. Fuck.

"Park, call my phone."

"What?" He glanced over the forkful of apple pie that was about to go into this mouth.

"Call my phone."

Parker took his phone out of his shirt pocket and dialed. After a few seconds they heard it. Jack followed the sound to the bedroom, under his bed. He pulled it out and killed the call. Annoying, but he'd be rid of it soon. At least if what everything he'd read and been told worked. He walked back to the kitchen.

"What's up?"

"It was under the bed."

"You leave it there for some reason?"

"Nope," he shoved his phone into his pants pocket.

"Ah," Parker paused. "Got some issues you haven't told me about?"

"Yup."

They mutually quit on the pie and Jack wrapped it back up to put away.

"And that's what the salt's for?"

"Could be."

"You gonna tell me or be an asshole about it?"

"Haven't decided yet."

"Fair enough," Parker leaned back in his chair, still holding his beer. "So, zombie apocalypse, huh?"

Jack smiled. "Yeah." They burst out laughing. Parker could always break the tension. He loved that guy. "Should've brought more beer."

Parker grinned a shit eating grin. "Check my car." Jack went out and brought in another six pack. "I didn't know if you were up for it, but I always come prepared."

"You, man, are the best!"

"I know, I know. Pop one open and worship me later."

They brought the beer into the living room and Jack sat on the sofa, leaning back. Parker stood, staring at the Ouija board that was still on the coffee table. He walked to the far end, gave Caesar a shove and sat in the recliner. He put his feet on the table, crossing his ankles. The silence was growing between them as the number of beers dwindled.

"We gonna talk about the 800 pound gorilla on the coffee table?" Parker asked.

"Eventually."

Parker nodded and let it go. That thing was becoming a raw nerve and he was not ready to poke it. If he had to, he would. Just not yet. Finally, Jack sighed. "No more beers hiding in the car, right?"

"Sorry, man. Think we've both had enough, though."

"Yeah, probably," he exhaled. "So... I've got this ghost..."

Parker laughed. "I think, at this point, that might be an understatement," he leaned in, closer to Jack. "What's been going on, man?"

Another pause. "Little things, here and there. My stuff being moved, disappearing from where I leave it. Turning up other places. Smells." Parker raised his eyebrows. It was then that everything came pouring out of him. The pauses were gone; he just had to tell someone. "Footsteps up in the crawlspace, nightmares. Someone, something, was pulling my comforter off one night. And..." He looked away from Parker for a second, then back. "I got punched in the gut the other night."

"You got attacked. Again. Here." Parker put his beer down. This was getting fucking serious.

"Yeah." Jack was looking at his beer bottle, turning it around in his hands. "This ghost has balls."

"I don't think it's a ghost, Jack. I swear it. Ghosts don't attack. Not like this."

"It's got to be."

Parker shook his head. "How do I convince you? You're getting attacked in your own house. It's invading your dreams. This isn't your normal, run of the mill poltergeist. This is dark, Jack. This is serious." They both sat, staring at the walls, waiting for the other to say…something. "And the Ouija board? Did you talk to this thing?"

Jack felt like a five year old being reprimanded for talking to strangers. You don't know if they are good or not. They could snatch you up and hurt you. They're bigger and stronger than you are and they aren't all nice. "You know I did."

"What'd it say?" There was no more lecturing. No more convincing.

Jack reached over for the voice recorder that still sat in the corner of the coffee table. He slid it to Parker. "Just hit play."

Parker did and waited as it went through Jack's tirade. Then, he caught it. That growl of a voice behind the words. He paled. "Did it say what I think it said?"

Jack nodded.

"You're fucked? It said you're fucked?"

"I even put it through the software, Park. There's no mistaking it."

"Son of a bitch." Parker paused. "Let's send this mother fucker packing."

Jack smiled. "Let's do it."

Parker grasped Jack's hand and shook it once, holding on for effect. "You know, I think you're a douche for bringing all this shit down on yourself, even if you don't realize what you've done. But I'm in it till the end, Jack."

Jack chuckled and started humming You've Got a Friend in Me from Toy Story. Parker let go of his hand. "Yeah, well it was YOU who poisoned the waterhole. Jerk."

"Can you cleanse a house under the influence?"

"Can you get a CUI?"

"What?"

"Cleansing under the influence. Keep up, man."

"So fucking corny."

"If I had better friends, I'd make better jokes. You just don't fucking rate." Park laughed, "But seriously. What are we doing?" He'd let Jack take the lead with it all. It was his house, he had to take control back from whatever the fuck was causing the problems. Hopefully, he'd be able to help and, between the two of them, send the shitter out.

"I've read about two different procedures," Jack informed him. "One, you spread a line of blessed salt across every doorway, across the tops of windows, all entryways into the home. The other, you mix it with some water and brush it across."

"We can do both. Cover all bases."

"Sounds like a plan. Plus, I want to sage again."

Parker nodded. "It can't hurt. Might as well do everything. Are you sure this will help?"

"Nope. Not at all. But it's my next step. Everything I've read said this should send an unwanted spirit away."

"And, if it's not a spirit?"

Jack sighed. "I don't know what to tell you. I don't even know if I believe in anything more than ghosts, Park. How can I say how I'd get rid of something that I don't even know if it exists?"

"Fine. We'll cross that bridge if it comes to it, deal?"

"Deal." They went into the kitchen and opened the bag the woman at the shop had given him. "Do you think it's enough?" The bag held about a cup and a half of sea salt.

"Yeah. It's not like you need to coat it up thick."

"True."

Park got a bowl to divide up the salt, and then mixed it with some water. "Do you have a paint brush?"

Jack pointed to the junk drawer. "There must be one in there." He had started looking up, again, the procedures for cleansing the house. He wanted to be sure, needed to be sure, that he was doing this right. It seemed too simple to him. Salt. Why should that work? "Hey, Park. Hand me a bowl. We'll need it for the sage ashes. Don't want to burn the house down."

Parker got a cereal bowl out of the cabinet and gave it to him. Jack rested his sage bundle in the bowl. "Okay. The way I see it, I'll do the sage. As I go through each room, you follow behind me and spread the salt water on the entryways. We can get through the house pretty quickly that way and then come back through and finish up with the dry salt." Jack looked at Park for reassurance, confirmation that this wasn't as nuts as it sounded and he was doing the right thing.

"You got it," Park picked up the bowl of salt water and the paint brush. "Ready when you are."

Jack nodded and took a deep breath, gathering his confidence and focus. He lit the sage and let it burn a minute before blowing it out. A nice thick plume of smoke rose from the bundle. "We start in the bedroom."

Jack walked through the bedroom, and bath, making sure the smoke of the sage wafted into every corner, filled every space. "Only positive energies are allowed in this house. Nothing negative will remain. Negativity is not welcome here." He even made sure to pass the sage under his bed. In case. Park came along behind him, painting across the doorways with the blessed salt water. He made sure to even cover the bathroom door. He didn't think it was important, but he wasn't going to take any chances. Doorways were doorways and he was going to cover them all for his friend.

Room by room, smoke and salt, they slowly covered the house. Park addressed each side of every doorway as they went. To be certain. Every window, including the small ones in the basement. He was thorough. If it would help his friend, he'd paint the entire house with salt. He was afraid that a nasty spirit was not what Jack was dealing with. Not at all.

They finished this "first round" at the side door, the main entrance into the house. "Only positive energies are allowed…" Park coated the inside and then the outside of the door. He put the bowl on the kitchen table. "I think you need to do the dry salt. Kind of wrap up the cleansing of the house strong and on your terms."

Jack agreed. "Come with me, though. Keep the focus strong." They made a last walk through the house, stopping at every door and window, placing a line of sea salt across each, and ending with the side door once again. He placed what was left of the dry salt on the table. The house was quiet. No more or less quiet than it had any other time, but they stood silently listening. Nothing.

Jack shrugged. "Should it feel different? Should we notice something leave?"

"I don't know. I'd think that it might feel differently? But maybe it just changes the dynamics of it all. You know, it's gone and everything is normal again?"

"Maybe. I hope so. Getting tired of this fucker."

"Well, if I was him, I'd leave. This place smells," he smiled. "What's next? Want to go out? A movie or something? It's still early."

Jack shook his head. "Nah, thanks. I really need to chill one more night. Just shaking this germ and I don't want to relapse it. Maybe tomorrow."

"You're such a lightweight. Fine, fine. I'm gonna go then. Maybe I'll find a little waitress for myself somewhere."

"Go, you jerk. I'll call you tomorrow after I hit the store. Gotta restock. You've eaten me out of house and home."

"Cool. I'll be sure to be over then. Get some premade dinners. I'm sick of your cooking." Park laughed. "See ya, buddy."

Park went out the door and Jack looked around. His house was salted, that's for sure. He felt a little more confident, but a little foolish. Hopefully it would all help. He'd have to figure out how long the salt needed to stay. Did you leave it a night and vacuum it off? Leave it forever? In the meantime, though, he was going to shoot Laurel a text. Thank her for the food and being so sweet. Maybe they'd get together this weekend, too. Now that would be fabulous. And, after he sent the message, he was getting into bed and having a nice, long sleep.

He woke. The only sound was Caesar purring beside his head. The sun was coming into the room through the cracks around his shades. 7:30. Wow. He must've gotten at least eleven hours. He stretched and felt…good. Not amazing or wonderful, but good. Not sick. Not sore. Just good. He gave Caesar some pets and stayed in bed, relaxing. He was in no rush to start the day. A slow Saturday was exactly what he needed.

When he did finally pull his body out from under the covers, he saw he had a message on his phone. From Laurel. *Hey, Jack. Glad you're feeling better. Working today, but should be off tomorrow if you'd like to get together. Hugs.* She always made him smile. He'd be smiling even more after his shower, too. He only had one aching muscle, and that could be remedied by thoughts of her and some long slow strokes. Stiff and getting harder, he went into the bathroom and turned on the water. Steam and a good cum would start this day just fine. He was starting to feel like himself again.

When he emerged from the bathroom, he smiled at Caesar who was sitting on the end of the bed. "Hungry, kitty?" Still wrapped in a towel, he filled Caesar's food bowl, giving him some pets. He shook the box of crunchies. Nearly empty. "No worries, Cees. I'm going to head to the grocery store and get us both some goodies." He went back into the bedroom and pulled some clothes out of the basket. Jeans, a tee. Yeah, he felt good. He toweled off his hair, brushed his teeth and was ready to head out into the world. He threw on a jacket, grabbed his keys from the bowl and went out the door. Glancing back, he saw Caesar sitting in the window over the kitchen sink. Now that was great. It had been a while since Caesar had ventured that far.

Jumping into the driver's seat, he put the key into the ignition. It turned and came to life with barely a complaint. Could things get any better? Had the planets aligned or something? He chuckled. It didn't matter, he'd take it. The day wasn't even overcast.

He turned out of his driveway. A quick run to DD for some coffee; a stop at McD's for a breakfast sandwich, and he was on his way to Walmart. This time, he'd even get a cart. Not his usual, but he needed to restock the house. He wasn't going to have to run back in for at least a week. Systematic this time, he went aisle by aisle, tossing items in when he saw something he might need. Milk, chips, toilet paper…paper towels. Damn. Early November and everything was Christmas! Decorations, snacks, gifts. Somehow, the store had transformed almost overnight from Halloween to Christmas. Everything started too early. There were even carols coming over the loudspeaker. He rolled his eyes. He wasn't ready for grandma to get run over by a reindeer. It was just too soon.

Back to his mental list. Juice, eggs, some frozen dinners. Laurel had already gotten him some sandwich stuff. Peanut butter, ketchup. Cat food, beer. The essentials. He maneuvered his cart in and out of the other customers, nodding at moms with their kids, trying to keep control of their sanity, and making his way back to the front of the store. He swung in to a checkout lane that only had one person ahead of him and put his things onto the conveyor belt. "Good morning," he greeted the cashier.

"Morning."

He watched as his items got run up, grabbing each plastic bag as the cashier filled them. He paid with a cheery, "Have a nice day." He left the cart in the cart return and took his bags to the car. Not bad. It was only 9:45. He'd be home and done, ready to put his feet up and relax, in short order. Another not too bad, non-tooth rattling start and he was on his way home. More and more houses had their Christmas decorations out. He was good with that, though. It could be really festive driving through his town. The lights were pretty and reminded him of when he was small. It kind of brought back the magic of the season to him.

He pulled into his driveway and turned off the car. A few rumbles and the car was settled. He took the bags out of the back seat and headed up his steps. Unlocking the door, he stepped inside. And stopped. Every drawer and cabinet was open and his kitchen table was on its side. The basement door was wide open and he could see that the living room was a mess. Torn apart. Furniture upended, moved. He put the bags on the counter and dropped his keys where the bowl should have been. He saw it, in pieces, on the floor at the other end of the kitchen.

Jack's first thought was that he was robbed, but in the next heartbeat he knew he was wrong. "Cees?" he strode into the living room, shocked at the chaos, but needing to know his cat was okay. "Cees!" He could hear a faint meowing and found him in the back corner of his closet. Safe. His bedroom, however, wasn't in such good shape. He let go of Caesar and took his phone out of his back pocket. He walked outside, sat on his steps and called Park.

"Hey. Can you get your ass here? Like now?"

"What? What's up?"

"Can you?"

"Uh, yeah? Be there in like fifteen, okay?"

"Yeah." Jack clicked to kill the call and rested his head on his arms. He stayed that way until he heard a car in his driveway. Park jumped out and walked up to him.

"I guess it didn't like the cleansing," Jack said.

"What?"

Jack motioned with his thumb over his shoulder for Park to go inside. He went in, moving slowly from room to room and then joined Jack on the steps. Stunned.

"So, we didn't make it leave, but we pissed it the fuck off."

They sat in silence for what seemed like forever. The cold air was seeping into Jack's jacket. Park asked, "What's our next move?"

"I guess I have to get the Ouija board out."

"The board! Fuck. We cleansed the damn house and never took out the board. What the fuck is wrong with us?! How did we miss that?"

"I don't know. I never thought about it. Never put that much stock into it... that it truly could be the source of it all. You know, nasty ghost, kick it the fuck out. Nothing more," he paused. "I'm going to drive it back to New Castle."

Park thought about it for a minute. "We could break it up, bury it."

Jack shook his head. "I want it gone. Back to where it came from."

"I'm not sure that'll do it, Jack. Some of this stuff, I know it sounds nuts, but..."

"But I'm going to do it this way. It seems right to me. If not, then we'll go on to the next step and the next until this fucker is gone."

"We could sage the damn thing."

"And salt the hell out of it."

"When do you want to go?"

"Right after I get my house straight." They stood and went inside. Jack had forgotten his groceries on the counter. They had started to defrost a bit, but no matter. He tossed them haphazardly into the freezer. Park started picking up the glass of the bowl that had shattered, gently putting the shards into the garbage. Jack turned the kitchen table upright.

When they finished in the kitchen, they moved on to the living room. Jack's sofa was slid away from the wall and the coffee table was overturned. "Where's the board?" Park asked. They looked behind the recliner, under the sofa. Nothing. It was definitely not in the living room anymore. Fuck. Jack walked into the bedroom as Park got the coffee table and its things settled.

"It's here." Jack walked into the living room with the Ouija board and planchette in his hands.

"Where was it?"

"The middle of my bed."

Park looked at his friend. "It's trying to fuck with your mind."

"Yeah. Let's get this done. I've got a two hour drive ahead of me."

"I'm going with you."

"You know you don't have to. I can handle it. Don't want to screw up your entire Saturday."

"You already have, asshole. And I'm going with you. Grab the end of the sofa, you lazy shit. I can't do this all myself."

Jack smiled. As much as this had shaken him, he knew it'd be okay.

"You're gonna buy me lunch, right?"

Jack took a pillow off the sofa and threw it at Park. "You're such a jerk."

"Yup. But I get lunch."

They worked on the rest of the house, putting odds and ends back where they belonged. Then, they sat at the kitchen table with the board. "Do you have the last of the salt?"

"Yeah."

They lit some sage and held the board in its smoke for a few minutes, passing it through, front and back, edges, everything they could think of...including the planchette. Finally, Jack put out the sage stick. He picked up the salt. Park got a bowl with a little bit of water and mixed in most of the salt. He then brushed it across the board, as thoroughly as they had saged it. The last bits of sea salt they sprinkled across the board and let it sit. They waited. For what, Jack didn't know, but they waited. Maybe to see if the house would start to shake or if the board would burst into flames. He'd watched too many horror movies, but at this point, just about anything could happen and he didn't necessarily know if it would surprise him. The house was quiet. The board sat on the table like, well, a board.

"Do you think it worked?"

Park sighed. "No idea."

"Let me check on Caesar and then we can go." Jack looked around and found Caesar back in the closet, sleeping on an old pillow. He gave his cat some pets and made sure there was a bowl with food for him.

Park was standing in the kitchen, staring out the window. Jack joined him, picked up the board and they walked back out into the cold. "Want to take my car?"

"No," Jack replied. He tossed the board and planchette onto his back seat. Somehow it didn't seem right to put the board in Park's vehicle. It had come home in his and, apparently, had caused all his issues. He didn't want to even chance unleashing something on Park. A turn of the key and the Subaru shook to life. "See? Smooth."

Park laughed. "Smooth as shit."

Jack turned out of his driveway. "Lunch on the way back."

"Cool," Park replied, and in a few minutes, "Beautiful day for a road trip."

"Shut the fuck up." They both laughed. He took the highway entrance and let the road roll out behind him.

The drive went quickly, and quietly. Jack watched the road, intent and solemn. He wasn't thrilled with the thought of returning to New Castle, although he guessed it wasn't much worse than what he had experienced at home. Much. Hah. Being held against a wall with no air in his lungs was pretty fucking worse. And, even though it had to be the same entity that had been in his house the last few weeks, he didn't care to be walking back in to where it all began. The pit of his stomach was in a knot. Double knot. Hell, it was tight.

Jack took the exit for the town of Freemont. As he maneuvered through the side streets, getting deeper into the outskirts of the town, his anxiety level rose a bit. He noticed his jaw getting tighter when he turned onto the overgrown drive that led up to the asylum. Park let out a long, slow whistle as they went up the twists and turns, finally pulling into an open space with the institution right before them. Jack drove nearly up to the building, putting it in park and sitting for a moment before turning the car off. It died in a few spurts and moans.

"Friendly looking place," Park muttered, getting out of the car and stretching.

"Wait'll you get inside. A homey little fixer upper," Jack leaned into the backseat for the board and planchette and felt a lump in his pocket. The selenite and tourmaline. "Hey," he called over to Park, holding out his hand. "For protection." Park looked confused for a second, but dropped them into his jacket pocket.

"You okay, man?"

"Nope. Not at all," he looked at Park. "Let's go." They walked inside, Jack taking the lead. Park followed, eyeing the place as they went. He had a feel for New Castle from going over Jack's photos, but pictures never did compare to the actual place. It was a cold November day and the cement walls seemed to suck the heat from him. He pulled his sweatshirt more tightly around him, shoving his hands deep into the pockets.

Jack gave a quick look around the main entrance room and then quickly went to the stairs to the second floor. He wasn't wasting any time. Getting in, leaving the board, and getting out were his main objective. Taking the stairs two at a time, he stood at the top waiting for Park, who was walking slowly and taking in the atmosphere. "Wouldn't want to show me the morgue, would you?"

"Nope."

They walked out into the second floor hallway. Jack's footsteps tapered off now, more cautious. He eased back to Park's pace. "Nice graffiti," Park commented. He dragged his fingertips along the wall, feeling the flaking plaster as he went. As cold as it was, Jack's hands were sweaty. They made their way farther down the hallway and, as they got closer to the darker toned area, he almost felt the board vibrate in his hands. It had to be his imagination, though. His nerves were getting the better of him.

"A little devil worship, I see," Park noted. "How the fuck did they carve that pentagram into the floor?" He squatted down to get a better look.

"No idea. If I had some holy water, I'd douse the whole damn area."

Park raised his eyebrows.

"For good measure," Jack responded. "In case it might work." He placed the Ouija and planchette as close as possible to where he had found them and stepped back. No sound, no grand dark acceptance of him bringing it back. The floor didn't open up and swallow them and the Ouija through the gates of hell. The only sound was his and Park's breathing. "There. Done."

"Ready when you are."

Jack nodded and they walked in silence back down the hallway they had traversed minutes before. Park was still fascinated by the graffiti, but didn't lag behind. They needed to get back to the car, if only for Jack's peace of mind. He knew his friend was struggling. It wasn't something he had seen before and it disturbed him. He wished Jack had listened to him on this shit.

When they stepped outside again, Jack took a deep breath. It was refreshing, renewing. He felt as if he had been holding his breath the entire time they were in the asylum. Damn. He didn't want to admit it, but it was good to be rid of the board. Really good. Almost as if something dark had been hanging over him the entire time it was in his possession. Surrounding him. Gripping him. Okay, okay. He had to stop. Getting overly dramatic was not his usual mental state. Thanks, fucker. He hated that thread of fear that had been driven into his heart by this thing. It was time to regain his confidence.

"So where do you want to go for lunch?" Park smiled.

Jack shook his head. "You never change."

They got in the car and Park pulled out the selenite and tourmaline. "What are these?"

"The lady at the Eclectic shop said they were for protection. Dispel negativity, stuff like that." Park made a move to hand them back and Jack shook his head. "Keep 'em. Maybe they'll do something for you."

Park tucked them back in his jacket. "Now, about that lunch…"

Jack laughed and started the car. "Okay, okay. Your stomach trumps all."

"As it should."

Jack negotiated the twists and turns down the drive to the main road. He found a small diner on the east end of town. "Good enough?"

"Yes, my good man. It looks tremendous."

Jack rolled his eyes. "Be thankful you're not yelling into a clown's mouth."

Park saluted him as they rolled into a parking space. "Maybe you can pick up a sweet little waitress here, too." He ducked as Jack went to hit him.

Inside, they sat in a booth by a window and Jack ordered a cheeseburger. Park asked for the same and then added a salad, onion rings and a milkshake to his order. "What?" he asked when Jack stared at him. "I'm hungry."

Jack smirked. "When are you not?"

Park nodded. "Yeah, you've got me there." He ripped the end off his straw paper and pushed the straw into his milkshake. "So, what are you going to do when we get back? Got plans tonight?"

"Nah. Laurel's filling in a shift. Probably chill with some bad television and do something with her tomorrow."

"Want to catch a movie? Mad Max, Star Wars or something?"

"Yeah, we could. That'd be cool. Not sure if I'm ready to sit home anyway."

"So I'm the fucking default?"

"Yup. At least you rate higher than the shit spirit that fucked up my house."

"Well, that's something. Do I at least get dinner if we're getting a movie?" Park almost couldn't keep a straight face.

"Are you fucking kidding me?!" Jack laughed. "You take the cake."

"If there was a cake, I would take it."

They both roared. They finished their meal; Jack sat sipping his coffee while Park slowly went through his onion rings one by one. Small talk and table chat, with silences between the words that were cavernous. The 800 pound gorilla was on both of their minds, but neither wanted to approach it and wonder out loud whether they had been successful. Or not. Jack felt good again, relieved, but doubt was nagging at the back of his mind. And fuck, he resented that.

The ride back to 11 Ridley was the same, with the spaces between their comments becoming more pronounced as they got closer to Jack's home. The final miles were driven in silence. Jack's apprehension was palpable; his jaw set in a hard line. He pulled into the carport, hand resting on the key.

"You know, we've got this. Whatever is in there, we've got this," Park offered up.

Jack nodded and shut off the car. It wheezed a bit, then died. They walked to the steps, Jack with his eyes down as if he needed to look at his key to open the door. He stepped inside, Park on his heels. Jack dropped his keys on the counter and looked around. Quiet. Peaceful. The kitchen was the way they had left it. The living room was fine and Caesar was sleeping on the sofa. He opened an eye and watched them walk in, then sleepily closed it again. They stepped back into the kitchen.

Park sighed. "Everything looks okay."

"Yeah, looks. It's like I'm waiting for the shoe to drop."

"I'm sure. But it should be gone."

"I hope so," Jack paused. "Gonna need a new bowl."

Park smiled. "Christmas is coming."

"You're so generous."

"Anything for you, dear," he laughed. "Hey, look, man. I know it's got you unnerved, but even Cees is chilling on the couch. You know if he's hanging, things are quiet."

"Yeah, I know."

"Do you want to stay here for a while or head out and catch an early movie? We can get dinner and hit a seven o'clock movie."

"You're fucking kidding me. There is no way that you could be hungry after that lunch. It's only been 3 hours!"

"Not yet, no, but by the time you decide, I'll be fucking starving. Thought I'd plan ahead!" Park grinned.

"Sure you don't have a tapeworm?"

"Fine, skip dinner. But I'm getting two boxes of popcorn at the movie. And Sno-caps."

Jack smiled. "Unreal."

"And fucking amazing. We going or what?"

"Yeah, let's go. I get to pick the movie, though."

"Okay, okay," Park acquiesced. "I'm driving. It's about time you got to experience a car that isn't having death throes at every turn." Jack took his keys and they left.

They got to the movie theater and Jack read the marquis while Park stood on line for snacks. "Hey, Jack!" Park waved him over. "Help me carry, man."

"Any of this for me?" Jack asked incredulously.

"Sure, sure. Whatever you want. I just like to be prepared," he grinned.

Jack picked up two tubs of popcorn and let Park get the drinks and Sno-caps. They made their way in to Mad Max: Fury Road. It was a great distraction. Jack let himself get lost in the story. His phone was vibrating in his pocket as the credits rolled.

"Laurel?" Park asked.

"You know it," Jack couldn't help smiling. He got entirely too excited when he saw her messages, and he loved that. *Am off tomorrow, if you'd like to get together.* Like? He chuckled. Not quite the word he'd use. *Hey, Doll. I'd love to. Why don't you come by in the morning and we'll figure something out?* He waited, anxiously, for her reply. Or maybe anxious wasn't quite it. With eager anticipation. That would be more accurate. *Sounds like a plan. Can't wait to see you.* He quickly typed: *Can't wait to have you in my arms.*

He safely tucked his phone back in his pocket and he and Park walked out of the theater. Tomorrow would be a great day. Rest, relaxation and one hell of a night to look forward to. Damn, things were looking up. He almost forgot, almost, his nerves as they pulled into his driveway.

"You sure you don't want me to come in?" Park asked.

"And hold my fucking hand?"

"If you want, but kiss me first."

"Asshole."

Park smirked. "Yeah."

"I'll be fine. I'll call you tomorrow. Maybe we'll do something before Laurel shows up."

"All right. Night."

"Night," Jack shut Park's car door and turned to his house. Everything seemed cool. Park was already backing out of Jack's driveway as Jack turned to give a short wave. He unlocked the door and dropped his keys on the counter as he walked in. He hit the switch for the kitchen light. It came on, but flickered and immediately went out. Fuck. He didn't have any more lightbulbs. He tried the switch a second time, but knew it wouldn't come back on. Damn it. Frustrated, he walked into the living room. If Park had seen it, he might have been concerned.

Only 9:45 p.m. He flipped on the television, and looked around for Caesar. Must be in the bedroom. "Meow?" he called. "Cees?" Nothing. Probably deep asleep on his pillow or something. He flipped through the guide, looking for anything that would just be background noise for a while, but nothing caught his eye. A little reading in bed then. Cozy and reading till he dozed off didn't sound half bad. Off went the television. He picked up his latest book and walked into the bedroom. No Cees. "Come on, kitty. Where are you?" Jack heard a faint meow from inside the end of his closet. "Are you back on that pillow?" Caesar walked out slowly, peeking around the closet door. Jumping onto the bed, he snuggled hard into Jack, as if he hadn't seen him in days. "Aw, lonely kitty? Sorry I was gone so long." Caesar kept up the rubbing and purring until Jack gave in and sat on the bed in his clothes. "Okay, okay. I won't go get changed." He fluffed his pillow and sat back, ready to read if Caesar would chill a little. He kicked off his shoes and settled in.

It was late when he woke. There was a vibration in his bed and his lamp flickered and went out. He pushed up on his elbows and stared. Was that a shadow at the end of the bed...uncoiling? It was in that split second that it rushed him, pinning him back on the bed. He struggled, but couldn't move. It was on him. Sitting on him.

The pressure in his chest was enormous and the breaths he could get were putrid. Rotting hell, he could taste the decay. He forced himself to try get away, to scream, but no sound came. He could feel hot breath on his face but could only make out a shadow form. It wasn't really holding him, there were no arms, but it enveloped him. And that's when he heard it. But didn't hear it. The sound was in his mind, yet all around him. That laughter. Maniacal. Evil. Terror overtook him. Not a thread of fear anymore, but terror to his core. The seconds were ticking and he couldn't move, couldn't turn, and he could feel the thing in his mind. Cold sweat was dripping down his face. A silent scream took over as it laughed. He could feel it laugh and it shook him. The last thing he felt was a backhand to the face. It hit with a force he couldn't have imagined and swung his face to the side. He blacked out as it hit and welcomed that darkness.

Hours later, he opened his eyes. At first, through his foggy head, he thought it was all just a nightmare. A horrible nightmare of terror and pain. But then he moved. Turned to get out of bed and felt it. His jaw. Fuck, could it be REAL? There was a trickle of blood on his pillow from...his nose? His mouth? No idea. He felt his jaw and didn't know if it was broken, but fuck it hurt. He slowly pulled himself from the bed to go look in the bathroom mirror. His left eye was blackened; his cheek dark and bruised. Fuck all. He had to get out. Had to find a safe place.

"Cee..." was all he could get out. His mouth was too sore. He looked around. The poor cat must be hiding in the closet again. A peek inside and yeah, there he was. Jack reached in to get him, but Caesar wouldn't have any of it. He arched back and hissed. "Okay," he managed in a whisper, barely moving his mouth. "Okay. I'll get you last."

He grabbed his jacket, tried to think. What did he need? His face was throbbing, making it hard to concentrate on anything else. His wallet. Some clothes? Fuck, was there even time to pack a bag? He shook off the thought. He didn't need a bag, he needed out. He fumbled to make sure he had his wallet, yeah. Good. Cees. Where was the cat carrier? The closet. It had to be in the closet. He walked over, leaning on the closet door to get his bearings. The rhythmic ache in his face was killer.

He heard a door creak open. What the hell now? He walked to the doorway of the bedroom and saw the basement door half open. Fuck. No. He was not ready for this. He dropped everything and strode into the kitchen. He was a soldier waging war on an invisible army and this was his fucking house. He slammed the basement door shut and locked it. Standing for a minute, breathing in rhythm with the pain, he was poised for an attack. None came. Maybe he was safe, for now. Maybe he could get his things and get out. Then, he saw it. On the wall. On the fucking wall. The Ouija board. He stared, for how long he didn't know. Finally, he turned, and as he strode back toward the bedroom, the next hit came.

It caught him from behind and threw him forward, almost knocking him from his feet. Luckily, he only tripped. He wheeled around, fists high, to... nothing. Fuck. He half ran back into the bedroom. The carrier and Cees weren't there. Damn. Maybe it was in the basement. To hell with that. He found where he had dropped his jacket, bent to grab it and almost lost consciousness. No. Not this time. He stood and waited for the blackness to dissolve from his vision. He shoved his feet into his shoes, fuck the ties, and jogged into the kitchen. He grabbed his keys and as his hand went to the door, something pulled him back. Yanked him by the neck of his shirt. He hit the kitchen table. Floundering for a moment, he pulled himself up. Where to run? If he couldn't get the fuck out, what could he do? His mind raced.

He breathed. It was quiet. Once again, he started for the side door. Slowly this time. As if he could sneak around it and not be noticed. His hand was shaking as he reached for the knob, his other hand gripping his keys so tightly he was almost drawing blood. He felt the cool metal of the knob, but before he could turn it, he was yanked back once more. He hit the floor and blood spurted from his mouth, his tongue now wrecked. He lay there, aching, terrified of this unseen attacker. He felt his pocket. Somehow, he still had his phone. If he could get Park, if he could get someone to come, he would be okay. He took it out of his pocket, trembling.

Barb Shadow

5

Parker's phone rang and he hit the speaker button. "Yeah?"

The signal was in and out; the voice broken. It was faint…a man's voice. It sounded like Jack, but hard to make out. "Jack? Is that you? You're breaking up. I can't hear you."

"Park." There was static, too, which didn't make sense. He should have had a crystal clear signal, for God's sake. He was within sight of the cell tower. The joys of living in a mini-city.

"Jack?" The signal was gone; the call lost. A second later, his phone rang again. Parker grabbed the phone, ignoring the "hands free" law. "Jack? What the fuck? What's up?"

"Park. Help, man. I need…" The words trailed off, but were unmistakable this time. Panting. Pain. "Park…it's killing me."

"I'm just down the street. I'm coming, man. Hang on." He tried to turn at the next side street but it was blocked off. Construction. They were routing all the traffic into one lane, diverting him farther away from Jack. He was getting agitated, leaning from side to side to try to see ahead, around the traffic. Looking for any way to turn, to U-turn even, to head back in his friend's direction. He was only about two miles away but it seemed like a million. "Come on, come on…" He hit his horn. It wouldn't do any good, but he might get someone's attention. "Come on, guys," he yelled out the window, "emergency here!"

The man holding the stop/slow sign jogged over to him.

"My friend's in trouble. I need to get around."

"Sorry, guy. You can't. There's no way to get past the machines. You're gonna have to wait. Call 911."

911. He hadn't thought of 911, but what could they do?

"9-1-1, what's your emergency?"

"My friend has been under demon attack for the last three weeks, and I think the damned thing may be winning."

"All right, Sir. You said demon attack? Give us the address and we'll have a team of certified exorcists on their way."

Or, more likely,

"What's your address, Sir? Where are you now? We'll have someone on their way to you with a nice, white coat. Very cozy. Like a hug."

Park was losing it. He'd get out of the car and run it, if he weren't still so far away. He needed to be there NOW.

Finally, as if by willing it, the construction guy turned his sign to "slow" and Parker drove on. It was still moving too gradually for him. He laid on the horn. He was nearly to the next side street and that one was blocked off. It was as if someone had strategically cut off his access to anything that would get him back to Jack. Could that even be possible? He knew in his heart it was. And that scared him more than anything. If he attempted a U-turn, he'd be right back waiting for Mr. Stop/Slow to turn his sign around. Everything was slowing him down. The clock wouldn't stop ticking. He didn't even want to imagine what his friend might be going through. Parker typed in 911 on his phone and let the call go through, shouting, "My friend is being attacked! 11 Ridley Road," and hung up. He didn't know how he would even help, but if he had to pull him out of the house on bloody stumps, he would. And he hoped that wasn't foreshadowing.

At the next intersection, and against the light, he swung a quick left. If he had the side streets straight in his head, in about half a mile he could pick up the far end of Ridley. It added a little distance, but at least he'd be on the right road. And, he'd straighten out the twists and curves. He hoped no one would be coming toward him. After holding his breath while the side streets passed by, he saw the sign for Ridley and gunned it.

Jack dropped his cell phone from his right hand and leaned against the kitchen wall. There was no leaving, no sneaking out. He had tried that earlier and all it did was leave his left arm broken, he was pretty sure. He didn't know how much longer he could take the attacks. Breathing in was painful, sharp and deep. A few ribs might be shattered. He didn't know. It didn't matter anyway. Another slam or two and he'd be dead; that was certain. This…thing…wasn't messing around anymore. It was a game of cat and mouse, or, more accurately, a game of lion and gazelle. Soon, it'd be going in for the kill.

He felt in his shirt pocket for a pen. If he could leave a note, a warning, for Park and any others, he needed to. Tell them to burn the house down, fry that goddamned Ouija board, do whatever could be done to stop this. Tell them. Document it. He winced as he brought out the pen and reached for his journal. The air temperature dropped around him and his stomach tightened. He was slammed low and hard, knocking him to the ground, and scattering the pen and notebook sliding across the floor.

"You bastard," he managed to spit out, along with the blood collecting in his mouth. He laid his cheek on the cool green tile and let himself pass out for a few seconds. He could feel the entity inside him, in his mind, and he tried to push back. Tried to shut it out, but he was losing grip. Drowning in the blackness. Giving in to the madness. He pushed off the wall with his foot and tried for one last go at the door. Searing pain jolted through him as something grabbed his leg and pulled him back. He turned his face to see his attacker and it finally manifested. A tall shadow with…eyes? Doubled over, holding on to his last shred of sanity, he asked, "What the fucking hell ARE you?" The darkness drilled into his mind and the only thing he could hear was a cold, cruel laughter echoing in his head. There was a slow tightening on his heart and, as it beat its last, he gave in to the entity. Jack's fight was over.

Parker cut corners on the road and drove like a maniac. As he pulled up, he could see the energy of this thing. The house almost seemed to be pulsing. Almost. Just on the edge of normal vision. The lights were flickering on and off, like in a bad horror movie. And then, as he jumped out of his car and ran to the door, the house fell silent. All he heard were the sirens in the background. At least help was coming.

He pounded on the locked door yelling, "Jack! Can you hear me?!" and stepped back to break it down. Two hits on the old door and he was through. The Ouija board was on the wall and he was halfway through the kitchen before he noticed Jack on the floor in a puddle of blood. "Jack, Jack," he cradled his buddy. "My God, man." He sat, absently rocking his dead friend, with shoulder heaving sobs.

The police arrived at the same time as the ambulance crew. A police officer took Parker to the living room to get a statement so the crew could check Jack. They started CPR; Park knew it was futile. He tried to watch from the doorway, but the officer kept redirecting him. He stood, shifting his weight from side to side, wringing his hands, pushing back the hair from his face. "He's gone. My God, he's gone." The officer took his name, his statement. Another officer stepped over and did the same. It was a blur. Parker sat in Jack's recliner, bent over. "This is a nightmare. A fucking nightmare." The tears were still streaming. He looked around. "Where's Caesar?"

"Who?" the officer asked.

"Caesar. His cat."

"Sir," a young officer called to the man beside Parker. Officer Sanchez, he thought he had heard. "Would you come here a minute?"

The man excused himself from Parker. The younger officer held something in his hand that he was showing to Officer Sanchez. His brow furrowed and he strode back to Parker.

"Mr. Davies. Would you stand, please?"

Parker stood. The officer took Parker's wrist and snapped on handcuffs. "Mr. Davies, you are being arrested for the murder of Jack Barnes."

"What?!" Parker was floored. He stood, unmoving, trying to comprehend what was happening.

"You have the right to remain silent. Anything you say can and will be used against you in a court of law. You have the..." The words faded off. He didn't know if he couldn't hear them or if they disappeared on their own. There was a rush in his ears. A muffled... laughter? Both of his hands were behind him, cuffed, and he was being led out of the house. Through the kitchen, that awful kitchen! The ambulance crew had gone and only an officer stood, waiting with the body, for the corner to arrive.

"I don't understand! He was my best friend."

"It's all here, Davies," the officer patted Jack's journal. It was tucked under his arm. Another officer was marking off the house with yellow crime scene tape.

"Wha..." Parker shook his head, as if trying to shake off everything they were saying. "That's Jack's investigation journal. What's that got to do with anything?"

"No, Sir. It's his journal of your abuse. He was in fear for his life and YOU are the one named."

Parker had no words. His mouth moved, silently, as the reality sank into his brain. He knew what the entity had done. It had stolen Jack's life and taken his own as a bonus. As they led him out the side door, he shot a last glance over his shoulder. The door to the basement, which had been ajar, swung shut and the Ouija board was no longer on the wall. He collapsed on the back seat of the squad car and never saw Laurel's car pull up or the confusion on her face as a police officer stopped her before she reached the house.

· Barb Shadow

EPILOGUE

A few years later

Willow Tree Weekly, June 24

This week, an infamous icon in our community has been given new life and a fresh start. New Castle Asylum, empty and abandoned for nearly forty years, is being transformed into apartments by a group of investors from New Jersey. Construction began Tuesday.

Although New Castle had a reputation of being haunted, it was truly only troubled by its horrendous history of mistreatment of its patients back in the day. Now, something positive will come from the soil and be a benefit to the local community.

Joe Paine took a sip of coffee and turned the page of his local paper. The steam rose up from the cup. People always thought he was nuts for drinking hot coffee in the dog days of summer. He didn't care. He'd drink it sitting on Satan's lap with a table of flames beside him. That's how much he liked his coffee hot. The owners of the asylum had the coffee pot fired up when he was there. He had met with those Jersey guys earlier in the week to interview for the apartment manager position and they had hired him on the spot. It was a good feeling. He guessed his construction background had given him a leg up on the other guys, since they were bringing him in early on the project. He'd be overseeing the different contractors, hiring and getting it all together. A liaison between them and the Jersey guys. Hopefully he'd get his basement apartment and office done quickly and move right in, while the other apartments came together. Joe took a bite of his bagel and turned the page.

Local Man Found Dead

Parker Davies, convicted murderer of Jack Barnes, was found dead Wednesday in his cell at the Aarondale Correctional Facility. Police have not yet commented on whether his death was murder or suicide. While this facility does use surveillance cameras, the one on Davies' cell had reportedly malfunctioned in the days prior to his death. Davies, 47, was serving life in prison.

He remembered that guy. It was all over the papers for weeks after he murdered Barnes. Damn, that house was a mess. Bet it took forever to clean up the blood. Pretty near everyone followed that trial and all were relieved when Davies was sentenced to life. Good riddance! They all plead innocent when they get caught. The poor guy who got killed had documented it all in a journal. Was a shame he hadn't come forward and told someone before the freak killed him. Davies deserved what he got. Should've gotten the death penalty.

Well, it was time to get back to work. He tossed the newspaper into his truck and went back to the worksite. He'd do another walk through while he waited for the roll off to be delivered and the crew to show up. Everything needed to go, then there'd be a lot of cleanup, a lot of work to convert the small rooms into larger, friendly apartments. His place would be downstairs, in the area still marked "Morgue." He smirked. Something about that seemed cool. Maybe he'd keep the sign on his desk. He walked inside and took a deep breath. The only area that he didn't like was the second floor. A few coats of paint would take care of the graffiti. He'd have the crew go up to take out the Satan shit. That stuff made him edgy. They'd have to cover that pentagram in the floor. A good indoor outdoor carpet would take care of that. As long as he didn't have to deal with it, that was fine.

Before he could head upstairs, the sound of a motor interrupted him. "Must be the roll off," he muttered and turned to go outside to show them where to put it. There, to the side of the entrance, leaning against the wall, something caught his eye. A Ouija board. What the fuck?

"Look at that," he bent over and picked it up. The planchette, too.

"Now where the hell did that come from?" He looked around, sure someone was playing a trick on him. He'd been in and out of that doorway any number of times and he was sure, well, fairly sure, it hadn't been there before. "Nearly new, too." He dusted off the board. He always wanted to try one of these things, see what all the fuss was about. Not that he believed in ghosts, but what the hell. It'd make a cool party game.

"I'll be damned," he said. He tossed it into his truck and went to greet the crew.

Barb Shadow

GLOSSARY

Apparition - the ghost-like image of a person or animal.

EMF Meter - measures fluctuations in electromagnetic fields. Many people believe that spirits can manipulate these fields, causing unusual "spikes" or elevations in the measurements. The Mel-Meter is an EMF detector with a temperature sensor.

EVP - electronic voice phenomenon. These are sounds and voices found on electronic recordings that are attributed to spirits.

Ghost box - a piece of equipment used for direct communication with spirits. It is generally a modified AM/FM radio that does a continuous scan through the band. It is believed that spirits can manipulate the energy and communicate through the device. Also known as a spirit box.

KII Meter - another type of EMF detector. The KII uses colored lights to indicate the intensity of the electromagnetic field.

Ouija Board - a flat board that has been painted with the alphabet, numbers 0 - 9, the words yes, no, hello and goodbye. Although marketed as a game for children, many consider it a communication tool for spirits. Also known as a spirit board or talking board.

Planchette - the small, usually heart shaped piece of wood or plastic used with a Ouija board. Participants place their fingers gently on its edges and wait for the planchette to slide across the Ouija board to spell out words, supposedly communication from spirits.

Portal - a crossing over point through which spirits can travel.

Barb Shadow

ABOUT THE AUTHOR

Barb Shadow is a paranormal investigator and researcher. She cofounded the Sullivan Paranormal Society, an investigative team in upstate New York, and has appeared with the team on numerous radio shows to discuss their experiences.

Shifting to Black, the sequel to *A Step Into Darkness*, will be released mid-2018.

To find out more about Barb and to get updates on her upcoming titles, visit barbshadow.com.

Made in the USA
San Bernardino, CA
22 March 2018